Hush My Mouth

A SOUTHERN FRIED MYSTERY

CATHY
PICKENS

THOMAS DUNNE BOOKS

ST. MARTIN'S MINOTAUR 🐟 NEW YORK

This is a work of fiction. All of the characters, organizations, and events portrayed in this novel are either products of the author's imagination or are used fictitiously.

THOMAS DUNNE BOOKS.
An imprint of St. Martin's Press.

www.thomasdunnebooks.com
www.minotaurbooks.com

Library of Congress Cataloging-in-Publication Data

Pickens, Cathy.
    Hush my mouth : a southern fried mystery / Cathy Pickens.—1st ed.
        p. cm.
    ISBN-13: 978-0-312-35442-8
    ISBN-10: 0-312-35442-8
    1. Women lawyers—Fiction. 2. South Carolina—Fiction. I. Title.
    PS3616.I27H87 2008
    813'.6—dc22

                                                        2007039948

First Edition: February 2008

10 9 8 7 6 5 4 3 2 1

TO MY HOME STATE OF
SOUTH CAROLINA—AND FOR THE FOOD,
THE FRIENDS, AND ALL THE QUIRKY WEIRDNESS.

AND, AS ALWAYS,
TO MY PARENTS, PAUL AND KITTY,
AND TO MY HUSBAND, BOB,
WITH MUCH LOVE.

Acknowledgments

Many thanks again to all who helped Avery on her way: Vickie Bottoms, victim/witness advocate; Patrick Merck, evidence technician; and Rhonda Morgan, victim/witness advocate are in the trenches every day. Thanks for the work you do and for allowing me a glimpse inside. I beg forgiveness for the places where I ignored what you said so I could tell a good story.

Thanks also to John Dickinson for site scouting and for my tireless readers, Catherine Anderson, Elizabeth Dickinson, Tom Dickinson, and the members of an extraordinarily mean bunch of women: Paula Connolly, Terry Hoover, and Ann Wicker.

Avery wouldn't get far without the teams at St. Martin's Minotaur and the Jane Rotrosen Agency. My deepest thanks to Ruth Cavin and Toni Plummer, Meg Ruley, and Christina Hogrebe for taking me under your wings.

One's eyes are what one is, one's mouth what one becomes.

—JOHN GALSWORTHY, *Flowering Wilderness* (1932)

Monday Morning

An eternal question: If I started sliding, would a sticky patch of roofing tar stop me from plummeting two tall stories to my death?

I inched along the steep roof with my knees bent and mentally rehearsed aiming my fanny into a quick sit should gravity threaten to draw me over the edge.

Of course, with my natural grace, a slip of the foot would grab a patch of roofing tar at just the wrong angle and send me flying over the leaf-clogged copper gutters, past the too-often-painted gingerbread eaves, and onto the patched sidewalk or wide brick steps below. No chance I'd be cushioned by the thorny holly shrubs. Nope, it would be the sidewalk. Headfirst.

I hunkered down near a badly curled shingle, willing the worn shingles underfoot to have enough grit left in them to withstand the gravitational pull of the earth. I dabbed the stubby, stiff brush into the tar pot and stippled the goo thickly around the damaged shingle edges. Just this one last patch to do. Then I could inch my way over to the ladder, ease a foot onto the rungs, close my eyes, and climb down.

I had watched roofers amble with a relaxed, limber-legged gait, bouncing on bent knees. They made it look easy, so I'd told Melvin I'd just patch the leaks myself in the former Baldwin & Bates Funeral Home, now the combined offices of Avery Andrews, Attorney-at-Law, and Melvin Bertram Capital Ventures. In lieu of rent payments, of course. Now I understood why the two estimates I'd gotten from roofing contractors had been so outrageous.

Yet another prime illustration of something that had seemed like a good idea at the time. What had I been thinking? Okay, I'd been thinking about cash flow. Now I wished I'd also thought about life insurance and whether, from this height, a broken neck was instantly fatal or a lingering end.

I glanced over the gutter to the sidewalk below and contemplated another eternal question: Is it an immutable law of nature that unexpected company and inopportune personal moments coexist on the space-time continuum? It never fails. Company will catch you at your worst. Too early to be my new client—I hoped.

Two guys and a girl milled around on the front sidewalk. The Victorian house was an eye-catching mauve and architecturally interesting, but they had turned their backs to the house, choosing instead to take pictures of the eight-foot stone angel that stood on our front lawn.

The angel was an unusual choice for a signpost. She'd been destined for life as a grave marker until a former client had chosen to bequeath her to me. AVERY ANDREWS, ATTORNEY-AT-LAW was now discreetly engraved on her pedestal. She was a beautiful piece of art, and I'd smiled at the thought of having her, with her head bowed prayerfully, hands resting against an obelisk, her wings folded, a reverential beacon in front of the former funeral home. When I'd accepted her as a gift, I'd seen her as a guardian angel. I now feared she might become a beacon light for weirdos.

'Twas the season, though—the start of summer, when all manner of folks drove up Main Street in Dacus and straight into the Blue Ridge Mountains, where the Southern Appalachian chain dips into Upstate South Carolina. I hadn't planned to turn the front of my office into a tourist photo op, the funereal equivalent of the World's Largest Ball of String or the Virgin Mary in a Piece of Toast Museum.

I inched over to the edge of the porch and opened my mouth to yell for Melvin to come hold the ladder when I heard his voice from the porch. "May I help you?"

The three photography bugs had the good sense to act startled when he spoke.

"Hey," the lanky blond fellow answered. "Hope you don't mind. We didn't step on the grass or nothing."

The pockets of his cargo pants and his multipocketed vest bulged with so much photography paraphernalia that it visually doubled his slight size. "There's somebody on your roof." He craned his neck back to stare. I didn't wave.

Melvin stepped out from under the porch eave and glanced up in my direction. In his most dignified radio-announcer voice, he said, "My lawyer."

The girl, waifishly thin with white-blond hair scraped back into a wispy ponytail, stared up at me, her mouth round with surprise.

I sat on my heels and carefully tied the wire handle of my tar pot to the end of a thin rope, waiting for Melvin to finish toying with the visitors.

"I'm Colin, but they call me Mumler." The talkative guy with the stuffed pockets stepped up to shake Melvin's hand. The girl's brother? I stared down at the top of his head, his spiky hair the same white-blond as the girl's and, from this angle, so thin he almost looked bald.

"We're ghost hunters," Colin announced with the same enthusiasm a kid might tell his parents he'd made the basketball team. "This is most interesting. We were wondering if you'd allow us to take some readings inside. We understand this used to be a mortuary, and—"

"No." Melvin's tone was polite but firm.

"We wouldn't disturb anything, Mr. Andrews. We'd just take some photogr—"

"I'm not Mr. Andrews," Melvin said, his voice still level. "This is a place of business. I'm sure you understand."

What the kids couldn't know was, before this was a mortuary, it had been Melvin's family home place. I didn't know much about Melvin's family, but they likely weren't the kind of people who'd hang around to haunt a house. They were Presbyterians.

Melvin took a step toward the trio, ushering them down the sidewalk. His graying sideburns and neatly pressed oxford shirt lent him a certain authority. However, the leader of the ghost-hunting threesome wasn't gently dissuaded or spooked.

"Do you know of other likely sites that might present paranormal activity? We take measurements, try to capture phenomena on film. In fact, we're hoping to get enough material for a TV pilot."

"Oh, really." Even though I couldn't see Melvin's face, I could tell from his tone that his mouth was crooked up in a wry grin.

"Yessir."

"Well, in that case . . ."

For Pete's sake, get on with it and get me down from here. Was this the vantage point disembodied spirits had? Hovering overhead, studying the tops of our heads and listening to inane conversations? No wonder they decided to shake things up and play pranks. I was about to manifest my tar pot off the roof.

"Why don't you try Highway 107 north of town? Toward Highlands. You'll come to a picnic spot on your left called Moody Springs."

Don't drink the water, I thought. *Nasty stuff tastes like tepid rust.*

"A couple of miles farther up the mountain, there's a pull-off on the right. A scenic overlook, though it's a bit overgrown now. A soaking wet hitchhiker appears out of the fog, either at the overlook or at Moody Springs, then disappears when you set him out at his stop, at the other location."

"Wow." Melvin's storytelling had hooked the girl.

"They say he piloted a small plane that crashed into the mountain back in the fifties. He prefers to appear in rain and fog."

And to somebody who was drunk or sleep-deprived.

"Wow. Thanks, man. Maybe we can get some readings."

"Or orb activity." The guy with the brown ponytail who'd been silent up until now spoke with reverence. He shifted from one foot to another, ready to go in search of an orb, whatever that was.

"Thanks." The girl waved back at Melvin. Her gauzy white skirt swirled about her legs as she followed the rest of the Ghost Squad down the sidewalk.

Melvin looked up at me, shaking his head. Nice to know he hadn't forgotten me and my precarious perch while he played ghost guide.

After I lowered the tar pot, I let the rope drop. Melvin held the ladder and I eased myself around until my foot found the rung. That first step was always the worst for me. Stretching into limbo, fearful the ladder would begin to tilt into space.

"I can't believe you sent those kids on a wild goose chase, Mr. Andrews," I said when I touched ground.

A wry half smile still turned up one corner of his mouth as he dusted his hands off. "Seems they chose a wild chase without any help from me. You really need to get a receptionist. So much coming and going around here. I can't be expected to be your greeter. Especially"—he cocked his head in the direction the trio had taken—"if you and your stone-faced friend here begin to attract the fringe element."

I handed him the sticky tar pot, its rope trailing along the ground. "If you'd take care of patching your own leaky roof, Mr. Bertram, perhaps I'd have time to greet the weirdos myself. You know where the ladder goes."

I took the porch steps two at a time. I had to hurry and get ready for the client who'd insisted on a morning appointment. I closed the front door without looking back. I knew Melvin would look dismayed, both at the tar-smeared pot in his hand and at the task of pulling down the extension ladder and hauling it to the huge garage around back, under the house. His penchant for order would be at war: leave the ladder in plain view of everyone traveling Main Street or risk getting dirty while wrestling it out of sight without my help. I knew if I glanced over my shoulder, I'd feel sorry for him and turn back to help. But I was a bit shaky-legged from both the physical and mental exertion of my roof walk.

Roof patching and other chores offset my rent payments even though Melvin might, at times, have been better served by paying professionals. But for the last three months, since I'd officially decided to set up practice in half the downstairs of his recently reacquired Victorian, it had been an amiable and mutually beneficial arrangement.

Today, though, my subcontractor work was interfering with my practice of law. I had a new client coming in just a few minutes. I'm not much of a primper, but I needed to shower, change clothes, and get back downstairs before Melvin had yet another count against me on the matter of no receptionist.

Melvin's consulting work doesn't entail clients coming to his office. When he'd invited me to share space, I wasn't sure he'd foreseen the effect of clients dribbling into my office. Dribbling, not streaming. It wasn't so much the quantity as it was the unpredictable but steady number of characters and odd cases that arrived, as this morning illustrated. I also had some doubts about my next appointment.

She'd called early this morning and needed to see me right away. Her sister was missing. When I'd suggested she call the sheriff, she cut me off, insisting it was more complicated than that. Now that I thought about it, maybe I should have asked the ghost hunters to stick around to help with the search.

Monday Morning

I made it back downstairs after my shower mere seconds before my new client stepped onto the deep, shaded porch. When she'd called early that morning, she hadn't given me much information, just that she needed help finding someone.

In the seven months since I'd returned to Dacus from a big firm specializing in trial practice, I'd choked back more than a few knots of anxiety. In my old life in Columbia, I'd known what I was doing and I was good at it. The tougher and more complicated the case, the more I liked it. Now, all too often, the bread-and-butter problems that walked through the door—the wills or property transfers or divorces—all had learning curves for me. Whether my clients knew it or not, I was frequently surprised by how little nuts-and-bolts law I knew.

On the other extreme, some of their problems were so simple,

I felt like a thief asking for my fee. Too many of those who found themselves on my doorstep had already been beaten up and sucked dry. Likely why some of the other lawyers in town steered them in my direction.

"Finding someone" fell outside my experience, but the young woman who now swung open my beveled-glass-and-oak door had been insistent.

"Ms. French?" I asked. "I'm Avery Andrews."

"Fran." Her heels made three businesslike clicks on the oak floorboards of the room-sized entry hall as she crossed to shake my hand.

Her slender fingers were cool, her handshake firm. She looked down at me, her green eyes curious, studying me just as I was studying her.

I led her to my back office and we settled in. The answering machine would catch any messages, and the two wing chairs in the window alcove would be comfortable and private. My outer office had once been a family parlor and later a funeral home viewing room. Beautifully furnished with a few carefully chosen chairs, my grandfather's oak desk scavenged from my great-aunts' attic, and my own collection of antiques, it lacked only one thing: the receptionist Melvin kept pestering me to hire. That seemed such a big step—both a financial and personal commitment to being here, to practicing law on my own. I kept putting off the decision.

Fortunately, Fran declined my offer of coffee. I'd forgotten to check whether Melvin had made any, and as a noncoffee drinker, I was completely inept at the task. "You said you needed help finding someone," I said.

"My sister Neanna Lyles is missing. To be truthful, she's not really my sister, but my parents . . . we were raised together as sisters."

The part of me always interested in others' stories wanted to settle back for a chat. The part of me that had worked on billable hours with a big firm knew to get down to business. If I couldn't help her, no point in dragging this out.

"Your sister lives in Dacus?"

"No. In Atlanta. We both do. We grew up there. She drove up here a couple of days ago. I haven't heard from her since Friday, and I'm starting to panic. She should have called before now. I called all the places I could think of—the hospital, the sheriff, all the hotels in the area. When I ran out of options, I got in the car and drove."

Her fingers tangling and untwining in her lap were the only physical hint at her disquiet. Flawless makeup on porcelain skin, chocolate-brown pants, cream silk shirt, bobbed auburn hair, wide green eyes, she looked like an Atlanta bank executive, which she might be when she wasn't searching for her not-quite sister.

"Was she here visiting someone?" The reasons to come to Dacus were limited, despite attempts by the Chamber of Commerce and the scattered bed-and-breakfasts to market the local charm. People mostly just passed through on their way to fish on the lakes or to camp or hike in the national forest or to travel higher into the Blue Ridge Mountains seeking cooler weather.

"She said she was coming to a concert." Fran untangled her fingers. "Nut Case, her favorite group. They were playing at some club around here."

"You know the name?"

"The Ranch? Or the Pasture? Something like that."

"The Pasture." I'd never heard of Nut Case, but the Pasture had been around for decades, a honky-tonk with a big pasture out back for occasional concerts.

"Neanna called on her way here last Friday, then nothing. It was easier to drive here than to sit home and worry. I couldn't help but see your angel sign when I drove into town. I appreciate you seeing me on such short notice."

"I'm not sure I'm the best person to help you. Dacus has a private investigator who is actually very good. I could put you—"

"No," she said, her tone sharp. "No. I've had enough of P.I.'s. You're from around here, aren't you." She wasn't asking. "You know people, know how things work around here."

"Yes." My family had been here longer than dirt.

She nodded at the confirmation. "I asked about you. People like your family. At least the people who work at the gas station on the north edge of town." Her smile acknowledged the unscientifically small size of her sample. "The story is difficult. You can hire whatever help you need, but I need someone I can trust, someone—who can handle a difficult case and move quickly."

"You can't know that about me from the gas station."

She smiled. "No, but they did tell me you were once a 'big fancy lawyer in Columbia.' After I called you to make the appointment, I stopped by the library to check you out online."

Hmm. I needed to check myself out sometime, see what popped up. "Okay, suppose you tell me about your sister. Then we can talk about next steps."

"Fair enough. To tell the truth, the concert wasn't the real reason she came. She came looking for her aunt, for information about her death."

She noted my surprise.

"Maybe you've heard about Wenda Sims?"

I shook my head. "I don't think so."

"I'm sure it was in the papers, but you'd have been young when she died."

Fran looked to be in her late twenties, a little younger than I was, but I let her tell her own story.

"Wenda was murdered here in Dacus in 1985. She was found stretched out on a grave marker in a cemetery."

The lightbulb came on. "I do remember that." I'd been in

junior high school. It had been all the buzz for a few weeks, just because it had been so strange how she'd been found in the graveyard. In the way of small towns, it had probably disappeared as a topic of conversation because she wasn't from Dacus and people figured she'd brought her trouble with her from somewhere else. "That was Neanna's aunt?"

She nodded, her expression somber. "She'd been strangled and displayed there, with her suitcase and makeup kit sitting on the ground at her feet. Neanna idolized Wenda—and, I'm afraid, idealized her. Neanna was only seven when Wenda died. She was Neanna's fairy godmother, her shining light in an otherwise dreary and sometimes frightening family."

"Seven. That's a tough age to—"

"Lose someone? Particularly for Neanna. She wouldn't talk about it for the longest. It just hurt too much. I think a lot of what she remembers about Wenda are her grandmother's stories about how much Aunt Wenda doted on her. Neanna still keeps the Raggedy Ann doll on her bed that Wenda gave her when she was a baby."

When she wasn't talking with her hands, they moved restlessly in her lap.

"Neanna's grandmother—we called her Gran—raised her after her mother ran off with some guy. Neanna was just a baby. Gran never said, but I assumed Neanna's mama had a drug or alcohol problem. They didn't hear from her after she took off. When we were in high school, Neanna finally found out her mama had died. It hit Neanna hard, finding out her mama had been dead for years."

"Had anyone looked for her mother?"

"Off and on. It's why I don't trust private investigators. I watched too many of them take Gran's money—and her hopes. She couldn't afford it, but they didn't care. Gran found out on her own that Marie had died in San Francisco a year or two after she left Atlanta. Gran found out our senior year in high school. Everything's so emotional then anyway. You can imagine how hard it was on Neanna."

"What about Neanna's father?"

"Long gone. He'd disappeared when Neanna was a baby, never to be heard from again."

"How did you know Neanna?"

"We've been best friends since kindergarten."

When she smiled, the fret wrinkles around her eyes eased. "We were in school together from then on. When we turned thirteen, Neanna's grandmother started having some health problems—gallbladder surgery, diabetes, I don't know what all. Neanna had always spent a lot of time at my house when we were little, and she stayed with us more and more whenever Gran had to go to the hospital. I don't think Neanna's teen years could have been much fun for Gran. Maybe she was remembering her own two daughters and how things hadn't worked out too well, one murdered, one just gone. Neanna had a rebellious streak, at least when Gran was the one handing down ultimatums. Neanna would do anything for my dad, though. Eventually she just moved in with me and my parents."

She paused, staring into space—or across time. "I wish I could say we all lived happily ever after, but after we graduated from college, Neanna drifted from job to job. She majored in art, but she didn't want to teach and she didn't have the business head to become a gallery darling. So she took retail or waitress jobs, just something to pay the rent. She doesn't even paint for fun anymore, which is a shame. If someone has a gift like that, she should use it."

"What do you do, Fran?"

"Besides wish I was as talented an artist as Neanna? I own my own advertising and sports marketing firm."

That helped explain the professional polish, the creased slacks, the pearly white teeth, and why she was so much better at articulating her case than many of my clients.

"You did have the business head, then."

"Yeah. Too bad we couldn't team up somehow, huh? We talked about it, but things just settled into a routine. Neanna is still a member of our family. She's there for Thanksgiving, Christmas, birthdays. And, I suspect, for the occasional loan from my dad."

She emphasized the word "loan" with crooked forefingers, hinting that her dad hadn't looked for or expected repayment. Judging from her lack of bitterness, I suspected her dad was generous with both his daughters. Fran had the confidence and presence of a child who has been well cared for. Fran could be my sister—or at least a cousin. My hair had more gold than red in it, but the similarities outweighed the differences.

"You said your family is from Atlanta?" I said.

The essential Southern questions: Who are your people? Where are they from, and how long have they been here? Those pre-Revolutionary War families eligible for membership in the Colonial Dames got bonus points, followed by the Daughters of the American Revolution and finally the United Daughters of the Confederacy. In some sections, such as Charleston, anybody who'd arrived after the Revolutionary War could expect a slightly raised eyebrow and a sniff of superiority from someone whose ancestors had fled England and France no later than the eighteenth century in the face of religious persecution—or legal prosecution. Time was honored; the reasons they came were graciously ignored.

The pecking order could be complicated—and in some places, it got so snobbish and tightly defined that if carried to its illogical conclusion, each clique would have but a single member. In the Upstate, we aren't quite so regimented.

People from outside the South take our questions as a rude intrusion or inscrutable put-down. Some raise their hackles at being called "Yankees," not realizing that's just a shorthand way of saying we might not know as much about you because we have limited ways to define you. To lots of Southerners, Ohio and New Jersey might as well be the same place, for all they know about either.

Fran knew exactly why I asked. She knew the cultural shorthand. "We've been in Atlanta or around there since before there was much Atlanta," she said, which meant they'd been there so long, it didn't much matter whether they'd begun as red-dirt farmers, as merchants, or as plantation owners. She carried the certainty of knowing what she could call home. Her background would have pronounced differences from mine, but we knew each other all the same.

"So you and Neanna grew up together. This aunt—Wenda—was Neanna's real aunt?"

"Yes. Her mother's sister. Gran's oldest daughter."

"Make sure I understand. Gran had two daughters—Wenda and Marie. Any other children?"

"No."

"Did Wenda have any children?"

"No."

"So Marie had Neanna, then left her with Gran."

Fran nodded.

"When Neanna was seven, her aunt Wenda died. In high school, she learned Marie—her mom—had died, what? Seventeen years earlier?"

"Something like that."

"And now Gran is dead."

She nodded, somber.

"Was Wenda living in Dacus?"

"No. She had a boyfriend who'd moved here or was doing some work here, though. Tank Smith."

I didn't recognize the name. "Aunt Wenda was murdered twenty-three years ago. What made Neanna decide to come here now?"

Fran shrugged. "I'm not quite sure—though it started after Gran's death."

"Which was . . . ?"

"Six weeks ago. She was Neanna's last real relative."

"That must have hit her hard."

"Harder than I would've expected." She glanced down at her hands, maybe remembering the emotion but not sharing it with me. "Anyway, Mama and I were helping her clean out Gran's house. When Gran passed away, she was still living in the same little house she moved into when she'd first married, so she'd accumulated a lot of stuff. Neanna found a scrapbook and that was the start of it all."

"Scrapbook?" I pictured one with multicolored pages and ruffle-cut trims and stickers and cute captions, but that sort of craft-store creation didn't mesh with the mental picture I had of a family with deadbeat dads and druggie moms.

"Scrapbook, as in scraps. Yellowed news clippings pasted in a dime-store scrapbook, all about Wenda's murder."

"A scrapbook. That's—" I caught myself before I said, *That's creepy.*

Something in her faint frown said she knew exactly what I was thinking—and she agreed. When I thought about it, though, it made sense. Of course she'd clip the articles and hold on to anything she could. Anybody would. Maybe it was just the idea of a scrapbook that struck me as weird.

"Most of the articles were from the Greenville and Dacus papers," Fran said. "*The Atlanta Journal-Constitution* really didn't cover it, I guess. Plenty of home-grown crime there. At first, the articles filled the front page, but it didn't take long for the story to shrink out of sight. A few follow-up articles on the first anniversary, but eventually nothing."

"The whole scrapbook was just articles about the murder?"

"The whole scrapbook. The only scrapbook. Gran had no photo albums—just pictures stuffed into drawers or a couple of shoe boxes. No baby books, no high school memory books or wedding albums. Just the one keepsake book. With the articles. And one photo stuck inside."

"Photo?"

Her shoulders scrunched as if she was drawing back from something. "Laid in the front of the album, loose. Of Wenda's body on the grave marker."

"You're kidding? Where did she—how—?"

"Who knows? We—Neanna and I—wondered the same thing. Where did she get it? A newspaper photographer? A passing motorist? Who knows? How would Gran get something like that?"

And why would she keep it? On some level, like the newspaper clippings, I could understand why she might. After all, throwing it away wouldn't put it from her mind. Maybe, like grief, it was more seemly when it was kept private.

"Do you have the scrapbook?"

She shook her head. "I guess Neanna brought it with her."

"What did the photo show?"

She closed her eyes, whether to remember or forget, I couldn't tell. Likely forgetting wasn't an option for her, any more than it would have been for Gran.

"She was lying on her back, her head lolled back with her throat exposed. She looked so vulnerable, I remember that in particular. She had a coat on—it made me think of a velvet opera coat, though I don't know why it brought that to mind. Her dress was gathered at the front." She swept her fingers across just below her collarbones. "Like one of those sixties' peasant dresses, a tie-dyed print. She wore dark ballet flats."

"She died when?"

"Nineteen eighty-five. I know," she said with a shrug. "A long way from the sixties, but other pictures I saw of her always made me think of hippies. She wore her hair long, parted in the middle and pulled straight back."

Trends tend to sweep Dacus anywhere from three years to a decade after the fashion's finished everywhere else. But Wenda hadn't been from here. Had her retro look been out of fashion or all the rage? I couldn't say.

"Her suitcase sat on the ground at her feet, with one of those hard-sided makeup cases that would have been old even then. You could see lots of brown leaves around her, covering the ground like it was late fall or early winter."

I couldn't quite picture the scene. "You said she was found on a headstone?"

"Not like a tombstone. I wouldn't have known that's what it was except that's what the news articles said. It looked more like a bench, with rolled stone arms at either end. Her head was tilted back over one arm, and her body stretched along the seat with her feet on the ground beside her suitcase."

"And no indication who took the photo?"

She shook her head. "To me, it looked as though it was taken at night. You know how black-and-white flash photos sometimes look both bright and dark at the same time? It reminded me of that."

I couldn't think of a gentle way to ask my next question. "In the photo, how did you know she was dead?"

She bit her bottom lip and studied the dark oak floor beside my chair before she answered.

"I saw the picture before I read the scrapbook, before I knew the details about what happened to her. At first, I thought she was wearing a heavy necklace." She blinked rapidly. "The articles said her throat had been cut, that she'd been cleaned up and dressed before she was carried to the graveyard and—left. That's why it looked like—" Her hand rose to her own throat.

In my bright, high-ceiling office, I felt a chill. Packed up and sent on her journey. Whoever left her knew Wenda wouldn't need whatever was in the suitcase.

"If her aunt has been dead twenty years, why would Neanna come here now?" I circled back. Lawyers and cops know that repeating questions can shake loose new information.

Fran shrugged. "She kept insisting she was coming to hear Nut Case play. Or, more particularly, their lead singer Gerry Pippen. But I've known Neanna for an awfully long time. Do you have sisters?"

"One."

"Then you know, don't you? She can't lie to you, can she?"

I smiled, not bothering to explain that Lydia's a horrid liar. I probably am, too, I just like to believe I'm better than Lydia.

"She loves acoustic music, and Nut Case is her favorite band. Even so, I couldn't believe she let it interfere with our annual trip to the beach. For the last ten years, we've rented a cottage on Jekyll Island for this week in June. At the last minute, she called to say she couldn't make it, that she'd join me after the first of the week."

"Did she ask if you wanted to go to the concert?"

"She knew it wasn't my thing. I'd really been looking forward to quiet time at the beach. Vegging out, reading, listening to the waves. Nut Case wouldn't have filled the bill for me."

"Did she go to the concert?"

"I don't know for sure."

"Anybody go with her?"

"Some guy hitched a ride up here with her from Atlanta."

"A boyfriend?"

"No. She got his name off an online ride board. Another Nut Case fan."

She must have read the concern on my face.

"She checked him out. Some friend of a friend, she said. Somebody to keep her company, help her with the gas."

"Have you tried to reach him? Is he back in Atlanta?"

She shook her head. "He planned to stay in Dacus for a summer job. That's why I decided to come straight here when I couldn't reach her on her cell. To find him or somebody else who went to the concert."

"Where was he going to work?"

"I'm not sure. Some park or something? Is there an amusement park around here?"

"No-o." Not even close, unless he was commuting back to Six Flags Over Georgia or to Carowinds in Charlotte. Two or three hours to either. Unlikely. "Maybe one of the state or county parks? Is he a lifeguard?"

"I don't know."

I made a note: *Call Edna Lynch.* "Back to Wenda. You said she had a boyfriend in Dacus?"

"He'd been spending time here. Odd thing was, he wasn't here when she was killed. He was in Tampa that week."

"Then what was she doing here?"

"That's always been one of the mysteries. According to the articles in the scrapbook, she was killed somewhere else and moved to the graveyard. But as far as I know, no one ever officially answered why."

Even in 1985, deducing that she'd been moved was simple enough, since cutting someone's throat deeply enough to look like a heavy necklace would have meant a lot of blood.

"Any speculation about where she was killed?"

"Not that I saw. I didn't read every article. They got repetitious pretty quickly—mostly rehashing how little the police knew."

"I imagine Neanna studied the articles pretty thoroughly."

"Heaven help us, yes. To the point I was ready to shred them."

"She didn't say anything about coming here because of her aunt. You just know she was obsessed with the scrapbook."

She nodded.

Canceling a long-standing trip with your sister seemed pretty significant—at least it was significant to Fran. What was it about a twenty-year-old murder that compelled Neanna to come to Dacus? Or was it really just the concert? Did Fran have a tendency to overreact? Too easily become overwrought? Being a trial lawyer had hammered home for me the problem with having only one side of a story—it was rarely the whole story.

"Can you get me a picture of Neanna, one I can borrow?"

"Oh. Yes." She reached for the saddle leather handbag she'd sat on the rug beside her chair and fumbled with the complicated brass latch.

"I also brought one of Wenda, just in case."

Would I have thought to bring photos?

Almost as though she read my mind, she said, "As I said, we had plenty of experience with P.I.'s."

I took a breath. I wanted to pick my words carefully. "I know you have, but all investigators aren't created equal. I promise it will save you time and money if you let me get in touch with Edna Lynch. She's thorough, she knows this area even better than I do, and she'll spend your money like it was her own—which is to say frugally."

She waved her hand as if shooing a fly. "As I said, hire whomever you need. But I prefer working with you directly. Here they are." She handed me some color snapshots.

The first photo showed a young woman with almost ghostly pale skin and hair standing next to a young man in a dark blazer and button-down shirt. They both held drinks. Her eyes were large in deep sockets, her skin smooth with a delicate freckle above her right lip. Her companion had a slurry, well-lubricated grin, but her expression was somber, as if she was trying to see inside the camera as it seemed to be searching inside her.

I looked up at Fran.

"That's Neanna," she said. At first glance, the next photo looked like another shot of Neanna, but on closer inspection the differences became obvious—hair not quite as pale, cheeks even more hollow, shoulders almost gaunt. She looked like someone who'd spent most of her money on feeling good and not enough on food.

"Neanna's aunt Wenda," I said.

Fran nodded, pleased that, despite their similarities, I'd seen their differences.

The photo of Wenda looked as though it had been snapped at a family gathering in somebody's kitchen. Around the edges, the photo captured bits of other people, an arm reaching across in front of Wenda, the back of someone's head glimpsed over her shoulder.

I studied her clothing. The isolated bits of other partygoers visible in the picture caught a wide shoulder pad or a wildflowered blouse typical of the early eighties. But Wenda's clothing made her look as though she'd arrived at the party in a time machine. She wore a white peasant top falling off one thin shoulder and a choker necklace of black ribbon, a small cameo in the center. She'd obviously found a style she liked and stuck with it.

"How old was Wenda when she died?"

"Twenty-nine."

I held the two photographs and compared them.

"They look like sisters, don't they?" Fran said.

I nodded.

"From what her grandmother said, Wenda and Marie—Neanna's mom—looked nothing alike. Neanna's mom was, shall we say, robust, with thick, curly dark hair. She wore it long. Neanna envied her mom's curviness. She thought she looked too boyish and flat-chested."

"We always want what we don't have, don't we?" I said, knowing what it was to covet your sister's bra size even as she envied my red-gold hair and petite height.

Fran gave a faint smile. "I always envied Neanna's ease at attracting boyfriends."

Looking at Fran, with her shoulder-length auburn hair and her crystal-green eyes, I couldn't imagine she'd sat home on prom night. But walking down her memory lane was stirring up some of those long-abandoned teenage self-doubts we all harbor.

"Who's this?" I pointed to the young man standing next to Neanna.

"Just some guy. She dated him a year or so ago." She reached for the picture and flipped it over. A date was penned in a tiny, shaky scrawl.

"Not someone she's seeing now."

"No. It wasn't anything serious."

"Are these the most recent pictures of Neanna?"

"No, but they're the best likenesses of her I could find."

"How old is Neanna?"

"Twenty-nine." An odd expression crossed her face. "The same age Wenda was." She indicated the photos in my hand.

The same age. I looked at the back of Aunt Wenda's photo.

The same tiny, careful hand had noted the date. "This was taken not long before Wenda died."

Fran glanced at the date. "That's right."

Wenda wouldn't have known she would see less than a month more of her life. But, looking at the picture, I knew, and knowing made her eyes seem sad.

I still hadn't gotten an answer to my earlier question, so I tried it another way. "You don't think Neanna really came just for the concert. Why did she need to use that for an excuse?"

Fran looked me directly in the eye. I forced myself to hold her gaze. I'd had to learn to do that. Not until I started practicing law, meeting people from all over the country, did I realize how my hill country upbringing had ingrained in me that it was rude to stare directly at someone. In my head, I knew a direct, unwavering gaze implied sincerity, but where I grew up, some age-old cultural instinct said it was just plain rude at best, an invitation to a fistfight at worst. Your past stays with you. By the same token, I've had liars look me right in the eye and spin me a web. Even though they know how to mimic sincerity, the blinking usually gives them away. Fighting against who you are is hard.

Fran took my measure—or searched her own fears—before she spoke. "She came looking for Aunt Wenda. I think she couldn't quite admit to herself what brought her because she was afraid of what she'd find. In the simplest terms, she came because of the scrapbook. And the insurance policy."

"What policy?"

"Going through her grandmother's things, she found out Gran had bought insurance on her—on Neanna. Life insurance, not a little burial policy. It really upset her. Like—" Her voice cracked. "Like she was betting on Neanna dying so she could get some money. With her own two children—Neanna's mom and

Aunt Wenda—both dying, Neanna figured Gran saw betting on her death as a better gamble than the slots at Harrah's Cherokee."

"How did she take out the policy without Neanna knowing?"

Fran shrugged. "Neanna never paid attention to details, to paperwork."

"Maybe Gran had some other reason," I said, wincing at the thought of a grandmother hedging her bets, gambling on her granddaughter's life.

"That's what I tried to tell her, though I really stretched to come up with a more charitable explanation than hers. She just wouldn't move past it. And she pored over the scrapbook."

"She brought the scrapbook with her?"

"I think so. I looked for it, when I was getting these photographs. I couldn't find it anywhere. I had teased her about having memorized it."

She frowned, maybe regretting she hadn't been more understanding, simply because it had been such a big deal to her sister.

"I want you to help me find Neanna," Fran said, making clear both her involvement and her expectation of success. "As quickly as possible. I suppose you have a fee agreement for me to sign?"

I got up from my chair, surprised at how stiff I was, probably more from the tension of absorbing Fran's story than from just sitting.

Over the few months since I'd set up practice in Dacus, I'd gotten better at being businesslike without office staff to handle the details for me. I had fee-agreement forms neatly filed in the bottom drawer of my grandfather's massive oak desk, but I still hated talking about money with clients.

On the form, I circled the hourly fee—one that usually made people in Dacus blink. Fran didn't.

"Do you want a check now? You'll have expenses, if you hire an investigator."

"That can wait." I immediately regretted waving off her checkbook. Cash flow might be a problem this month, and I loathed dipping into savings to float my rejuvenated law practice. At the same time, I wanted to make sure Edna and I could deliver.

"As a next step, I need the name of the fellow who hitched a ride with Neanna."

"Skipper Hinson. That's all I know. Here's my cell phone number." She'd written it on the bottom of the signed agreement. "Or you can reach me at the bed-and-breakfast. I've forgotten the name. Off Coffee Road north of town."

Liberty Lodge. I knew the place. Good Sunday brunch there. "I'll keep you posted."

"I'll do the same for you," she said as she stood and smoothed out her slacks.

I had a warning twinge. She didn't need to be wandering around town asking her own questions. I wasn't used to clients hiring me, then working their own cases, but her level gaze said trying to talk her out of it would have the opposite effect. She'd driven from her Jekyll Island vacation cottage to find her sister. In her place, I wouldn't sit idly twiddling my thumbs, either.

"Why don't you call the hospitals again?" I suggested. Best to focus her efforts. "Try Greenville and Anderson, as well. And the Highway Patrol. Then give me a call."

She nodded.

"We'll find your sister," I said.

Everything she'd told me said we needed to hurry.

Midday Monday

My sense of urgency over finding Neanna didn't have anything with which to vie for attention. My calendar was clear except for a final divorce-decree hearing scheduled for first thing in the afternoon. Simple enough, and I'd already overprepared for that, so I could turn my attention to Neanna.

I hunched at my desk absentmindedly tracing my pen over the words where I'd taken notes. Which path to follow first? How about the easiest?

I spun my chair around, got the phone off the credenza behind me, and dialed Rudy Mellin. Chief Deputy Rudy Mellin. Fran said she'd checked the likely places, but maybe she hadn't checked with the right person.

He answered his office phone on the second ring.

"Rudy, have you by any chance arrested anybody named

Neanna Lyles? Or found any amnesiacs wandering around? Anybody unidentified end up in the Camden County Hospital this weekend? About thirty. A very pale, very thin blonde."

Rudy gulped something. Probably coffee. He didn't switch to Diet Pepsi until the afternoon.

"Heaven help us all. You've turned psychic on us."

"You have her?" I couldn't believe it.

"We-ell," he drawled. Not in his teasing way though. "I don't exactly have her. You want to tell me why you're asking after her?"

"Her family's looking for her."

"You know the family?"

"Just her sister. She's here from Atlanta trying to find her."

"Atlanta, huh? So how do you two know each other?"

"We don't, Rudy. She hired me."

"Oh." He got that reserved tone he gets when he's playing cop. "Why'd she think she needed a lawyer?"

"Not the kind of thing you call an accountant about, is it?" I didn't want to mention the drawing power of my giant stone angel.

"So why didn't she call us, if she was worried about her sister? She involved in something she didn't want to draw attention to?"

"She did call the sheriff's office, Rudy, along with the hospital and everybody she could think of. Nobody gave her any information." I let that sink in. "Besides, she doesn't know the area. For Pete's sake, just because you hang around with crooks all day doesn't make everybody one."

He was quiet so long I wondered if we'd lost our connection—or if he'd hung up on me. Finally, he asked, "You got a picture of this lady? Any identifying marks?"

Uh-oh. "I have a photo. And she has a small freckle or mole just over her lip, like a beauty mark." I took a breath before I asked, "Why?"

"Meet me at the Burger Hut. I was headed out for a quick bite."

"Sure."

Burger Hut had neither good burgers nor did its blocky brick-and-glass boredom look anything like a hut. But it sat across Main Street from my office, in a parking lot next to a long-empty grocery store, so it had the advantage of convenience.

I labeled a file *Neanna Lyles,* stuck the loose sheets with my notes inside, and wrote Fran's cell number and home mailing address inside the cover. Even though my caseload was light, I found the detritus generated by even the simplest cases could quickly build into toppling stacks if I didn't label it and beat it into submission. My little niece Emma had dropped the hint to her mother—my sister Lydia—that I needed a label maker of my own after she'd spent a Saturday afternoon helping me with my filing. Where does a seven-year-old—especially one related to me—learn to file?

I sharpened some pencils before I strolled across the street and still beat Rudy there. But he'd had farther to come: a stroll out to the Law Enforcement Center parking lot and the four-block drive to the Burger Hut.

The three picnic tables outside were already occupied, so I loitered until Rudy whipped into the lot in a marked sheriff's patrol car. He glared at the table occupants, all enjoying what might be the last bearable day before summer blasted in to stay.

We ordered, got our cardboard trays, and I followed Rudy's lumbering bulk back to the cruiser. I sometimes forget just how tall he is. He'd played on our high school football team, but he seemed bigger now—not just heavier.

"Don't spill anything in here. We're having to clean these things out ourselves now."

I didn't ask who used to clean up their fast food and doughnut messes. I didn't want to hear about County Council budget cuts or intradepartmental mutiny.

"You got that photo?" he asked just before he bit off half of his first hamburger. A creamy mustard-mayonnaise blob landed in the cardboard tray in his lap.

I settled my half-unwrapped burger back in my tray, slipped Neanna's party picture out of my purse, and held it up for Rudy to see.

He chewed and kept looking long after his expression said he'd seen what he needed to see.

"So?" I asked as he swallowed and reached for his foam cup.

"You don't have a weak stomach, do you?" he said after a loud slurp.

I crooked an eyebrow to emphasize the irony before I took a bite of my greasy hamburger.

He pulled a plastic folio from under his seat. The cruiser's front seat held a dash-mounted computer, a shotgun sitting upright between us, and various other high- and low-tech gadgets, so storage space was scarce. Thanks to the prisoner cage, he couldn't throw stuff in the backseat, where I carried most of my worldly possessions.

He pulled out a picture. "Cleaned up but only a little. You sure you don't mind identifying it?"

I was afraid I knew what he meant by *cleaned up,* but I'd handled medical malpractice defense in my earlier life. I'd seen plenty of gruesome photos.

She lay on her back, her damp-looking hair swept away from her forehead. The dull steel table made it clear she wasn't in a hospital room. The delicate birthmark, right below where her cheek would crease if she could smile, was dark on her bloodlessly pale skin. Neanna Lyles.

"She's the one you're looking for?"

32

I nodded, my mouth too dry to speak.

He slipped the photo back into his folder.

"What happened?"

"How do you know her?"

"I told you. I don't. Her sister—I have clients, you know. Just clients."

"We don't know for sure what happened." He took another bite and looked out the windshield, watching the people in line at the Burger Hut window.

"You don't have to spare my feelings, you know." What was with him? He wasn't usually so protective or so reticent.

"It was a tough scene," he said. "One of the rookies on routine patrol spotted a car parked at the overlook early Saturday morning."

I didn't ask which overlook.

"He figured he'd interrupt a couple in flagrante delicto and send them home." He rolled out the Latin in his thick drawl.

"The driver's window was down—actually shot out, as he discovered. He could see the driver slumped over the wheel. The view he had was much worse than the photo you saw. Exit wound did a number on the left side of her skull. From the initial description of the body, sounded like she'd managed to give herself a perfect kill shot."

"Give—she shot herself?"

He half shrugged, half nodded. "Can't say for sure. I reckon the autopsy report will give us a better idea."

"I take it there wasn't a note."

"No. No ID either, so they're working up a sketch or some computer version—something a bit more presentable than that photo—to put online and release to the media, see if someone recognized her."

Two plus two equals four. "Why didn't somebody do the math and put it together with the call from her sister?"

"That," he said with a touch of disgust, "is what I intend to find out."

That didn't bode well for whoever had worked the desk when Fran called.

I took a deep breath. "Wow." I'd been so intent on the hunt. I never expected this. "What's the next step?" I hoped he would tell me a cop would break the news to Fran.

"We need an official identification, especially since she didn't have any ID on her."

"Can her—sister give it from that photo, without having to—"

"Probably."

"She's going to have a lot of questions. She's not going to buy that it was suicide."

"Nobody ever wants to. But sometimes, them's the facts."

We crunched through the last of our hot French fries in silence, and I wiped my fingers on a tissue-thin paper napkin.

"Thanks for the lunch invite," I said as I opened the door. "Wish I could say I enjoyed it."

"Same," he said with a wry grin. "You reckon you can bring her by midafternoon?"

"I'll call her."

As he fired up the cruiser's big engine, I leaned in the open window.

"Rudy, how sure are you about the suicide? I mean, is there any question?"

"You mean, would I tell her sister that she killed herself? At this stage, it's not for certain. Not until the ME has finished."

"Did you work the scene?"

"Personally? No. A new guy did it, with help from Lester Watts."

I gave him a wary eye. Lester Watts was notorious for his poor crime-scene photos.

"Lester's got a new digital camera. And he's a damn good cop."

Rudy was trying to convince himself and me at the same time.

"No need to tell her anything about the circumstances just yet," he said. He knew all too well how difficult breaking such news would be. He was telling me I could let myself off the hook. "Nobody wants to believe a loved one would do such a thing."

I didn't want to believe it, either. I gave the door of his cruiser a farewell pat and jaywalked across the four lanes of Main Street to my office, the lights at the end of the block shining favorably for me. I hoped it was a good omen.

Monday Afternoon

I was only partially relieved when the ringing phone transferred to Fran's voice mail. The delay in talking to her would give me more time to plan what to say, but also more time to dread her reaction. I left her a message asking her to call me and hoped my voice gave no hint what our conversation would be.

I brushed my teeth, touched up my pale lipstick, and tucked the file folder for the Swindell divorce under my arm for the short walk to the courthouse.

I didn't expect the hearing to last long. The Swindells had already worked out their property settlement amicably between themselves and had been separated for almost the requisite year well before Mrs. Swindell called me a month ago and asked if I'd represent her at the final decree hearing. Mr. Swindell would have no lawyer, she said. I'd told her the judge would have to question him, to make sure Mr. Swindell wasn't being flimflammed. South Carolina law doesn't allow a lawyer to represent both parties in a divorce, but those who've already settled their property division can opt to have one side unrepresented, to save money.

In our initial conversation, I'd questioned her about their separation and gave my usual spiel: explained that separation meant no sex or cohabitation; told her that if they didn't stay separated, they'd have to wait another whole year; asked if the property as divided still held roughly the same value; and asked her to have a character witness at the hearing.

Shouldn't take more than half an hour, I thought as I entered the courtroom, my mind leaping ahead of the hearing to fret over talking to Fran French.

The hearing progressed as the other domestic cases I'd watched had. Because I'd spent most of my lawyer life as a trial attorney defending corporations and physicians, I'd had to spend the last six months boning up on all kinds of law I'd never practiced—real estate closings, simple incorporations and business formations, simple criminal procedural cases, and domestic cases.

Everything was moving as expected until the judge asked Mr. Swindell what should have been a simple question: "Mr. Swindell, have you and your wife been separated and living apart for a full year?"

Mr. Swindell hesitated for long enough that the judge looked up from his note-taking. I glanced at my client, who intently studied a spot on the table where we sat.

"Yes, Your Honor." He bit his bottom lip. "Except for Tuesday a week ago."

The judge had been doing this so many years that the routine cases were probably nothing more than background noise. He now sensed a schism in his quiet, predictable universe and fixed his gaze on Mr. Swindell, who sat below him and to his left.

"Mr. Swindell, could you elaborate? What took place last Tuesday?"

The witness leaned closer to the microphone, to make sure everyone, including his wife's mother who'd come to serve as a character witness, heard what he said. "We had sex." His big ears flushed red above his snug shirt collar.

Was it my imagination, or did he sound particularly proud of that?

Judge Lane turned his baleful eyes in my direction, as if I had personally served as their pimp. "Miz Andrews?"

"Yes, Your Honor." I stood beside the not-soon-to-be-divorced Mrs. Swindell, who was rubbing her index finger back and forth along the table edge.

"Does your client refute the testimony of this witness? Is your client aware of the consequences?"

"A moment, Your Honor."

I sat back down and leaned close to whisper in her ear. "Is that true?"

Her nod was almost imperceptible.

"Did he force you or coerce you in any way?" Not that that would change anything.

She looked up at me for the first time, her eyes startled wide, She shook her head.

"Whose idea was it?" I asked that question only to determine whose neck I was going to wring after the hearing ended.

She blushed and looked down, then leaned close without looking at me. "It—just happened. He stopped by and . . ."

I waited, but she wasn't going to finish the sentence.

"Did you remember what I told you? That you wouldn't be able to divorce for another year?"

She shrugged, pinching her skirt between her fingers, then gave a half nod.

I stood and faced the judge. "Your Honor, my client will not refute the witness's testimony."

"Mrs. Swindell, would that be your testimony?"

She bobbed her head and squeaked, "Yessir."

The judge gave a dramatic sigh, magnified by the microphone in front of him, as if the failure of this marriage to dissolve had personally cast him as Sisyphus, eternally shouldering the same divorce up a never-ending hill.

"You will file the proper affidavits and order of dismissal, Miz Andrews. Get your client and the petitioner into marriage counseling. Do I make myself clear?"

"Yes, Your Honor."

"This hearing is adjourned." The gavel cracked with finality.

I took Mrs. Suellen Swindell by the elbow and practically lifted her out of her chair. I wanted to grab her cock-of-the-walk husband by his outsized ear, haul them both out in the hall, and knock their heads together.

Lou Swindell followed without me having to grab hold of anything. I knew I shouldn't be angry. Maybe they'd saved their marriage. That was wonderful news. But they'd wasted the judge's time, and that could haunt me in future cases.

"Why didn't you tell me? Call me ahead of time, so I could postpone the hearing. Tell me in the hallway before we went in. Something."

The two of them stood staring at their feet like a couple of teenagers caught making out in the back pew at church.

Mrs. Swindell kept nervously bunching a handful of her flowered skirt. They both wore neatly pressed Sunday-go-to-meeting clothes. Had she also pressed his shirt and freshened his polyester sport coat when he stopped by her trailer?

I stared at them, trying to decide if their goofy ingenuousness was real on both sides. I wanted to be sure Lou hadn't tricked her into having sex so he could delay a final decree—a popular trick if one spouse didn't want to see the other spouse and half the assets leave. Lawyers routinely warn their clients not to succumb to blandishments. The Swindells had already divided their assets, though, and neither party had sought alimony. Maybe I was witnessing a miracle—a couple that had gotten to the brink and redeemed themselves.

"Both of you, look me in the eye. You understand what the judge said? The clock started ticking again when you—um, ceased to be separated."

They both nodded and cut their eyes at each other. Suellen looked like she wanted to giggle, but bit it back when she saw I wasn't in a giggling mood.

"Do you want to withdraw your petition for divorce? Or do you want to proceed?"

Lou's face got serious as he turned to his wife. "Suellen?"

Her eyes actually sparkled. Her heavy face, which had looked older than her thirty-five years when I first met her, glowed through her dime-store makeup.

She reached for his hand and nodded. He looked ready to let out a war whoop.

True love triumphs. How often had the institutional beige hall outside the Family Court chamber seen that? While we'd talked, a few people had walked past, some studying signs on doors in search of an office, others moving with purpose, at home in the courthouse annex. None of them knew they'd passed that close to a miracle.

"Listen to me. Both of you." I tried to channel my mother and great-aunt Letha to make sure I was stern enough. "You two have to see a marriage counselor. You understand?" I should send them to my mom for counseling. She'd jerk the knots out of them right quick.

They glanced at each other and nodded, still holding hands.

4 1

"Do you know one?"

They looked hesitant.

"Here's my card." I handed it to Suellen. "Call me and I'll give you a name. The judge is going to insist."

She nodded.

I had to smile. They were so goofy, like junior high schoolers. Who could stay mad at them just because they'd ticked off a Family Court judge I'd have to appear in front of time and again in other cases?

"Good luck and best wishes to you. This is certainly a happy ending."

They floated off down the hall toward the back parking lot, still holding hands. I left by the front door, turned right, and crossed Main Street to my historically accurate mauve office building, my ears still burning from Judge Lare's displeasure.

The phone started ringing as I unlocked the doors into my office.

"I already know." Fran's voice was steady but husky, as if she had been crying.

"I'm so sorry." What else could I say? How had she found out so quickly?

"I went by the newspaper, to see if they would run an article about Neanna. Someone had just delivered—this picture."

The police sketch. "I'm so sorry. I'm sorry you had to find out like that."

A tiny part of me felt miffed. Why had she bothered to hire me if she was going to run around town on her own? Checking in at my dad's newspaper, for Pete's sake.

Instead of airing my pique, I asked, "What can I do?" She'd have more details to contend with than she might realize, making arrangements for the funeral and to transport the body.

"I want you to find out what happened."

42

"What—"

She cut me off. "How she died. Where she was, everything that happened after she left Atlanta."

Uh-oh. She didn't know everything. "Fran, we need to talk in person. You want to come here or—"

"What's there to talk about? She was found shot."

"Fran, we need to sit down face-to-face."

"Avery, what are you trying to tell me?" Her voice shook with emotion, whether anger or fear, I couldn't tell. "Just tell me, dammit. I'm tired of all this bullshit."

"Fran."

"Tell me!"

Best to spit it out. "It's not official, but the cops are considering it might be suicide."

The silence on the phone line was exactly what I had dreaded. In person, I could have at least offered a consoling arm around her shoulders.

"Bullshit! That's—just—bullshit."

The venom burned through the phone line.

"Don't even start to fall for that pile of—who do I talk to? Take me there right now. There's no way Neanna would do that. There's no way she'd leave me—" Her voice broke into husky sobs.

"Fran, I'll be right there. It won't take me five min—"

"No," she barked. "I'll come there."

The line went dead. No time to ask if she should be driving. Had Neanna been this volatile? This pigheaded? I checked myself. To be fair, I wouldn't be anywhere near as lucid and decisive as Fran was if I'd just learned my sister Lydia was dead. Thinking about it tightened my throat into a painful knot. If somebody said she'd killed herself, I'd move out to do battle, just like Fran. Come to think of it, Fran's reaction wasn't so extreme after all, though still painful to face.

43

When she swung open the French door, I was waiting in my outer office, car keys in hand. No way I was going to ride with her. She was too mercurial right now.

"First," she said, "we need to find Skipper, the guy who hitched a ride from Atlanta with her. Any idea how to do that?"

Oh, now she was asking my advice. Maybe now she'd also listen.

"Edna Lynch. She has connections all over the county and she's painfully ethical." Edna was a grandmotherly, soft, short black woman who'd look more at home on the third shift in a cotton textile mill than on a bar stool sipping Barcardi with Philip Marlowe, but she had brothers and cousins who could whip ass and take names—and they were all afraid of Edna. As was I.

"Fine. Call her. Tell her what we know about him. Tell her to move as quickly as she can. I want to know—just . . ." She finished with a helpless gesture of her hands.

I left Fran in my front office and went to my desk to call Edna. It didn't take long to tell her the little we knew.

"Okay," Fran said when I rejoined her. "I want you to take me to the Pasture."

"Right now?"

My grandfather's ebony mantel clock said 6:15.

"It's a bar, isn't it? They're barely getting cranked up."

"Ye-es, but . . ." I hesitated. She was holding her grief at bay by rushing into angry activity. Reminding her that she still needed to formally identify the body and make arrangements to have it transported to Atlanta once the autopsy was complete seemed cruel. She'd recently helped Neanna deal with Gran's death. She knew better than I did the overwhelming number of details. She was simply choosing to ignore them.

"What?" She stood with her hands on her hips, a manic glint in her eyes.

"Let's go." If retracing Neanna's steps helped her deal with what had to be a crushing loss, who was I to question it? "My car's around back."

Monday Evening

The Pasture had survived several incarnations and police raids, and when I was in high school, it had been a shrine for a certain group of my classmates—the place they'd discovered sex, drugs, and local groups trying to play rock and roll. About that same time, I was clogging on Friday nights at the state park and learning to race my car down the mountain from Highlands. Decidedly tamer pursuits. Then again, I'd also managed to finish high school without getting pregnant, doing jail time, or getting shot. Life's full of options.

Strolling up to the Pasture for the first time, I couldn't help but be disappointed. The mystique had been so strong. In the harsh light of a long summer evening, it looked like what it was—a weathered, rambling, low-slung barn bounded in the front by an enormous gravel parking lot and, in the back, by a broad, weedy field that hosted concerts by local bands hoping for the big time or national acts long past their prime.

Inside, stale cigarette and beer smells did battle with a co-conut odor that I finally traced to electronic scent machines that periodically released tropical deodorizer.

The summer sunlight slanting through the few greasy windows did nothing to improve the scarred wooden tables and chairs crowding the large room. The only nod to decor—other than the once-red carpet—was the wall leading to the restrooms, covered with eight-by-ten candid shots of patrons and past acts in a mishmash of frames bolted to the paneling.

Fran had been right; this was about as far from "cranked up" as I could imagine. Not a soul in sight, no customers or employees.

We ambled toward the bar, the carpet sticking to my shoes with each step. The dark carpet had seen so many footfalls and spilled beers that it had melded into a dark goo. I wished I hadn't looked down. Even low light and lots of alcohol or drugs wouldn't make this place bearable, much less exotic. Yet another mystique-shrouded high school icon cracked and broken on the reality of wide-eyed adulthood.

"Hello?" I called, listening for sounds of life from the kitchen galley, which opened through a window to the bar.

"Can I help you?"

Fran and I both started at the voice behind us.

The Pasture's greeter was a too-often tanned middle-aged man with long strands of blond hair stretched from his receding hairline. He was taller than I was, close to Fran's height. His swagger said he thought he had a great deal to offer both of us.

"Ash Carter," he said, offering Fran his hand and me his smile.

Fran glanced at me, perhaps hoping he wouldn't notice that

she was trying not to laugh. Didn't look as though the debonair aging redneck playboy was going to find a slot on her dance card.

"A special table for you two ladies?"

Fran bit her bottom lip. Ash Carter cut a cartoonish figure as an aging swinger, but I hoped she could control herself.

"No. Thank you, though. Are you the owner, Ash?"

"Um, one of them."

Bad start, Avery. Something in his eyes went cautious. Maybe I sounded too much like a salesman—or a health inspector.

Stepping closer so I'd have to look up, I poured on my best sorghum syrup voice. "I was hoping you could help us. Fran's looking for information about her sister. She came up here from Atlanta last week to attend a concert, when you all had Nut Case up here? We're not sure where she headed after that. So we thought we'd start here, see if anybody remembered seeing her."

The caution around his eyes and mouth didn't relax much. Of course, I'd gone from threatening his business with an inspection to threatening his business with bad publicity over a missing girl.

"Well." He rubbed his chin as if conjuring a thought. "I'd sure like to help. That concert was sold out, you know. The pasture out back was jammed. Nobody turned a young lady in to lost-and-found afterwards, I can tell you that."

His weak laugh said he regretted his joke before it was out of his mouth. He looked away from Fran, smoothing the back of his hair.

"Maybe you could take a look, in case you remember seeing her that night? Maybe who she left with?"

I pulled the photo Fran had given me from my pocket.

He respectfully studied it for a time before shaking his head.

"No-o. I can't say's't I do remember her." He gave Fran a smile full of teeth too bright in his sun-damaged face. A golfer? Probably. I couldn't picture him as a hiker or a hunter, but I could

49

see a younger incarnation at the Myrtle Beach Pavilion. He'd probably shagged away some long-ago summer nights—the South Carolina beach dance, not the euphemism for what the sexy, slow swing-step conjured up.

"Everybody leaves with somebody," he said.

He handed the picture to me and avoided meeting Fran's narrowed eyes. Fran's jaw muscles knotted as she gritted her teeth, but she didn't let his insensitive comment distract her from her mission.

"Is there anyone else around who might have seen her that night?"

"Not right now. Later, of course. Folks start coming in after they get off work. Mondays aren't big nights. You girls are welcome to stick around. A beer on the house? Maybe some white wine?"

Fran bit her lip again. I'd better get her out of here before she snickered in his face or her lip started bleeding.

"That's very sweet of you," I said. "We'll take a rain check."

He fumbled in the pocket of his wild print rayon shirt. "Make sure you look me up. Here's some drink coupons. To help get the party started."

"Thanks." I accepted for both of us, not trusting Fran's reaction. My mama had raised me to be gracious, no matter what—which I'd found went a long way in getting help or information when I needed it. The part of me related to Aunt Letha wanted to braid poor Ash's remaining strands of hair into a knot on top of his head. Hence the source of many a Southerner's schizophrenia: Should I fight or be polite?

"Could you by any chance tell us where Nut Case is playing now?"

He shrugged. "Not right off the top of my head. Edmonds might know. He'll be in later."

50

I got the full benefit of his expensive dental work. Someone should have told him years ago that sunscreen is the fountain of youth.

"You talking to me?" A voice came from the kitchen, followed by the creaking of the double-swing door.

Ash licked his lips. "Lenn. There you are. Didn't know you were here." His voice grew loud with hollow welcome. "Meet our guests."

I extended my hand to the tall newcomer. "Avery Andrews. This is Fran French."

"Lenn Edmonds. Nice to meet you." His melted chocolate-brown eyes warmed with his smile.

I could see why Ash might not be anxious for us to meet his partner.

"The Lenn Edmonds who played football at the University of South Carolina?"

He ducked his head with practiced modesty, pleased that I knew.

"Long time ago." He patted his slightly padded midsection. "Sure can't run like that now."

"Um, they're looking for Fran's sister," Ash said. "She was supposed to be here Friday."

I held out Neanna's photo. As he studied it, I noticed a middle-aged woman in a tight T-shirt pass by the other side of the galley window. Probably a waitress getting ready for a slow tip night.

"You remember seeing her?" Fran asked.

Lenn stared at the photo and slowly shook his head. "No. Not Friday. She sure looks familiar, but I don't think I've seen her here. What did you say her name was?"

"Neanna Lyles."

He shook his head again. "No. That doesn't ring a bell. She's awfully pretty." He handed Fran the photo.

"You didn't see her, Ash? Ash works the crowd, usually," he explained.

"No." Ash slid his hands in the pockets of his too-tight jeans. "Not that I remember. Big night, Friday."

"Whew, it sure was. Which means tonight'll be dead."

"Excuse me." Fran had just spotted the woman at the far end of the bar. "Excuse me, ma'am." She strode toward her, holding out the photo. "Did you happen to see this woman last Friday night?"

The waitress met Fran halfway, reaching for the photo but studying Fran. Her brassy blond hair was brittle, and her makeup only emphasized the deep wrinkles and sags.

"No-o." She shook her head. "Can't say that I did."

Lenn looked disappointed. He gave Fran a consoling smile. "I hope you find her soon. You must be terribly worried."

Having Lenn Edmonds working the crowd would be good for business, I thought.

"Oh, we've already found her," Fran said. The barb in her voice wasn't lost on either Ash, Lenn, or the waitress.

"She's dead. The police found her body early Saturday."

I tried to watch the two men for their reaction, but found my gaze darting back to Fran. She was too close to the edge and she worried me.

"Oh, my. I'm so sorry." The sun wrinkles around Lenn's eyes softened in concern, and he raised his hand as if he wanted to hug her but then thought better of it. The tip of Ash's tongue flicked out as he glanced at Lenn. He rocked up on his toes, his hands still jammed in his pockets.

Fran looked from one to the other without really seeing them. Her anger over the reality of her words had taken over.

Lenn looked as though he wanted to ask what had happened, but he was astute enough to read the tight set of Fran's jaw and the tears pooled around her eyelashes.

"I'm so sorry," he said.

I stepped to Fran's side and put my arm around her waist.

"Thank you," I said. "If you think of anything, please give me a call. We sure appreciate your time."

I handed both Lenn and Ash one of my business cards and steered Fran toward the door.

A car and a small pickup truck crunched into the lot as we climbed into my car. Probably the hired help. Even though the sun was setting, this place wasn't somewhere people came for an early supper after work. They came here to meet other needs; judging from the jangle of odors inside, eating would not be high on the list.

Fran slumped in the front seat of my vintage Mustang.

"The inn's on the way back into town," I said. "I'll just drop you off and meet you early tomorrow for breakfast. You can get your car from my office then."

She nodded.

I was grateful she hadn't argued about leaving her car. I didn't want her wandering around alone playing Nancy Drew in the middle of the night. Maybe it was her grief. Maybe it was because she felt she could count on me to be the adult so she could take a break from that role, after being the adult for both herself and Neanna—and perhaps for Neanna's Gran. Or maybe she was used to being the pampered, headstrong child. Whatever the reason, her inner child ran the risk of interfering with what she'd hired me to do. I needed to do what I could to prevent that.

I turned onto the winding two-lane road toward Dacus. We passed scattered brick ranch houses and house trailers, some with roadside mailboxes bearing familiar family names. A few cars met us, headlights on now as full dark fell among the hardwoods and pines lining the rural road.

"Avery?"

Fran stared straight ahead. "I want you to understand something. Neanna didn't kill herself."

I didn't reply.

"She didn't. I know you think that's just nutty denial. It's not. I knew Neanna. Sometimes better than she knew herself. I knew the good *and* the bad. She didn't, Avery."

We drove in silence the last few miles to the inn. I pulled slowly into the rutted drive and stopped at the bottom of the front steps.

"I want you to find out what happened. I want you to find out why she's gone. It doesn't matter what it costs."

Now I knew she was talking crazy. No client ever said, "No matter what it costs," not even the well-heeled corporate ones.

"Fran, don't worry. I know the officer who'll be in charge. He's good. We'll find out all there is to know." I patted her on the forearm and studied her profile in the dim light.

When she offered no response, I said, "I'll see you for breakfast in the morning. We can talk about what else needs to be done."

She unlatched and pushed open the long, heavy car door.

"Call me if you need anything tonight, Fran. Promise?"

She leaned down to look in the car and nodded, solemn, before she closed the door and climbed the steps between the gargantuan white porch columns fronting the inn. I hoped she'd find tea, cookies, and comfort inside—something more genteel and less sticky than the Pasture.

Tuesday Morning

The next morning, I parked my car in the area tucked discreetly at the side of the inn and followed the gravel drive around to the grand front entrance.

Fran hadn't come downstairs yet, so I picked up a paper from the stack of Monday's Dacus *Clarion,* dropped some coins in the jar, and sat on a bench in the hall leading to the dining room. At the bottom of the front page, I found the two-paragraph story about the discovery of the body at the overlook.

Noah Lakefield, the *Clarion*'s new—and only—field reporter, quoted a sheriff's department spokesperson saying the death was under investigation. I'd been skeptical when Noah had first accepted the job in Dacus, and amazed when he'd seen the business that brought him to town finished and decided to stay. With his exuberant hair and his lithe build, he had equal amounts of charm and bluster, depending on which he needed to get a story. His talent and drive should have taken him on to a larger, more prosperous paper, but he also had a boyish naivete that could be contagious—and seemed unusual for someone who had been a fire-breathing investigative reporter.

The paper comes out midday on Monday, Wednesday, and Friday, so Noah would be hard at work on tomorrow's edition. With the death listed as a suicide, he wouldn't be chasing after Fran. That would violate the editorial policy for both Walter, the editor, and my dad, the paper's new owner. The thin ten-page paper was filled with high school sports, elementary school science projects, civic group meetings, and yard-of-the-week photos. In a small town, embarrassing personal stories were told elsewhere.

I folded the newspaper when I heard footsteps descending the creaky staircase.

"Avery, I hope I didn't keep you waiting."

Fran looked fresh, as though she'd managed to sleep. She saw the paper in my hand, and her mouth tightened. "Is there any mention?"

"Just a small piece about finding her."

She nodded, her face solemn. After a pause, she held out her hand. I turned the paper so she could see the article, discreet and innocuous at the bottom of the page. She seemed relieved.

"What's this?" She pointed to another small article in the space above the two paragraphs about Neanna. Before I could read the headline, one of the B and B's owners greeted us with a cheerful, "Good morning. Two for breakfast?"

I followed Fran to our table, biting the inside of my lip to keep from laughing at the news article she'd pointed out:

ARE YOU HAUNTED?

A group of paranormal investigators from Charlotte, North Carolina, needs your help.

Does your house exhibit signs of paranormal activity? Do you know places in Camden County where evidence of such activity may be investigated? The group will be conducting investigations in Dacus and Camden County in the coming weeks. Please contact Colin "Mumler" Gaines for information.

The article included a phone number and an e-mail address.

Fran and I sat, listened to the instructions about breakfast, and ordered tea to drink—iced for me, hot for Fran.

"That's odd, isn't it?" Fran said, indicating the article.

I didn't want to laugh, out of respect for her and her grief, but the ghost-hunter plea struck me as ludicrously funny.

"I wouldn't want to be answering Colin Gaines's cell phone for the next several days," I said. "This will draw out every nut in the tri-county area." What kind of nickname was Mumler?

Fran nodded with a faint smile. I was glad to see her smile, though it did little to ease the tightness around her eyes. She headed toward the table filled with fresh fruit and berries while I went for the hot food.

I spooned buttered grits onto my plate and chuckled at the thought of what Mumler would find in his voice mailbox. The lady standing across from me shot a glance through her heavily mascaraed eyelashes as if she feared my lithium had worn off. Probably visiting from a big city, where crazy people were scary because she didn't know them, and only crazy people chuckled to themselves. In bigger cities, maybe the nuts feel they have to straighten up and fit in because all they have is a first impression. In small towns, nuttiness can just hang out in plain view.

I ate my eggs Benedict and let Fran guide the conversation. She talked about the weather and how she hated driving in the traffic on I-85. Maybe she wanted to avoid eavesdroppers in the crowded dining room, or maybe she just needed to pretend life was normal for a while. I couldn't imagine how much her heart must hurt.

All day yesterday and this morning—and likely in my dreams—Neanna had stayed at the edge of thought, coloring my mood with a sadness I couldn't shake. I hadn't known Neanna, but I kept trying to imagine what had been in her head. What drives someone to kill herself? How impotent and angry Fran must feel, thinking she could have done something. How would I feel if I lost my sister Lydia under any circumstances? Especially if I was left wondering what I should have done to stop it.

After we finished eating, I got another pot of tea, and we carried it to Fran's room where we could talk in private.

Before I could sit the pot down, she said, "Avery, I've got to go back to Atlanta. To make arrangements." She stopped, unsure of her voice.

I poured dark tea into a dainty rose-patterned china cup for her, to give her time.

"Avery, you'll find out what happened to Neanna. She didn't kill herself. I—know that. I know I keep repeating that, but I want you to believe it."

With those last words, her reserve broke. She hid her face in her hands and sobbed.

Nothing I could say would ease her grief or save her from the hurt. This was just the next step: denial, anger, bargaining, depression. Before long, I hoped, some acceptance.

I sat on the arm of her overstuffed chair and put my arm around her. Her tears soaked through the shoulder of my shirt, and I thought the force of her sobs would crack one of her thin ribs.

Eventually, when her tears slowed, I went into the bathroom for the box of tissues and a warm washcloth.

"I'm—so—sorry." She hiccuped each word as she wiped her nose.

"I'm glad to see you cry. You were worrying me." She knew what I meant. Her hiccuping breaths slowed as she buried her face in the warm washcloth.

"I want to know what happened," she said, her voice husky. "I can't keep wondering, imagining things that . . ."

Imagining things neither of us could express, about what might have been.

My cell phone buzzed in my pocket. I couldn't put a name to the number, but it looked familiar. Someone I'd called recently. I stepped into the bathroom to answer it, using it as an excuse to give her some space.

"You need to get someone to staff your office."

Edna Lynch, my demanding grandmama private eye.

"Before nine in the morning?" I returned her irritation with my get-serious tone.

It didn't work. "Ever hear of an answering service? Sumbody can track you down? Get you to take your messages?"

She had me there. I hadn't checked my answering machine since yesterday afternoon.

"You have something?"

"I'm standing in the church parking lot in my choir robe calling you, aren't I? I found Skipper Hinson."

"Already?" I didn't ask what her choir was fixing to sing about on a Tuesday morning.

"Yesterday." She wasn't letting up on my laxness. "He's working maintenance and such at the state park this summer. He'll be working in the gift shop today. It opens at ten."

"Thanks, Edna. That was quick."

She gave my compliment a derisive snort, her way of saying, *Of course. You doubted me?*

"The funeral's starting. They're waving us in the back door." The phone clicked off.

She knew where to send the bill.

I stepped into the bedroom. "I know where her hitchhiker is. I can talk to him—"

"Where?" Fran sat up like a bird dog on point. "Can we talk to him now?"

"Um, in a while," I said. "But don't you have to go—"

"I can still make it to Atlanta by midafternoon. How far is it? I just need a few minutes to pack."

"Not far—about twenty minutes. Um, I'll let you pack. Be back in a few minutes to pick you up."

"I'll be ready." She carried the mascara-stained washcloth into the bathroom.

I needed to change shirts. No need to wear a tear-soaked shirt around all day, and I'd just noticed an eggs Benedict blotch.

True to her word, she was pacing in the side yard when my Mustang tires pulled onto the gravel drive twenty minutes later.

I backtracked to Main Street and turned left. The road quickly began the climb into the southern end of the Blue Ridge Mountains.

"You have any music?" Fran indicated my in-dash AM radio, standard equipment in 1964.

"Some bluegrass is all." I had wired a portable CD player and updated the primitive speakers in my vintage Mustang—my grandfather's late-life splurge pulled out of mothballs for me by my dad, when I'd left my large Columbia law firm and my leased BMW.

"That would be nice."

Fortunately the song that came on was "Foggy Mountain

Breakdown," a banjo number, lively and optimistic. Neither of us needed to dwell on a mournful mountain ballad. As a Texas friend of mine had once observed, mountain folk music is full of murder and dying. I tried to argue otherwise, offer a defense of my people. But after listening to some CDs with her ears, I had to admit she was right. Lots of murder and dying. Too much for Fran—or me, right now.

Today, though, the banjo music and the thick green, sun-speckled shade, and the car's eagerness to gobble the curvy road provided some buoyancy. At least for me. Even though the edges of my mind kept asking *what if* and *I wonder why* questions.

I turned into the state park and eased slowly toward the campground store. Waves of nostalgia hit me. Summer day camps, school and church picnics, weekend square dances. I hadn't been here in years, but the weathered wood buildings, thick trees, and narrow, rough asphalt lanes hadn't changed.

Finding Skipper wasn't hard. In the shotgun-long store that served the campground with everything from charcoal and milk to diapers and ceramic toothpick holders stamped SOUTH CAR-OLINA, he was the only lanky, bored-looking clerk. In fact, he was the only human being inside the store.

He was younger than I'd expected, probably college-aged. He showed that lack of interest in anything not playing on a computer or game screen, traits indigenous to guys his age. But he was clean-shaven, with buzz-cut hair, and his khakis were neatly creased.

"Skipper Hinson?"

"Uh—yeah." He raised an eyebrow in surprise.

"I'm Avery Andrews. This is Fran French. She's Neanna Lyles's sister."

"Oh." An uptick in interest thawed some of his bored ex-pression.

"You and Neanna rode up from Atlanta for the Nut Case concert? You went to the concert together?"

He nodded, his wariness growing with his interest. "I rode with her. A bunch of us went to hear the band."

I cut to the chase. "Neanna died over the weekend, and we're trying to learn everything we can about what happened after she left Atlanta. I'm sure you understand, so her family can know."

His gaze flitted to Fran and back to me, maybe not wanting to see too clearly the questions in her eyes.

"What happened?" He looked me in the eye, his brows knit together.

"She—" I took a deep breath. That wasn't my news to share.

"We don't know what happened," Fran said with finality.

His eyebrows met in a wrinkle and his jaw was slack, as if he'd been hit in the stomach. I felt bad cornering him at work with the news. He was just a kid, but he was also the last one who'd seen her.

"What kind of mood was she in?"

He shrugged. "Fine. We talked. I mean, I didn't know her. We hooked up on this ride board. Online. I had this job that started this week. And the concert. She seemed fine. She was really funny. We just talked."

"When did you last see her?"

"At the concert."

"Did she give you a ride here, to the park?"

"No. Another guy who works here, him and me rode here after the concert."

"Did you talk to her after that?"

"No-o. I mean, she had a boyfriend in Atlanta. She told me that. So I didn't want to get into any of that. You know."

"Did she plan to meet anybody at the concert?"

"I—don't know." He drawled his words out, thinking.

"Did she run into anybody, introduce you to anybody?"

"She talked to Gerry Pippen. She was really into Nut Case. Knew all this shit about Pippen. The guitarist. She totally wanted to meet him. Thought this might be a good place, since the Pasture was a smaller venue. You know."

"So she met Pippen?"

"Yeah. I saw them talking some while the band was on a break."

"Did she leave with him?"

"I don't know. I don't think so. She showed me her signed CD. She didn't say anything about hooking up."

"Did you see her with anybody else?"

"Naw. Not that kind of crowd. Bunch of greasy old guys. 'You look like somebody I know' or 'You'd look good on me.' Cheesy lines like that. She totally wasn't interested."

"Any idea where she was staying that night?"

"Uh-uh."

"Why was Nut Case playing there? Aren't they pretty popular?"

He shrugged. "Yeah, I guess. That's not really my kind of music."

"What do you like?"

"Bluegrass, mostly. I just went, you know. Hook up with my friends. Get up here. I don't have a car, yet." He emphasized "yet" in the face-saving way of car-less boys.

Fran stepped into the pause. "Was she drinking? Did she do any drugs?"

He didn't seem surprised by the questions, though I was. She hadn't said anything about Neanna having a drug problem, even though Neanna's mother apparently had. Skipper just shrugged. "I don't know. I didn't see her do any. She seemed straight."

"Were there drugs there? At the concert?" she asked.

"Sure."

I didn't quite trust his answer, if for no other reason than he wouldn't want to admit he'd been out of the know.

"Did they sell alcohol to minors?"

He shrugged again, increasingly uncomfortable. "I dunno. Just beer. Someone would get it for you."

Her questions were too hard for him to answer truthfully. You have to make the truth easy and acceptable—or inevitable. *It's okay, everybody does that.* Or *I have a photo of you taking a hit on a pipe.* One or the other.

The bell on the doorknob jangled.

"Thanks, Skipper," I said. A man wearing a white T-shirt stained a faded gray, with an energetic little boy in tow, headed for the milk cooler at the back.

Skipper looked relieved. He resumed his slumped sentry duty at the cash register, his eyes focused on something not in front of him. Maybe we shouldn't have questioned him at work. Even though they hadn't been friends, he had recently shared laughs and a journey with a girl about his age. A girl who was dead. That isn't easy for the very young to contemplate, or for anyone.

"Thanks again," I said.

Outside, Fran climbed into the car and didn't speak until I'd turned onto the two-lane road down the mountain.

"She didn't have a boyfriend in Atlanta," she said. "That was over. She must have said that to scare Skipper off."

Nothing I could say to that. Fran seemed to insist that a lot of things other people knew about Neanna just weren't so.

She didn't speak again for the twenty-minute drive down the mountain to the inn.

"Find out what happened. You know the police here. Keep pushing them."

She turned in her seat to face me as I stopped beside her silver

Honda. "She didn't kill herself. I don't care what you think, she didn't. Find out what happened."

She unzipped her cordovan leather clutch. "Here's a check for a full week's retainer at your regular rate."

The fee I'd quoted had been my *you don't want to pursue this* fee. Fran wasn't easily discouraged. If the check didn't bounce, she could apparently afford to get her way. Now wasn't the time to argue with her. I'd ask some more questions, follow up with Rudy, and return most of her money later.

"The cops here are pretty good," I said.

"Not good enough to solve Aunt Wenda's murder."

"Different cops."

"They'll do an even better job if they know somebody cares." Her gold-flecked green eyes searched my face. "I also want you to see what you can find out about Aunt Wenda's death. That—was important to Neanna. I'd like to—"

"I'll check on that, and I'll be in touch." I hoped answers, even if they weren't the ones she wanted to hear, would give her some peace.

"Thank you." She sounded as though she meant it.

She climbed into her car for her two-hour drive to Atlanta, and I headed to my office, accompanied by the sad edges around my thoughts: *Why?* And *what if?*

Tuesday Morning

As soon as I got back to the office, I took a detour to answer the ringing phone. What was with this phone lately?

"May I please speak to Miz Andrews?"

"This is she."

"Oh. Um. This is Tolly Mart. I—um—I think this is my one phone call."

"Yessir." I tried to sound businesslike while my brain flooded with inappropriate responses, such as, "Are you finishing the weekend up late or starting next weekend early?" Calls to my office from the jail usually start after Friday or Saturday night miscalculations of one sort or another. A Tuesday morning call was a first. "What's the problem, exactly?"

"I—well, I've never done this before?"

No kidding. "Yessir? What exactly?"

He sighed. "None of this. Never been arrested, never been in jail, never called a lawyer. None of it."

"I see."

"One of the fellows in here, he said I should call you. He said you were real good."

"Um-hmm." *Then what's he doing in there, if I'm so good?*

"He said you helped put him in here." That answered my question. Tolly Mart must be reading my mind. "But then he admitted he put himself in here. That's what his therapist said."

"Did he tell you his name?"

"Dells."

Ah, his court-*ordered* therapist. Dells was *back* in jail, for violating the restraining order I'd gotten to keep him away from his wife. He kept showing up where he wasn't supposed to be. He hadn't permanently injured her, but the word "yet" echoed in my head whenever I thought of him. Maybe he was learning something. Not enough, but something.

"How can I help you?"

"I want out of here. There's been some misunderstanding and I—" His voice quavered. I hoped he wasn't about to start crying. The public phone outside the intake cell wouldn't be a good place for that.

"I take it you haven't had a bond hearing yet?"

"No, ma'am." He almost whispered it.

"Tell the officer I'll be there in twenty minutes to have a client conference." That way, he could probably stay in the likely-near-empty holding cell.

"Yes, ma'am."

"I'm on my way."

I could've made it in five minutes, but I needed more caffeine.

As soon as I met him, I knew Tolly Mart was not my standard jailhouse client. Not that I'd had all that many, in the few months since I'd returned home. The ones I did have, though, were those the other attorneys in town were willing to throw my way. Court-appointed cases where the fee wouldn't cover my time. Never the rich kid's DUI and certainly never a guy who could pay his own bill.

Tolly Mart was a pressed and proper forty-year-old, a new breed of criminal client for me. He must have shaved this morning. His short brown hair was carefully combed, and his open-collared oxford shirt and dark slacks weren't wrinkled.

With a firm handshake, he held my hand in both of his, as if he were clasping a life preserver.

"Have a seat," I said.

The deputy had agreed to let me talk to Mr. Mart in an interview room rather than in the usual prisoner-visitor area.

"Start at the beginning. Tell me what happened."

He shrugged, his hands open on his thighs, his gaze direct. "The police showed up at my work this morning and told me I was under arrest."

"This morning? At work?" That explained the fresh-pressed look, but why arrest him at work? Why not pick him up at home and avoid the humiliation?

"What's the charge?" I watched his face, wanting to gauge how he narrated this difficult news.

"For making harassing phone calls to my wife." He dropped his gaze. "And for violating a restraining order she swore out on me."

He wiped his palms down his thighs and back. "But I didn't. Call her. I haven't. I told them that when they first served the order." His voice was urgent, his gaze unblinking.

"You need to start farther back, with you and your wife. You're separated? Divorced?"

"Separated. Getting divorced."

The initial interview is so much easier with guys who've been through the drill before. If this guy had been my first criminal client, we'd both be at a loss. Fortunately, I'd had a couple of good teachers over the last couple of months—guys who'd showed me how things work, from the inside.

"Tell me about the divorce."

I lost his gaze again. He shrugged. "You know. Married for ten years. Then it's over."

"Her idea? Or yours?"

He wiped his palms again. "Hers."

I leaned forward to let him know I was serious, but I kept my voice gentle. "You're going to have to talk to me. I can't help you otherwise."

"She left. She said she thought I had a girlfriend. I swear I didn't—don't."

"Okay. How long have you been separated?"

"Six months?"

"And?"

"Then she got the restraining order."

Restraining orders aren't granted on a whim, as his prison buddy Dells could tell him. Tolly Mart's wife would have had to show evidence of threats or abuse to get the initial order, as well as present evidence of its violation to have him arrested. He wasn't telling me everything.

"Who's your divorce lawyer?"

"I don't have one."

My turn to look surprised. "And hers?"

"Jackson Spurlock."

I knew him only from his ads on the back of the phone

book. His main office was in Greenville, an hour's drive away, but he apparently wallpapered all the small towns for a sizable radius, offering to handle car accidents, personal injury, divorces, and other ills that may befall.

"Why didn't you get a lawyer?"

"Because I didn't want a divorce. I thought she'd come to her senses. No need wasting that money twice."

"Twice?"

"I'd already paid her lawyer."

"Is she still living in your house?"

He nodded.

"And you're living where?"

"I'm renting a room over at the tourist home."

I had no idea it was still in business. Renting a bedroom with a shared bath in a lady's house, with breakfast and dinner included, seemed a nostalgic concept.

"For the last six months?"

He nodded. He looked slightly sick at his stomach. Could he really be this dim? Or was he really good at acting dim?

"Mr. Mart, look at me."

His brown eyes locked on to mine like he hoped I'd toss him a treat.

"You've been calling your wife, harassing her." It was a statement, not a question. A tried-and-true cross-examination technique.

His eyes moistened, but he didn't blink. "I swear."

"What kinds of calls does she claim you've made?"

"According to the warrant, she told the police I'd called her a hundred times, mostly in the middle of the night."

My turn to blink. Would a judge issue an order just on a wife's say-so? I had to admit I didn't know, but I couldn't imagine that even a mass-production lawyer like Jackson Spurlock would

71

seek an order based on nothing more than a soon-to-be ex-wife's say-so.

"Why did your wife think you had a girlfriend?" I circled back to that topic, hoping to catch him by surprise.

His gaze didn't waver. "I don't know."

I pretended to study the legal pad where I'd scribbled scarce few notes. He'd gotten a recommendation for a lawyer from a guy who'd been helped into jail by that very lawyer. He had a naivete that, inside the concrete block walls of an interview room, almost had to be a lie. But who'd make up a story that weak? He didn't look like a kook.

"Sit tight. I'll be right back."

I went into the hall and got the attention of the young officer who was keeping watch over the prisoner.

"Is Rudy Mellin in this morning?"

"I don't know, ma'am. I can check for you."

Ma'am. For Pete's sake, if I was looking that old, I needed more rest.

I stood in the hall while he walked down to a wall phone. I needed to think for a couple of minutes, away from Tolly Mart's moist brown puppy eyes.

The officer strolled back down the hall. "Chief Mellin can see you now, if you'd like."

I was surprised Rudy was in his office and not in a booth at Maylene's, hunched over sunny-side-up eggs with sides of bacon and sausage.

"Can you keep Mr. Mart in there for a while longer?"

"Yes, ma'am." He didn't act like my concern was unusual—or misplaced. Probably saved him some paperwork.

"Thank you."

————

Rudy's office was around the corner, past the main entrance and information desk, and down another short, nondescript beige-green hall.

"Hey." He didn't even look up when I knocked on his open door. "What's up?" He continued scribbling his signature on a stack of letters.

"I hate to show my ignorance to anybody but you. How long's it take to get a bond hearing?"

"For?" He kept scrawling, his dishwater-blond head bowed over his task.

"Violation of a restraining order."

He looked up at that. "You're here to get a wife beater out of jail?" His tone was part surprise, part derision.

"No." Mine was all derision.

He cocked an eyebrow and held his pen, waiting for the story.

"He was ordered to stop calling his wife."

"Any violence?"

"Not that I know of. I haven't seen the paperwork." I didn't want to confess the extent of my inexperience, even to an old friend like Rudy. I had, after all, only heard one side of the story—and limited vision is always fraught with peril.

"The magistrate who sets bond is out today. One of the judges is handling the bond hearings, but he's moved them to this morning before the lunch recess. Just call the clerk."

"Okay." The clerk should have the paperwork filed in the case up to this point. I also needed to get my client to sign a contract of representation. More paperwork. My least favorite thing. "Thanks."

I turned to leave him to his signing, but then stuck my head back in the door. "You gonna be here awhile?"

"Yeah," he said. "Having a little trouble getting through with all this. Interruptions, you know." He didn't look up.

I patted the door frame. "See you later." I wanted to see if he had any more information about Neanna Lyles, but I first needed to get a bond set for Mr. Mart.

The young deputy outside the interview room assured me that he could leave Mr. Mart in the interrogation room for a while longer.

At the courthouse two blocks away, Alma, the court clerk, said the judge had set the hearing right before he took his lunch break.

"Always a sandwich in his office," she said, smiling over the purple glasses perched on her nose.

"Thanks." I gave her my cell phone number, in case things moved more quickly than she anticipated. "Do you have the copy of the petitioner's file in the Mart divorce case? Mr. Mart has recently retained me."

I needed to explain my fee arrangement and get Mart's signature on a fee agreement. At least I'd finally gotten smart and stuck several in my briefcase so I didn't have to run down the block and across Main Street to my office. I put the photocopied sheets Alma had given me into my slender case and walked the two blocks back to the Law Enforcement Center. Might as well take care of some other business while we were waiting on the judge.

Mr. Mart sat twiddling his thumbs in the bare room. He nodded numbly as I explained our business details, and he carefully penned his signature.

"Would you like something to read?"

He shook his head. "No, not really."

I'd rather be hung by my heels than left without book or paper and pen, but I slipped out and left him to study the stained Formica tabletop.

Rudy was nodding into the phone, so I stopped in the doorway.

He waved me in and kept nodding and muttering, "Mm-hm, mm-hm," then, "Okay. Thanks."

Fascinating conversation. No wonder he hadn't minded me listening in.

"Yes'm, what can I do for you?"

I didn't tell him not to start with the "ma'am" stuff. He'd never let up if he thought it bugged me.

"Any news about Neanna Lyles?"

I plopped down in the chair across the desk from him. His office could barely hold its furniture: a large desk, two thinly padded chairs for visitors, a bookcase, and a credenza behind his desk. The only window faced out into the hallway.

"Has the ME finished?" I asked.

"Autopsy's done. Report isn't. Should get the tox report today. If we need more, a full run might take weeks. Good news, her sister didn't have to view the body. The coroner accepted her ID of the photo."

I was glad Fran had been spared seeing Neanna's body. Seeing a loved one is upsetting enough after the mortician has replaced the color drained from the face and covered what would haunt dreams and shouldn't be seen.

"What do you think? Did she kill herself?"

He settled back in his chair. "Lots says she did."

"Such as?"

"Single gunshot wound to the head. A killshot, disrupted the brain stem. Gun in the seat beside her. A positive GSR—gunshot residue—test on her hand."

"A note?"

"No note. Not yet, anyway."

"Not yet?"

"She could've mailed one to somebody. Or left a journal or something."

"Who saw her last?"

Another shrug. "Dunno. She had a concert ticket stub in her pocket and a signed concert CD by the same group in her console."

"Have you talked to her sister Fran? Or to Skipper Hinson?"

"I haven't. It's technically not my case."

"Oh." That surprised me. Was I treading on tender territory here?

Rudy gave a deep sigh. "A'vry, we just got this, okay. Things take time. There are other crimes around here that people also demand we pay attention to, you know."

More important than signing letters asking for donations to the Police League? I didn't say that out loud since I didn't want him to know I'd been reading upside down, curious about the surprising amount of paperwork he'd been signing.

"Would you let me see the file?"

He stared at me over the cluttered expanse of his desk. "When we get a file, Avery, I surely will."

My cell phone buzzed.

"Judge Lane can see you now." Alma's rich drawl didn't waste words.

Judge Lane? Oh, no. Not him. Not twice in two days. Why hadn't I bothered to ask which judge was holding the bond hearings today?

"I'll be back." Rudy didn't act heartbroken when I took my leave.

Dang. The judge moved quicker than I'd expected. I hadn't had time to read over the few pages Alma had copied for me on Tolly Mart's divorce.

I tried to glance through them as I half ran back to the courthouse. Good thing I hadn't worn heels today. For Mr. Mart's sake, I couldn't risk being late.

The only people in the courtroom to witness the judge's displeasure were Mr. Mart and a very young assistant solicitor I didn't recognize. Probably fresh out of law school—could she have just finished in May and be here handling cases on her own? Alma sat in the clerk of court's chair waiting to take notes on whatever was making Judge Lane look so dyspeptic. My guess? Something to do with what I hoped I'd misread on my way up the courthouse steps.

"Am I to understand that you are asking me to set bond for Mr. Mart?"

"Yes, Your Honor."

He sounded incredulous, as if bond did not exist, as if the Magna Carta itself had never seen the pen of King John.

"Miz Andrews." His frown deepened, directed only at me. "I realize you've come to town with quite a reputation for courtroom—" He paused.

My adrenaline pumped and I fought the urge to tighten my muscles, relaxing and shifting easily on my feet. Fight-or-flight responses could backfire in a battle of wits if those primitive instincts weren't channeled.

"—fireworks," he said finally. "Some successes, certainly." His acknowledgment was grudging. "But I must say, in our two short meetings, I fail to see evidence of the courtroom prowess of which I've heard."

I kept my gaze steady, shifting my stance only slightly, my version of a fighter getting the feel of the ring. No way I'd let him think he'd landed a blow.

"First, you failed to effectively counsel a client about the law prior to a hearing held at taxpayer expense. Then—" He leaned forward, as if to get in my face even though I stood a good ten feet away.

"Then you come in here in my very next court session and

ask me to set bond for a man who, despite my stern warning and his professed understanding of the consequences, has persisted in phoning his estranged wife, the petitioner in the case, a total of—" He stopped more for effect than to actually read the number. "One hundred twenty-seven times!"

Exactly as I'd feared. I hadn't misread the paper.

"Not only that!" The judge's face had bloomed into a burgundy hue. "He persists in denying that he's done this, despite overwhelming—" His voice squeaked at that point. Judge Lane had never been a trial lawyer, and family court judging likely hadn't allowed him to develop an oratorical timbre.

He cleared his throat and took a long breath. Some of the redness faded from his cheeks. "—overwhelming evidence in the form of telephone company records showing these calls at all hours, day and night. Made from his phone to the petitioner's home phone number. Does your client deny he was at his residence at 2:00 A.M. on Sunday night? Just to pick one instance."

Before I could respond, Mr. Mart was shaking his head.

"No, Your Honor," I said.

Judge Lane took another deep breath, an angry one. "Miz Andrews, I suggest that you do whatever necessary to present yourself and your clients in a better light the next time you appear in this court. Because of the repeated nature of the offense, the lack of acknowledgment or remorse, and my concern over the petitioner's welfare, bond is set at fifty thousand dollars. Court is dismissed."

He whacked the gavel with such force, I feared the head would fly off. Even the court reporter flinched, her eyes wide as she spoke her final words into her dictating mask. The judge swept through the door behind his bench in an angry swirl of black robe.

I sat down next to Mr. Mart. My legs were shaking too much from pent-up anger to stand. I released it in the only direction I had.

"A hundred and twenty-seven times?" I leaned close, my voice low.

He looked like he wanted to either start crying or throw up. He showed none of the flash of anger I'd felt at the judge's berating. He leaned forward, his elbows propped on his knees, his fingers knotted together.

"I haven't." He looked up, still shaking his head. "I haven't. How do I prove I haven't?"

His voice trembled, like lava sending up a tiny vapor stream through a fissure. I liked the anger, glad he didn't let it flare out of control but glad it was there. For me, it pointed toward his innocence. But then, I can be duped.

"Wait here for just one sec," I said, mostly to the police officer waiting to escort him away.

I caught the young assistant solicitor just outside the courtroom and introduced myself.

"I'm April," she said, her handshake mostly limp fingers. She had heavy brown hair that swathed her shoulders and porcelain skin that shows up in retouched ad photos more often than on real people. In her very high heels, she towered over me. A distinct disadvantage.

"I just got this case this morning and wanted to make sure I had the latest phone records and other information from your files." I wasn't asking a favor. Prosecutors are required, thanks to the U.S. Supreme Court's *Brady* decision, to turn over all evidence—including exculpatory evidence that might free a defendant. Most do it without a formal *Brady* motion, but many have to be reminded.

She hesitated, looking first at the creased brown accordion file under her arm, then at me. "Um, I think you do?" When her experience level caught up with her polished looks, she'd be quite formidable. By then, though, she'd be long gone from the Camden

79

County solicitor's office and hired on with a first-rate firm, making real money with her criminal court trial experience.

I pulled a business card from my jacket pocket. "I'm not certain that I have everything, especially the phone records that precipitated the arrest this morning. The judge didn't seem to be in the mood to talk about the evidence. Don't know what blew a breeze up his robe."

"No-o." She actually twittered, looking nervously around. Embarrassed for Judge Lane, for me, or for herself because she witnessed it?

"I take it Mrs. Mart's attorney supplied those records?"

"Um." She rolled her eyes up, thinking. "I believe so. I can check."

"Would you mind faxing over what you have? I got the file from the clerk's office this morning. I'd appreciate seeing anything you have as soon as you can get it to me."

"Sure." She nodded, her luxurious hair cascading as she wrestled with her bulky files and extended her hand. I shook her birdbone fingers.

Mr. Mart still slumped in his chair at the defendant's table. The deputy sat in silence near the courtroom door.

"Okay." I slid into the chair and leaned close for privacy.

"I don't have fifty thousand dollars," he said, looking heartsick.

"A bail bond usually requires ten percent and it doesn't have to be in cash."

His expression said fifty thousand and five thousand were all the same to him.

"I'll try to find out what's going on with these phone records. Meanwhile, it wouldn't hurt for you to talk to a bail-bond company." His cell buddy Dells could probably give him a name or two.

"I'm sorry."

He nodded. He might be new to this, but he wasn't stupid.

"The judge didn't order any restrictions on your phone use in jail, but they'll be monitoring your calls."

I didn't want to scold him and tell him to behave himself, but I sure didn't want him to do anything stupid. I stared at him, hoping for an insight. I'd believed him when he said he didn't know about the phone calls. Just how crazy was he?

He studied the oak wood grain on the judge's bench and gave an absentminded nod.

"Call me if something comes up. I'll be in touch with you. Also, I want your permission to hire a private investigator."

His gaze snapped around to me but his slump didn't shift.

"Her fees are reasonable and she's quick. I'm afraid I won't be able to get the bond reduced just based on you saying you didn't do it because it's apparently your word against some phone records. We need to find out what's going on here, okay?"

"So I can't go back to work."

Who is this nut who'd gotten my number from a wife beater in a holding cell?

"I'll see you later," I said and reached to shake his hand.

The act of reaching to accept my handshake roused him a bit.

"What can I tell my boss about when I'll be back at work?"

Good question.

He shrugged, with a look that said he knew he didn't have many options.

Midmorning Tuesday

As I strode down the block toward the Law Enforcement Center, I dialed Edna Lynch to give her the particulars on Tolly Mart's case. When I had trouble walking and flipping through the few pages Alma had photocopied for me, I sat on the weather-worn cement steps cut into the hill leading up to the county agriculture extension office and balanced the file on my lap.

"The complaint says one hundred twenty-seven calls," I said, the bad news confirmed in writing.

Edna's *harrumph* needed no elaboration.

"I'll fax you the phone company records as soon as I get them."

"How 'bout you just leave them at your office for me to pick up?"

"Mm, I could, I guess." I was trying to think where I would be later in the day. Nothing today had worked out as I'd planned.

"I probably won't be back there to make copies until mid-afternoon."

"You say they came and arrested him as soon as he got to work this morning?" She didn't sound happy—but then, Edna seldom does.

"Yes'm."

"I'll get back with you." My phone went silent.

I sat watching the occasional car pass, feeling for the first time the warm cement on my thighs and the increasing stickiness in the air as the sun moved higher. Nobody ever used these steps because the parking lot was around back, so a couple of the drivers slowed and stared, checking to see if I needed help or, more likely, to see if they knew me.

Just past the graveyard, in the direction of Rudy's office, the sidewalk lay in shade. Using the metal handrail, I pulled myself up and turned toward the shady sidewalk.

At the Law Enforcement Center's front desk, I said to the young woman on duty, "Chief Deputy Mellin, please."

"Your name?"

"Avery Andrews."

She eyeballed me as she picked up the handset, probably making use of the identification skills she'd studied in a textbook at the academy.

"Chief Deputy Mellin is not in his office." Her tone said she expected that to be the end of the matter.

"Could you page him for me, please?" I smiled sweetly.

She held my gaze a moment, then reached for the handset again. Maybe she feared I was a stalker, a dangerous ex-girlfriend, or head of a citizens' complaint committee—in short, bad news for Chief Deputy Mellin and, as a result, bad news for her.

I paced about on the polished institutional tile, watching the heat shimmer on the car windshields in the parking lot. Civilian cars. The official vehicles were parked around back in a separate lot, both for ease in transferring arrestees and for security of the vehicles—vandalized police cars were hard to explain to the county commissioner's budget committee.

I glanced at my watch. *Dang.* Rudy had probably headed out the back to lunch.

The switchboard set buzzed about the time I turned to the guardian of the gate to call off the search.

She covered the receiver and whispered, "Your name again?"

Less than a minute later, Rudy leaned around the door and motioned with a manila file folder for me to follow him.

"You ready for lunch?" he asked over his shoulder.

"Sure." If you want to talk to Rudy, being ready to eat on command was a prerequisite.

He tucked the folder under his arm and led the way.

Rudy, the bulked-up remains of a successful 3-A high school right tackle, still works out sporadically, but he's not running any wind sprints. He's what my daddy calls a right big ol' boy, the kind who can lift a perp up by the throat should the need arise, but he couldn't easily turn and look over his own shoulder.

He rounded the corner and stopped so quickly I almost plowed into him. He'd almost collided with a guy also wearing a deputy's uniform, this one with a slight build and a challenge on his face.

"Chief Mellin." His tone said he might spit on Rudy's shoes.

"Rodney."

"I was coming to see you."

"I'm heading out."

The officer didn't budge, his shoulders drawn back. The set of his jaw said he was looking for a fight.

Rudy stood solid. The officer noticed me standing behind Rudy. My presence didn't make him dial down his intensity.

"I hear you're messing with my case."

"I'm doing my job. Nothing stopping you from doing yours." Rudy leaned forward, emphasizing his height advantage.

"I'm going to the sheriff."

My eyebrows shot up. He sounded like some kid running to tattle to the teacher.

"You got an extra set of balls, you go for it."

He stepped past Rodney, opening the way for me to follow. I couldn't bring myself to look at Rodney, offering only a curt nod. His fury whistled through his clenched teeth as I passed.

Maylene's still had some breakfast stragglers. Rudy must not have made it in for breakfast this morning, since he was hungry so early.

We slid into a back booth, with Rudy facing the door, and placed our orders.

"What was that all about?"

"Dumbass doesn't have sense enough to wet his finger and see which way the wind is blowing. Thinks L.J. actually hired him and his book learning to be a detective."

"He's mad about you looking into Neanna's death?"

"He ain't seen mad."

I let it go. Rudy was a big boy and knew how to take care of himself. Most important, he knew how to take care of L.J. and keep things from blowing back on her. Which is what really mattered to L.J.

"So, you got a present for me?"

"I signed out the evidence file. You wanted to see it for yourself." He didn't hand it to me. "First, though, tell me about her sister."

"What's to tell? She's grieving. She misses her sister. She feels guilty, wondering what she could've done to prevent it. She's smart, very polished, and driven to find out what happened."

Rudy focused on buttering a biscuit from the napkin-lined plastic basket. "You know they aren't really sisters."

He watched for my reaction.

"Yeah." Quick work by the sheriff's department. "But they thought of themselves that way. That's what matters."

His turn to be surprised, that I already knew.

"So what brought her here from Atlanta? The dead sister."

I winced at his callousness, even though I knew Rudy, like any cop, medical malpractice attorney, doctor, or nurse—anyone who deals with human difficulty had to develop self-protective calluses.

I took a sip of ice tea, wanting to buy a moment to think. No need to let my friendship with Rudy blur the lines of my client's confidences.

"The concert," I said. "And curiosity. You know her aunt—Neanna's real aunt—was murdered here."

Rudy nodded, his eyes hooded. He'd wanted to know if I knew.

"Neanna was—curious." I'd hold the rest of my cards for now.

"Why'd her sister hire you?"

"Answers."

"She doesn't trust us?"

He read enough on my face to draw the conclusion he'd expected.

"Some of that," I said. "Face it, her aunt's murder is still unsolved. She doesn't know anybody in Camden County. How would you react, if you were her?"

He slid the folder across the table. I opened it on the bench seat beside me, blocking it from view so no idle passerby could get a glimpse that might ruin his lunch.

The photos were held in plastic-sleeved sheets. The first photo showed the rear of a dusty blue Honda taken from twenty feet away. The car sat on rough-patch asphalt littered with gravel and debris. In the second and third, the camera moved closer with each shot.

To the right of the car ran a silver guardrail, dented and pocked with rust. Beyond the guardrail, treetops were visible, so the ground must fall away steeply on the other side. The car had a Georgia license plate.

"Where is this?" I hadn't asked exactly where they'd found her. Judging from the photos, I guessed a pull-off on a steep, little-traveled mountain road.

Rudy studied me a moment with narrowed eyes. "The overlook above Moody Springs."

"You're kidding."

Of course he wasn't. Rudy could tell I was surprised by the news. "Um, we—some of us were just talking about Moody Springs yesterday," I explained. "Odd coincidence."

"We're trying to keep it quiet. Don't need a bunch of sightseeing ghouls up there getting theirselves run over."

Ghouls—or ghosters. I hoped the newspaper article had yielded more promising haunted places for them to visit.

"That's a busy road," I said. "An odd choice. And such a beautiful spot. How . . ." I trailed off into my own thoughts. Who drives to a spot like that and thinks, *This is a lovely place to die?* Had Gran's death and the breakup with her boyfriend and her obsession with Aunt Wenda's death piled up into a depression she couldn't push aside? Had she dwelt on the fact that she was now the same age Wenda had been when she died?

I flipped to the next picture. The photographer was standing close behind the car. The headrest on the front seat blocked the view but, after some study, I could make out a body, leaned slightly to the right, slumped over the steering wheel. I could also guess what was obscuring part of the left side of the windshield.

The next photo, taken from maybe ten feet away on the driver's side of the car, showed the body clearly through the open window, although what remained looked human only because I knew what I was seeing.

"I didn't bring all the crime-scene photos, just the key ones. They aren't all in the book yet. Too much trouble hauling everything around loose."

Something in Rudy's tone made me look up from the photos. I kept the file on the seat beside me. He took a gulp of his tea, so I couldn't read on his face what the loose photos implied, but I knew the case book would be Rodney's responsibility, the irate would-be detective. The clear tea glass looked tiny in Rudy's hand.

Rudy, whose hair often sticks up in a cowlick in back, was scrupulously well organized when it came to managing the few criminal cases each year that called on him to be a detective. Rodney better make sure he got his act together.

I flipped quickly to the next shot. "Thanks," I said. "This is plenty of pictures." Maybe too many. Sadness washed over me in a wave.

The next photo showed a close-up of the car's window frame. Bits of glass—the thick, almost round balls of safety glass from a broken car window rather than the shards that plate glass or a mirror would produce—lay along the edge of the window. Of course. The window was open because it was broken. Not rolled down. Shot out.

The next photo showed the ground, with enough of the car visible to give it visual reference. A few bits of glass dotted the ground underneath the door.

The waitress—new to Maylene's, which wasn't unusual because the turnover here was legend—plopped our plates and another plastic basket of biscuits and giant squares of cornbread down in front of us and smacked our checks onto the table.

I stayed twisted around in the seat, thumbing through the last few photos. Most were the scene-setting variety, not the close-ups with the right-angle ruler to measure the smallest bits of evidence or to show the wound details. These photos recorded the body's position before she was removed, washed, and probed inside and out.

I paused at one of the photo sheets. One shot taken through the open passenger door showed the gun on the front seat. An automatic pistol, solid black and ominous. The next, a close-up of her hand, showed dark flecks dotting the side of her forefinger and back of her hand. Her palm was clean, her fingers delicate and waxy.

The next picture captured the view through the passenger door. If you could ignore the ominous dark spatters and avoid wondering what was on the door frame and headrest behind her, you could almost believe she was sleeping. Her shoulder-length pale hair fell over the lower part of her face.

I closed the file folder, hiding the photos from view. That was enough for now.

"Where did she—shoot herself? You called it a kill shot."

"Behind the right ear and the right ear canal, into the brain stem. She died instantly."

Kill shot.

"You gonna eat your tomatoes?" He reached for the three bright red wedges decorating my lettuce salad without waiting for an answer.

I picked up my fork and stirred my bleu cheese dressing. The macaroni and cheese smelled good, crusty and brown on top.

A misspent youth, immersed as a young lawyer in medical records, physician textbooks, and photographs of the violence doctors can do to a human body trying to save it—or what an incompetent doctor can do in the name of "practicing" medicine—had left me able to distance myself from gruesome photos and the aftermath of injury. For some reason, though, I couldn't as easily separate myself from Neanna's private and devastatingly final act. Was it because of her sister, because I had a sister?

"Did you look at all of them?"

"No, not quite." I was still tossing my salad to mix the lumpy dressing. I'd known Rudy since kickball in grammar school. He was good at a lot of things, but he wouldn't be much help figuring out my emotional reaction to Neanna's death.

He stared at me, waiting. No food in his mouth or on his fork. "Look at the last ones."

I put my fork down, flipped the file open, and turned the stack of photos over to begin at the end of the stack. These photos were of the inside of the car trunk. I kept turning until I found the first in the series: a view of the open trunk from several paces away, with each photo moving progressively closer.

Inside the trunk was a battered blue American Tourister hard-sided suitcase. When had those things been popular? Before some wise man put wheels on the bottom and made them small enough that we could lift our own. I remembered the last time my mother's college roommate came to visit when I was a kid. Her bag, one just like this one, had weighed a ton, full of gifts for Lydia and me.

The suitcase lay open in the trunk, clothes strewn about—something lacy and pink, some jeans, a red sweater, a black bra. I glanced at Rudy. He was chewing now, slowly, watching me.

The last photos were close-ups of the suitcase itself. The blue lining was loose. I studied the close-up shots of the two halves. The lining had faded in spots but didn't look as though it had rotted or shredded from age or wear.

"The lining was torn out of the suitcase?"

He gestured with his fork. "Great minds thinking alike here."

He cut off another hunk of crispy fried flounder. It looked better than my "vegetable" plate: carrot salad, lettuce sans tomatoes, bleu cheese dressing, macaroni and cheese, and boiled crookneck squash.

"Where was her purse?"

He bowed his head as if acknowledging that his pupil was on track. "In the trunk. Down in the wheel well. Maybe I didn't include that photo."

"Also dumped out and ripped up?"

He nodded, chewing.

"Why would she do that?" I didn't need to say that out loud.

"I'm guessing we both got a guess."

"That she didn't."

"That'd be my guess."

I sat a moment, digesting the implications. "Didn't you say she had no ID?"

"They found it when they worked the trunk. Down under the spare tire."

"Did you find a scrapbook?"

"No. Should we?"

"She had one with news articles about her aunt's death. Her sister thought she brought it with her."

We both sat silent for a moment, then I said, "Back up, Rudy. How come you decided she committed suicide?"

"You're talking to the wrong person."

I scooped up a forkful of macaroni. "Suppose you start talking now."

"You met our new baby detective."

I covered my mouth with my hand so I could talk around my food. "He's the one who worked the scene."

He nodded.

I turned back to the file folder, looking again at those final two shots.

"He's a detective? He can't be much younger than you."

"He's been to the FBI Academy." Rudy emphasized the last words with raised hands and eye rolls and a body wiggle that put the disdain in his voice into motion.

"At any age, you wouldn't have missed a ransacked suitcase." I cocked my head to the left, toward the file folder beside me.

He shrugged and pushed his jealousy or disgust or whatever was going on with him and the baby detective out of sight as quickly as it had appeared. "Cop years are like dog years," he said. "They go by quick, age you quick. He'll learn."

"Meanwhile?"

"Meanwhile, I got L.J. to put me in charge of this. After she saw these, she agreed."

Sheriff L. J.—Lucinda Jane—Peters had been a high school classmate of ours. If there had been a senior class superlative category for "most likely to break the law," L.J. would have won hands down, a qualification that surprisingly made her a pretty good sheriff, if you overlooked her tendency to bully people.

"That going to cause more hard feelings when the new kid finds out you squeezed him out of his case?"

"I'll work with him, but if he messes up, then who the hell cares whose feelings get hurt?"

We ate in companionable silence. I had to rearrange some things in my brain.

"Okay, so what do you have so far? No suicide note, a positive GSR test. The window glass was blown out. No way somebody could've shot her from outside, on the driver's side?"

"Naw. I called the ME after I saw those photos, just to double-check. Entry wound is on her right, exit wound on the left."

"But—" I paused, the significance of the photo of the driver's side door crystallizing for me. "Explain the glass. If the bullet came from inside the car, wouldn't the glass fall outside on the ground?"

I knew from experience how much glass a broken car window left and how much vacuuming it took to clean it all up; someone had broken the window in my firm-leased BMW when I worked in Columbia.

"Good eye," he said. "That attracted everyone's attention. Most of the broken glass fell inside the car, but the window slopes in slightly, which could explain why it fell inside rather than outside."

On TV, somebody would gather the glass and glue the whole window back together to check which side showed exit beveling, just to make sure. Maybe Rudy could suggest that to the baby detective. Something to keep him busy.

"Was it her gun?" I asked.

"Don't know. Stolen in a home robbery in Birmingham four years ago."

I couldn't see somebody with Fran's privileged background buying a hot gun on the street from a fence, but Neanna had lived life closer to the edge, maybe had run with folks who could have gotten her a stolen gun.

"Any word on the tox screen?"

"A little pot. Some alcohol. A lot of Xanax."

Two thoughts running on different tracks collided in my brain. My emotional first response was, *No, don't tell me she'd been using. Like mother, like daughter?* The second, more rational response, I asked aloud. "Could she drive on that?" Even if she'd acquired a tolerance, could she navigate unfamiliar mountain roads?

"You'd be surprised the crap some of the folks you meet on the road got in themselves."

He studied his empty plate for a forlorn moment, then asked, "You see the gun?"

I nodded.

"You ever handle one of those? A .40 caliber?"

"Yeah, once. At the range." Dang thing almost unhinged my right shoulder.

"That model's heavier than mine," Rudy said. He could see he didn't have to lead the witness any farther.

I lifted my right arm, elbow stuck awkwardly out to the side, an imaginary muzzle pointed at the base of my skull, the spot where a bullet disrupting the medulla oblongata would stop everything. Instantly. Breathing, muscle movement, everything.

"That would be a difficult shot," I said. The weight of the gun, the angle, her small hands.

He nodded, proud of his pupil.

"Any dessert?" The waitress whisked up our plates, Rudy's wiped clean, mine only half-eaten.

"Peach cobbler," Rudy said without pause.

Maylene's desserts were usually the best thing on the menu, but I wasn't in the mood, even for warm peach cobbler and rock-hard vanilla ice cream. I turned sideways in the padded booth, my back against the wall and my legs stretched out across the bench seat.

I could feel Rudy staring at me. Was he willing me to say it out loud so he wouldn't have to commit himself?

I didn't turn to look at him. "You saying you don't think she killed herself?"

He slid his ice tea glass back and forth between his hands. "Not saying anything for certain. Just raising questions."

"Too many questions."

He glanced at me before his attention fell back to the puddle of condensation spreading from his sweating tea glass.

"It's worth digging into, don't you think?" I asked. "Just to make sure? It's probably suicide, but I'd hate to be wrong."

He shrugged. "That's what I'm thinking."

"It bothers me about that window glass on the inside of the car. I can see how that could happen, given the curve of the door, but at the same time . . ."

He nodded.

"You think we could find a car like that? Do an experiment?"

"You been watching too much TV."

"I was just thinking, Pun's junkyard probably has a car like that." Pun was always helping my dad track down parts for my Mustang. He probably wouldn't ask many questions—or mind if some window glass got broken. "I can check, if you want," I said.

"Maybe." Rudy wasn't going to let himself look too excited—or too committed. Playing it close to his beige uniform shirt? Or was he worried about looking foolish, if Detective Boy found out?

"Do y'all still have her car—Neanna's?"

"Yeah." His tone was cautious.

"Can I look at it? Or is it still—whatever?"

"The crime-scene guys have finished with it, if that's what you mean. But we can't use it for any kind of experi—"

"No, no. I know that. I just wanted—can I see it?"

He shrugged. "Don't know why you'd want to."

I couldn't quite answer that, even for myself. Whenever I'd tried large civil cases, I'd liked to conduct witness interviews myself, see the scene, touch the evidence, read the original hospital records before they were photocopied—even when I couldn't in good conscience bill for that time. I liked to know my case, personally.

"I just want to give her sister some small sense of—" Not closure. Something like this is never over and shut away.

"Understanding?"

I nodded. "Something like that. Too many open questions just makes it that much harder. Maybe it will help convince me that we have the right ending for her."

"I can take you tomorrow, if you want."

"Thanks. Would you all still have the file on her aunt Wenda's murder?"

"Should have. It's still an open case. Reckon you want me to dig that out, too. Anything else, Miz Andrews?"

With his attitude, he made a mighty poor Della Street. No good as Archie Goodwin, either.

The peach cobbler brightened his mood, if only a watt or two. He hunkered over it, using his left arm to protect it from a sneak attack from across the table.

I needed to change the subject. "You ever think about quitting? Doing something different?"

His brow wrinkled in a frown, and he looked at me as if I might know something he didn't. "No-o."

I shrugged. "Just wondered. You know. What else you might find interesting."

"Well, let's see. What could I do? Work in a mill? Everything's heading to Mexico. Nobody pumps gas for a living anymore. Fixing my own car makes me cuss, so my mama'd be by regular to knock knots on my head. Maybe the feed-and-seed store?"

"You ever thought about running for sheriff?"

He snorted. "My wife has. You both gotta be kidding. Kissing be-hinds on county council? Listening to an irate mama scream because a deputy abused her crackhead son? No thanks. I like what I do just fine." He narrowed his eyes. "What makes you ask?"

"Nothing. Just wondered." L. J. Peters, Rudy Mellin, and I had started kindergarten and graduated from high school together. I'd never heard him say how he liked working for L.J. No gracious way to ask how it was to have her for a boss, so I changed the subject.

"You heard about the ghost hunters in town?"

He spooned in a heap of golden crust and peaches Maylene had frozen last summer, dripping with half-melted ice cream. The smell of cinnamon made my mouth moist. "Heard something about it."

"Not a big crew or anything. Three kids. You see their article in yesterday's paper, asking anyone who had paranormal goings-on around their houses to call them?"

He covered his mouth with a filmy paper napkin and gulped, shaking his head in disbelief.

"Isn't that the craziest thing?" I said. "Ghosters running loose."

"Seems to me if you were psychic or whatever," Rudy said, "you could ride around and find ghosts on your own. Shouldn't have to advertise for them like you were looking for a used mobile home or a single white female."

"You believe in ghosts?"

He graced me with only a shake of his head. "Used to like to scare people who did, though." His smile grew as he enjoyed the memory.

"Okay, you can't keep that to yourself. What?"

"Just kid stuff." He wiped his mouth and pushed away his empty bowl. "You know that little cement bridge that turns off the highway north of town, a mile or so before it heads up the mountain?"

"I—think so."

"No side rails, just raised curbing at the sides. You might not even think of it being a bridge. Bottomland pasture on both sides of the road, with a little creek."

I nodded.

"Some of us were out one night, after a football game or some such. Telling ghost stories. Must'a been near Halloween. We drove across the bridge and stopped to see if we could hear the baby crying." He shook his head, smiling at the memory. "Ol' Campbell decided he'd impress his girlfriend, so he got out to walk back across it."

"What baby?"

"You never heard tell of the crybaby? Suppose to hear a baby crying if you walk across the bridge at midnight under a full moon." He snorted.

"I take it you didn't hear any crying."

"Only crying I heard was that dumbass Campbell." He smiled broadly. "Jennie Lee was sitting in the front seat of that old Plymouth I used to have. I got out to watch Campbell, she slid over in the driver's seat and put that sucker in gear. I barely got the back door open. She was moving when I jumped in. But not before I heard it."

He laughed out loud, one of his contagious belly laughs.

"Not the baby," I said.

"Naw. Campbell. Screaming like a girl. He must'a run a good half mile, chasing us and yelling before she stopped the car."

He pinched the bridge of his nose. His eyes had teared up. "We saw a ghost, all right. Campbell was white as a sheet."

I shook my head. High school pranks, whether five years ago, fifteen, or fifty, whether funny or frightening or angst-ridden, always have an intensity about them that survives. Our own little ghosts that haunt us.

"I remember that car," I said. A twenty-year-old hand-me-down from his grandmother, that car had been lavished with most of Rudy's money and affection. The rest he'd reserved exclusively for Jennie Lee, a well-endowed, sweet little girl.

I realized how little I knew about Rudy's private life. We hadn't been close friends in high school, so I hadn't gotten regular reports over the years from my family. When I'd come back to Dacus seven months ago, we'd renewed our acquaintance because both of us spent way too much time eating at Maylene's, but that's where it stayed. He wore a wedding ring, but I knew little else about his life away from his chief deputy job. Rudy was like most guys I'd worked with over the years, able to compartmentalize. Then again, I didn't talk about my personal life, either.

"Did you and Jennie Lee get married, even though she tried to steal your car?" As soon as I asked, I knew I'd gotten it wrong.

A cloud passed over his expression. "Naw. That was a high school thing." He didn't elaborate, and I didn't probe further. It might not be a fresh wound, but it looked like it still hurt. High school pranks weren't the only things that created an energy that didn't dissipate much over time.

"Reckon I better get going," Rudy said, slipping the checks out from under the bread basket and handing mine to me.

As we stepped out on the sidewalk, I heard a familiar buzzing sound, like a swarm of angry flies. Donlee Griggs zizzed down the opposite side of Main Street on the scooter he'd acquired a few months earlier—about the same time he'd acquired the tiny girlfriend whose matching round pumpkin-orange helmet mashed into the small of his back as she held on for dear life.

Another poignant trip down memory lane. While Rudy had dated cute girls like Jennie Lee in high school, I was attracting the likes of gigantic, slow-witted Donlee. The crush he had on me had resurrected itself when I'd helped him out pro bono on a drunk-and-disorderly charge back in November, but his unwanted attentions had evaporated like morning mist on a tree-shrouded creek as soon as his little motor-scooter mama had appeared. Maybe she'd brought the scooter with her. Either way, Donlee drove by, looking neither right nor left as he passed us.

Tuesday Afternoon

"If you expect to have anybody wants to hire you, you got to get you a receptionist. Totin' a cell phone around, answering it on the fly, don't cut it. You need a receptionist. Somebody make this like a real place of business."

Edna Lynch had walked in my front room lecturing and didn't stop to catch her breath until she'd backed me into my inner office.

"Uh—"

"My niece Shamanique is available. She can do what you need done. You want her this afternoon?"

"Uh—"

"You don't have to pay her but minimum wage. She's on probationary work release right now."

My eyebrows shot up in surprise. I didn't even get *uh* out.

"Bad checks, thanks to a worthless boyfriend'a hers. She ain't gonna have to worry about having her probation revoked. She gonna have to worry about me beating her sorry ass to within an inch of her life, she messes up again."

Edna's voice had taken on the lilt of a street preacher. Somewhere back along the line, I suspected she and my great-aunt Letha had been separated at birth—even though Edna is black and closer to my mother's age.

"I'd be glad to meet her." How could I say no? If I did decline, Edna and Melvin might gang up on me.

Edna had refused the offer of a chair, so we both stood in front of my desk. "Just stopped by on my way to the clerk's office," she said. She glanced up at the crystal chandelier. I needed to dust it, maybe bleach it or something.

"I take it what I hear is right, this Mart divorce is a bad breakup, mostly on her side?"

"That's what I understand," I said. "Of course, I only have Mr. Mart's side of the story."

"Most folks seem to be taking his side, from what I hear. That duhn't excuse driving somebody crazy with hundreds of phone calls."

"No."

"He was arrested at work instead of his apartment. The cops tell you why?"

I shook my head.

"Because she told her lawyer she didn't know where he lived, just where he worked."

I frowned. "Surely—"

"Can you check that with your client?"

"Yes, ma'am." It's a small town. How could his wife not know where he was living? Why would he keep that a secret from her?

"I'll get Shamanique over here this afternoon," Edna said over her shoulder as she passed into the front parlor, her brown polyester pants whistling faintly on her thick thighs. Edna, with her close-cropped mini-Afro, was shaped roughly like a bowling ball—thick, not tall, plenty hard.

I stayed in my office and glanced up at the chandelier. Nothing I could do with either Neanna or Tolly Mart and, as usual, I felt frustrated by inaction. Cleaning the chandeliers could count toward my work-for-rent deal with Melvin. Resealing the toilets could wait.

I checked a couple of home-repair books about the best way to clean crystal chandeliers. As usual, I'd end up calling Mom or Dad when I found the instructions inadequate. The chandelier had accumulated grime for many years, wood smoke from the fireplaces, and probably cigarette smoke from the now-gone days when people saw life through a softly filtered haze of burning leaves. The more I studied it, the more I feared it would be an all-out project.

I gathered my supplies—glass cleaner, bleach, a bucket of warm water, some smooth cotton cloths worn full of holes, and a space-age duster. In short, everything I could think I might need. I changed into overalls, knowing I'd need the pockets, and maneuvered my ladder into place. About the time I climbed to the top, the bell hanging on the front doorknob jangled.

Edna appeared at the foot of my ladder, her hands on her hips, her lips pursed, studying me with that mixture of disappointment and pity I've come to expect from her. In tow, she had a young woman. Her creamy milk-chocolate face was much lighter than Edna's. Her long legs looked graceful when she stood still, but when she sauntered over to the front window to look out, she moved with that sassy, hip-popping stroll that looked as though she had a techno beat playing in her ear.

"Hello," I said, backing down the aluminum ladder from my twelve-foot ceiling. I never notice how loudly a ladder groans until I'm heading down from a height.

"This is Shamanique. She's here to help you in the office."

Shamanique turned back to us and stood with one hip jutted out. She wore a denim skirt that, on somebody with short legs like me, wouldn't have looked so short. But she had giraffe legs. Her gold hoop earrings hung almost to her shoulders, and her hair was lacquered into an elaborate pile on her head.

Edna turned her disapproval laser on her young niece, who got the message without a word spoken. Same as I always did. Edna has loud thoughts.

Shamanique extended her hand. "Pleased to meet you," she said with rehearsed politeness.

Her Fu Manchu nails were airbrushed with artful swoops, and her eyes danced with a sassiness that could spell trouble or fun. Which surfaced depended on the circumstances and her mood, I was sure.

"You interested in doing some office work?" I asked.

She cocked her head to one side in a half shrug. "Sure."

"You type? Do bookkeeping? That sort of thing?"

In the tiniest uptick at the corner of her mouth, I could suddenly see the family resemblance. She was thinking, *Duh, 'course.* But she said, "Yeah. Yes, ma'am." The last was added quickly, her eyes cutting toward Edna.

"She can do what you need. She's smart, when she sets her mind. You need a more professional—setting." Edna's disapproving gaze covered me from my paint-splopped sneakers to my overalls sprouting tool handles from every pocket.

"Great. Um—when can you start?"

She gave her lopsided half shrug at the same time Edna said, "Now. That's why she's here."

Great. Having someone work for you requires having work for her to do, which means thinking it through, planning priorities, training her. And deciding how much I could trust her. That would take some time to determine and some private conversations with her, without Edna around ready to grab us both by the nape of the neck and shake us like bad puppies at the slightest provocation.

"Great. Well. Let's head back to my office. I'll show you around and we'll decide what to tackle first."

"What time will you need a ride home?" Edna asked, talking to Shamanique but looking to me for the answer.

I stopped myself before the words "Oh, whenever" came out of my mouth. "Um, five o'clock?"

"I'll just call Gabe, Auntie. You don't have to—"

"I better find your little self on the front porch waiting for me at five. You think I'm so dumb, I don't know Gabe?"

She spit his name with blistering derision, shook her head, and turned for the door, muttering to herself. I caught something about *Gabe* and *lick of sense* and *no count*.

"Well." I rubbed my hands together, my brain racing. I had an employee—one I was expected to pay—and no idea what she could do. She sure wasn't dressed to climb the ladder up to the twelve-foot ceiling.

"Let me give you the grand tour." That wouldn't take long. The ornate Victorian had a rather simple floor plan: off the entry hall, which was larger than most living rooms, two parlors opened on either side and an age-darkened oak staircase swept up to the second floor. The parlors had served as entertaining spaces both for Melvin Bertram's grandfather when he'd built and lived in the house and, later, for the Baldwin & Bates Funeral Home.

"That's Mr. Bertram's office." I indicated the French doors

that opened into his office suite—the former front parlor and dining room, which mirrored my two-room office suite. Fortunately for me, Melvin and his venture capital/financial adviser work didn't require a lot of books, so I got the former library and its matching front parlor, both with lavishly detailed floor-to-ceiling cases for my inner sanctum.

"Living quarters are upstairs, so that's private space." I didn't elaborate on the fact that Melvin and I had apartments upstairs. Separate apartments. This was a small Southern town, so I don't flaunt the arrangement, and I still wasn't sure living here would last. Living so close to work had its drawbacks, but it was more convenient—and better insulated from heat and cold—than my grandfather's lake cabin.

"Back here is the restroom." Ah, something I could delegate. "Occasionally, clients come in here. If you could make sure it's stocked with paper and soap, that would be a help. Mr. Bertram hires a cleaning service, but they only come once a week."

She nodded. We continued past the restroom tucked underneath the staircase—probably added by the funeral home—and past the door to the basement stairs, which led to what had been the embalming rooms. We kept that door locked, and I kept my treks downstairs to a minimum. I didn't explain its existence to Shamanique, or describe the drains in the floors or the stainless-steel sinks and counters and the lingering laboratory smell.

"Back here's the kitchen. Bring whatever you'd like to eat. It's just the three of us. Help yourself to the Cokes. Coffee, tea, and sugar up here."

The kitchen stock was really pathetic, considering it wasn't just an office kitchen, but also the kitchen for both of our apartments. Melvin kept some fresh fruits and vegetables in the refrigerator, and canned soups in the cabinet. I kept only popcorn and ice cream on hand because, whenever I was hungry, I had a good idea what time my mom, my great-aunts, or my sister would have a meal on the table.

"These are the stairs down to the parking lot in back. There's room back there, so you don't have to park on the street." Not that finding a place in front of the old house was difficult, except on the first morning of a court session. Until they got the jurors sorted out, cars were parked in the trees on this end of town.

The kitchen completed our tour—the only main floor room the Baldwin & Bates renovation decades earlier had left untouched. Clean but shabby, with faded linoleum and yellow Formica countertops scrubbed colorless in spots.

"That's all of it," I said.

Shamanique looked unimpressed.

We stared at each other for a blink away from uncomfortable.

"Okay." I led the way back down the hall. The dark wood floors popped underfoot.

The postman dropped the day's collection through the slot beside the massive dual front doors.

"You can get started with the mail. Separate it here." I indicated the round table in the center of the entry, probably left behind because it was too large to get out the door. "If Mr. Bertram's office door is open, just leave his mail on the table inside his office. He's not here right now, though."

Off in Atlanta or Florida on business, I forgot which. "When he's gone, leave his mail in the basket next to the refrigerator." We each had a basket, and the system had worked well so far.

For me, what hadn't worked so well was getting the mail where it belonged once it found its way into my office. Always something I had to think about or wait on or didn't know what to do with. So I lived with stacks of papers. I liked things visible, so they'd remind me what needed doing, but my stacking habit was obvious as soon as anybody entered my office. No matter how many file folders I labeled or where I'd worked, my horizontal filing system remained a constant. Good assistants had been the only thing that saved me from chaos.

Still no reaction or questions from Shamanique.

"Open the mail and sort it into two stacks: one if it looks important and one if it looks like junk. If in doubt, put it in the important stack." I might toss the junk stack in the garbage with scarce a glance.

I sat the mail on my desk and turned to look at her. "Okay." Again we stared at each other. Her face was impassive. Not challenging or angry. Pleasant enough. Just not—interested? No. Just—passive.

"What say we sit for a minute. Get to know each other."

She scooped her skirt under her as she sat, demurely perched on the edge of one of the two wing chairs in the windowed alcove of my office. My reading nook. The drum table—the top rotated and the sides held small books—had been my grandfather's. The collection of leather-bound literature shelved around the drum had also been his. The stacks of mail, legal magazines, and case printouts on top were all mine.

"Are you in school?"

She shook her head, her earrings rocking. "Took some classes at Tech. Thinking about going back."

"What were you studying?"

She gave a right tilt of her head, her version of a shrug. "Nursing. But mostly general courses."

"That what you want to do? Nursing?"

"No, ma'am."

She was well spoken, her voice soft and rich. But reaching down her throat to pull out every word was tiring.

"Tell me about your family. Any brothers or sisters?"

A borderline question: close to the questions one couldn't ask in a job interview. Not that she'd sue me for discrimination, not when she could just sic Aunt Edna on me.

"One brother."

"Older?"

She nodded.

"So. If not nursing, what would you like to do?"

She ducked her chin and picked at one of her elaborate fake fingernails. "Be an investigator."

"Like Edna—your aunt?"

She gave another half shrug. "Or a probation officer. Or a counselor. Like that."

I nodded. "Good." The most animation I'd seen out of her.

"What kinds of things can you do on a computer?"

The shrug. "I'm not very technical."

"But you know how to use one?"

"Sure."

"What kinds of software? What have you used the computer for?"

"You know. Word processing, spreadsheets. Some database. I've helped Auntie Edna do online searches and skip traces." She pronounced aunt like a long "ah" with a "t" tacked on as an afterthought, not like the word "ant."

"I'm good at finding stuff," she said.

I suspected she was more computer-savvy than I was. Why was she so danged hard to have a conversation with? I needed to unleash my mother on her. Never failed, she could get anybody chattering away—their hopes, dreams, fears, history, the works.

"Well, I guess we'd better get busy. One thing, Shamanique." I leaned toward her to emphasize what I had to say. "The things that go on in this office, the things you read or overhear, must stay in this office. Everything is confidential. You can't talk about any cases, to anybody. We clear?" My standard speech for years to all my law clerks and secretaries. The same speech I'd been given on my first clerking job.

"Yes, ma'am." She looked me straight in the eye. "Auntie Edna says the same thing." She shrugged. She was probably thinking, as I had: *Who would I tell? Nobody I know is interested in any of this stuff.*

"Great. Let me know if you have any questions."

She went to the desk in the front room, picked up the letter opener, and started methodically slicing open what would be mostly junk mail.

I climbed the ladder to study the chandelier. Some of the dangling crystals could be unhooked. Others couldn't. I climbed as high as the ladder safely allowed and pulled up on the chandelier's upper chain, trying to get a sense how much the thing weighed.

The answer: a lot more than I could lift. Two plans ruined. One plan had been to unhook the crystals, soak them, dry them, and return them. The other was to lower the whole assembly and soak the dangly parts in the bathtub. Two problems with that: It was much too heavy and, on close inspection, I was certain no bathtub—not even the deep claw-footed tub in my bathroom upstairs—could hold it. I braced my thigh against the top rung and fiddled and studied.

"I wouldn't use the bleach, if I were you. It might etch the crystal." Shamanique's quiet voice startled me. "That dust wand is a good start," she said.

"Think that'll work?"

"It'll catch most of the dirt. Then you can use a vinegar-and-water solution. Got any cotton gloves? You can wet one glove in the vinegar water and keep the other dry. That'll polish it up nice. Except your arms'll get awful tired. I've finished with the mail. I could help you with that."

I stared down at her.

"I've helped my mama do it. That's what she does. Clean houses."

"Okay, then. Why don't you lock the door there?" I pointed to the French doors. I wasn't expecting anybody this afternoon, but then again, I hadn't expected Edna to show up bringing Shamanique, shaman of arcane cleaning knowledge.

By five o'clock, we had a gleaming chandelier.

"The whole room looks brighter," I said.

"Yes, ma'am. What time you want me tomorrow?"

"Um." I couldn't very well say, *I wander downstairs whenever I wake up, some time between 4:00 A.M. and 10:00.* "Let's say 8:30?"

She gave a little wave, her earrings swaying with her graceful spin.

Wednesday Morning

The next morning, Shamanique bounced up the front steps promptly at eight-thirty, her hoop earrings and short skirt swaying. I took only a few minutes to show her the phone and my oak filing cabinets—from my grandfather's office, refurbished by my dad. I left her making labels to file a stack of papers. I'd stayed up late last night sorting and identifying stacks with sticky notes. How was I going to keep a secretary busy? At least I could go to Emma's soccer game this evening without feeling guilty about untended mounds of paper.

Rudy and I rendezvoused at Maylene's at nine o'clock. No need to head out on our somber mission unfortified.

The crowd was predictable. At a large table in the center of the room sat a couple of lawyers, a pharmacist, a couple of retired farmers, and other assorted pundits, dissecting yesterday's news and offering their own none-too-optimistic predictions for the future. Other tables held a group of highway workers wearing Day-Glo orange vests, a wildlife officer studying the newspaper, and three guys dressed in camo, in from a morning spent fishing. A normal day.

What Rudy ordered for breakfast was equally predictable. I opted for oatmeal and walnuts.

"Any blueberries?" I asked the waitress—another new one.

"I'll check." Her tone didn't offer much hope.

As she turned to the kitchen, still scribbling on her pad, I asked Rudy, "You have a chance to look for Wenda Sims's file yesterday?"

He poured half the sugar jar into his coffee cup and stirred, the spoon gritty on the bottom of the cup.

"I called Evidence. Carl said he'd look. Doesn't sound promising, though. We used to put some of our long-term storage in the basement of the old courthouse. It flooded, you know."

Rudy offered my disappointment a twig of hope. "Carl's been around here forever. He said Vince Ingum handled that case. Said Vince had retired to Myrtle Beach, but he had a number for him."

"Great." Provided he didn't mind revisiting a case he'd never solved, talking to a live person could be better than reading an old file, waterlogged and mildewed or not.

"Carl said what stuck in his mind was they chalked it up to a domestic case. She had a boyfriend back home who liked to use her as a punching bag."

"Oh." Fran hadn't mentioned any of that. Most crime boiled down to the tawdry, but it still surprised me. I somehow expected something so life-altering—or life-ending—to be worthy, or at least complicated. "They couldn't make a case?"

Before he could answer, movement behind me drew his attention. The commotion also attracted the attention of the rest of the restaurant. Even with my back to the door, I heard the chatter stop.

114

The cause for the disruption suddenly presented itself at our booth: Colin "Mumler" Gaines and the ghosters, in person. Colin huffed to catch his breath.

"Deputy Mellin? We were told you could help us."

Rudy, his hand around his thick, white coffee cup, didn't say yay or nay. He just waited.

"I'm Mumler Gaines. This is Quint and Trini." He acknowledged me with a nod, probably remembering my face but not that he'd seen me hovering overhead when he'd visited my angel.

"We went out to the Heath house. We're doing some paranormal research in the area and were told that house would be an excellent subject. While there, we were attacked."

He waved his arms to emphasize the enormity of the offense.

I coughed. My ice tea had gone down the wrong way. The Heath house. I could see the train wreck coming.

So did Rudy. "Someone told you to go out there?"

"Yessir. Somebody called, in response to our newspaper story."

I glanced at Rudy, but he didn't take his eyes off Colin or his photographer's vest and its bulging pockets.

"Exactly what happened?"

"We tried calling, but they don't have a listed number. So we went out there this morning, to see if we could set up a visit for this evening. They stole our camera!"

"Stole it?" Rudy's professionalism kept the sarcasm out of his voice. I didn't dare drink any more tea for fear I'd spew it out my nose.

"Well, they took it from us and wouldn't give it back. This big guy with a rag tied on his head. Big guy."

Ah, my old buddy Clyde. Or Do Rag, as I preferred to think of him, though I certainly never called him that to his face.

"Another guy rode his motorcycle down the porch steps and started buzzing around us, trying to run us down."

The members of the Southern Posse motorcycle gang had recently settled in the pre-Revolutionary War Heath farmhouse. If one of the motorcyclists had wanted to run Mumler down, he'd be in the hospital, not in Maylene's flapping his arms like a blue jay defending its trinkets.

"Did you ask them to give your camera back?" Rudy's voice was mellow-sweet as he smiled at Colin. With Rudy, that mellow-sweet voice is usually a sign to step out of the way.

"Not—exactly. We . . ." Colin didn't seem to have an answer for that. "We went to the police station." He waved over his shoulder toward the front door. "They said it was outside their jurisdiction. They said we could find you here."

"The city police?"

"Yessir."

Chief Deputy Sheriff Rudy nodded. Rudy's revenge on the city cop would be sweet.

"You can go to the county Law Enforcement Center—the sheriff's office—and file a report. Somebody will be back in touch with you. It might be best if you all stayed away from out there at the Heath house."

"Yeah." Colin nodded but looked forlorn. "That was one of our best leads, though."

Rudy pursed his lips and gave a good imitation of a commiserating nod. "You boys know about the crybaby bridge? Just north of town?"

Quint, the other ghoster guy, drew closer to the table. He and Colin exchanged glances.

"No."

"Some real activity there. Ask over to the county library. I'm sure it's been written up and all."

The group came to an almost immediate, albeit silent, agreement.

"Thanks."

"Best time's around midnight. Be careful. Don't get run over out there."

"Yessir."

They turned without seeing the smile at the corner of Rudy's mouth. I covered mine with my hand. The laugh I tried to choke back came out as a snort. Good thing I'd stayed away from the ice tea.

"Who the heck sent those innocents out to visit Mad Max and his motorcycle gang?" I asked.

"I don't know, but it's not funny." He snorted anyway. "They could've lost more than a video camera. Now, thanks to some wiseacre's idea of a joke, we get to send a deputy out to retrieve their camera."

"The crybaby bridge?" I said, shaking my head.

"They wanted ghosts." The grin on his broad face showed how much he enjoyed the thought of the three ghosters trying to capture the illusive baby's cry.

"You finished?" He stared at my empty bowl, perhaps feeling pity that it sat alone in front of me, no other crockery to keep it company. "They'll be waiting for us at impound."

As we walked to the register to pay, one of the three fishermen threw up a wave at Rudy. "Chief. How's it going?"

Rudy stuck out his hand. "Cuke." He shook hands with Cuke's two buddies with that kind of smiling grapple that always looks like guys are testing whether one could take the other in a fight. I eased on through the tables to pay my check.

The impound lot turned out to be nothing more than a fenced-off portion to the side of a towing service and auto body shop. The gravel and dirt had been compacted and glued together with crank case drippings for so many years, while so many grease-stained hands had touched the doors and equipment that the whole place had a gray-black tone to it.

Four garage bays stood open with cars parked inside, hoods up or tires dangling from hydraulic lifts. The guys working inside, all with at least one greasy rag hanging out a back pocket, gave us only cursory glances. Just another DUI coming to get her car, for all they knew.

The fifth garage bay sat next to a pen encircled by a ten-foot chain-link fence topped with concertina wire. A battle-scarred, dingy white pit bull shot out of his tar-papered doghouse straight toward us, moving like a heat-seeking missile. He didn't bark. He just danced along a well-worn track inside the fence and, head turning and bobbing, kept us in view with his one eye. The other eye had been stitched shut. I hated to think where he'd gotten the gouges and brown scars that patchworked his face. Was this the retirement home successful fight dogs long for?

Rudy rummaged around in his pants pocket. I realized the dog wasn't on a chain. How did those who were allowed entrance get past him?

Rudy walked to the edge of the fence, made the same sappy "good boy" kissy sounds he gives Aunt Letha's rottweiler, and poked something through the fence before he turned to unlock the garage bay.

Two large Milk-Bone treats. The dog dove for them, his eye fixed on me. He stood at attention, holding both treats in his mouth, until he saw me step toward the garage bay and away from his fence. Only then did he turn toward his house, with one final check over his shoulder to make sure I was behaving.

I studied Rudy's broad back as he flicked on the garage lights and punched the button that sent the door rattling shut. Both the dog and I knew, it's good to have friends.

"So this is separate from the body shop." I'd wondered how they maintained chain of custody using storage on private property.

Rudy, standing at the passenger door, fixed me with that look that said something between *you're so dumb* and *don't bring your city smart-ass back here.*

"Safer here than parked in the patrol car garage. Some'a those numbnuts'd have the thing stripped and selling pieces on eBay."

Rudy stepped to the back of the car and popped open the trunk. Inside, the lining was missing, leaving only gray rough-coat metal and glue spots holding stray bits of gray felt.

"Guess the lab took everything, huh?"

Rudy pulled the trunk lid down with two fingers, trying to avoid the sections with the heaviest dusting of fingerprint powder. "Reckon so."

He unlatched the passenger door and swung it open. "You wanted to see."

We stood beside the red car, dusty black with leftover powder. The metallic smell of dried blood hit me. I blinked. I can get myself ready for the sight, but the smells always take me by surprise.

"Well, Sherlock? Or is it Dr. Phil? Any insights?"

I didn't take the bait. The driver's side of the car, predictably, contained most of the aftermath. Bloodstains and stuff I didn't want to think about had spattered as far as the left rear window. The darkest blood, though, had pooled on and beneath the driver's seat.

Rudy rummaged in the pocket of his khaki pants and pulled out a flashlight. He flicked the beam around the car's interior roof, along the frame of the driver's door window where bits of glass glistened, and settled the light on the driver's floorboard.

"They vacuumed most of the glass," he said.

119

"Somebody going to glue it together?" That was mostly a joke.

He shook his head. "For somebody smart, you sure must watch a lot of TV."

I didn't bother telling him I didn't own a television set. My niece Emma and I used to watch *America's Most Wanted* together at her house until her mom decided that wasn't acceptable fare for a seven-year-old.

"Can I get in?"

Rudy frowned as though I'd suggested something unseemly.

"Here." I pointed at the passenger seat. "I won't mess anything up."

Still frowning, he stepped back so I could slide in.

Someone with long legs had been sitting here. Skipper was tall. Had he been the last person in this seat?

I looked out the front window at the smudged gray cement block wall. What had Neanna seen? Had she sat at the overlook as the sun set over the valley? Could she see the trees, with the leaves now hard-green for summer? Could she see all the shades of green, or had it been too dark?

"When did she die? What time of day?"

"Best guess is sometime after midnight, roughly six hours before she was found. Food in her stomach, but no one to say when she last ate, so internal body temp is our best guess."

"So it was dark." I looked over at the Honda coupe's dashboard. I'd never driven one of these—or even ridden in one.

"Were her headlights on?"

"Don't know. Can check the report."

I shook my head. "Just curious."

I quit trying to imagine what she'd seen, what had been in her head. I studied the inside of the car. The dashboard, steering wheel, doors, all the hard surfaces were dusted gray with powder. Even though the car was older and smaller than Fran's sedan, with fewer gizmos, the fingerprint powder was the only dirt in the car.

"Can you show me exactly where she would've—held the gun?"

Rudy raised his right arm, using his finger to point behind his ear but not quite as low as his earlobe.

"Like this?" I tried to mimic him. He bent over and pushed my right elbow back, directing my finger at a sharper angle behind my ear.

"Of course, to hold the gun, her hand would've been about here, not with her finger jammed against her head." He pulled my arm back a few inches. A sharp muscle spasm made my arm jerk out of his grasp.

"Where would her head have been?"

"On her shoulders?"

"Smarty. Was it on the headrest? Was she leaning forward? Was her arm resting here?" I patted the headrest of the passenger seat.

"Don't know for certain." He stooped over, his hands on his knees, and studied the seat. "From the looks of things, I'd say she was leaning back on the headrest."

"Do you have your gun? Could we try it? Is it about the same size?"

He looked dubious.

"Just unload it. It'll help to think it all through. Was she about my size?" The image of her small, pale hand in the crime scene photo flashed to mind.

"About. She might have weighed less."

Never crossed Rudy's mind that was something no female, however clinical, wanted to hear.

He unholstered his pistol, popped out the clip, and pulled back the slide to make sure no round had been chambered. He left it open. "Keep your finger off the trigger."

Surrounded by the smell of stale blood, I was glad he was maniacally safety conscious.

I hooked my index finger into the trigger guard and tucked it safely behind the trigger, then hefted the pistol. Even without the clip full of bullets, it was an unwieldy weight.

"No, farther back." Rudy pushed my elbow and tried to guide the muzzle to the sweet spot behind my ear.

"Oww!" My arm jerked forward in a self-protective reflex. "I don't bend that way."

Rudy studied me, then wrapped his hand around both the pistol and my hand. "Try this."

He slid my thumb into the trigger guard, twisting and pulling just short of dislocating my shoulder. I could feel that the muzzle still wasn't quite in the spot he'd pointed to earlier.

"Could you pull the trigger like that?" He let go of the gun. I tried squeezing the back of the trigger guard, but I couldn't hold the heavy weapon. It slipped from my grasp. Rudy stood close enough to grab it before it slid out the open door onto the concrete floor.

"Maybe her arms were longer than mine."

Rudy cradled the pistol in his hand, lost in thought.

"Maybe." Rudy reached in his pocket for his gun clip, reloaded, and holstered his gun. The holster snap sounded loud in the quiet garage.

I leaned back against the headrest, studying the inside of the car. Except for the gore and its sick-sweet metallic odor, the car was immaculate. Worn, but free of clutter. Unlike mine, which still served as a second home as I shuttled between my parents' house, my new apartment over the office, and the lake cabin. Would the cops have cleaned out any clutter, gum wrappers or old newspapers? Maybe.

Over the rearview mirror, the cloth lining on the roof was wrinkled. My gaze kept passing over it, noting it because it fell at a demarcation between where the fabric was blood-spattered and where it wasn't.

I reached out to touch it, a reflex I have for straightening things. When I brushed the fabric with my fingertips, a four-inch section gaped open at the edge, quite the opposite from what I'd intended.

"Oops." I started to tuck the fabric back under the plastic band around the windshield when I felt something underneath.

"Hey, be careful," Rudy said. "Don't mess that up."

I ignored him, slid my index and middle finger into the opening, and pincerlike slid out a rectangle of stiff paper.

Until I saw it clearly in the light from the open door, I thought it was a torn piece of cardboard interliner.

Rudy leaned in the door. "What's that?" He wasn't going to mess up a case over a stupid chain of custody issue.

"The photograph." I held it by the edges and turned it so Rudy could see.

"This has to be it," I said. "The photo Neanna found stuck in her grandmother's scrapbook."

Rudy took it by the edges and stood, studying it.

"Who keeps a photo like this in the family photo album?" he said.

I now had a visual for the phrase "deathly pale." Never again would I use that to describe something that gave a meek imitation of reality. Just as Fran had described her, Neanna's aunt Wenda reclined across a stone bench, her feet on the ground. Twenty-three years ago, the camera flash had reflected at just the proper angle, freezing her lifeless face in stark detail.

The only color on the photo came from tiny droplets of blood that had soaked through the headliner and left rusty dots on the paper.

Rudy said, "I'm more curious about where she got this than why she kept it."

"Neanna's grandmother had it."

"So where did she get it?"

"Beats me."

He stood outside the passenger door, his head bowed over the photo.

"I need to get Fran French to identify this. Can you get her into the office?"

"She's back in Atlanta."

He kept studying the photo. "Somehow this doesn't look like a crime scene photo. Maybe I'm just used to looking at Lester Watts's atrocities."

"Maybe a news photographer snapped it." I couldn't imagine why, or why anyone would offer it to the victim's mother. "Maybe that's what they used to identify the body, so her grandmother didn't have to endure viewing the body in person."

"Maybe. We don't let them keep the photos as souvenirs, though. Can we fax this to your client? Make sure this is Miss Lyles's aunt?"

"Sure. Or we can scan and e-mail it."

"Not on the equipment I have. You can do that?"

"Sure." I swung my legs out the door and stood, careful not to touch anything. We were both smudged with graphite powder.

"Let's go by your office and reproduce it," Rudy said. "Then I'll log this in with the file. Maybe give the guys who went over this car some lessons on where smart people hide things."

"Dear Lord." I remembered the photos he'd shown me at lunch. "Hiding things. Whoever tore up her trunk and her suit-case was looking for something."

I looked at the photo Rudy held. "Looking for that." My voice was almost a whisper.

"Probably so," he said and reached down to lock the car door before he pushed it shut.

Wednesday

"It wasn't exactly part of the scrapbook," Fran said when I called after faxing the photo. "It was stuck in the front, just loose."

"This was the only photo like this?"

"The only loose one. The newspaper articles were pasted in. Of course there were pictures in those, but no other loose photos."

She was quiet a moment. "It was like Gran wanted to know everything, to capture everything. Then one day she just stopped. I guess the newspaper quit covering it. Things just petered out."

We were both silent, thinking about a woman who'd tried her best to hold together her daughter's life and who'd pieced her death together as best she could.

"Avery, why would Neanna hide that picture in her car?"

I hadn't told Fran about the rifling of the car trunk. The

circumstances of identifying the photo offered enough difficulty for one phone call. She didn't need to know any more right now.

"I'd like to have a private investigator check out Neanna's last boyfriend. Is there anybody else in Atlanta we should talk to?"

"Gran had a cousin she was close to. I don't know if that would be helpful. Sidalee Evans. But I told you, Neanna and Dirick broke up. Some time ago."

"That's been known to provoke some guys. If nothing else, I'd like to mark him off the list. It shouldn't take long."

The line stayed quiet for too long.

Finally, she said, "His name is Dirick Timms. I don't know his phone number, but he lived in an apartment near Georgia Tech, last I heard."

"You happen to know his birth date?"

"Um—no. Yes. October 31, Halloween. Easy to remember."

"Okay."

"I was also thinking," Fran said. "Can you find Nut Case and that guy she was so interested in meeting? He might know something."

"The police can locate him. I'll—"

"It won't hurt for you to talk to him. I'll feel better if you do."

"Sure."

"Avery, while you're looking at boyfriends, have you learned anything about Aunt Wenda's death? I just have this feeling—it's not right." She stumbled, searching for words. "Somebody knows what happened to her. I see these cold cases solved on TV all the time. Maybe enough time has passed. Maybe you can find somebody who'll talk now. It was so important to Neanna. I just want—to do that for her."

Tears thickened her voice and she paused for a moment. "Since you're so interested in boyfriends, Aunt Wenda was dating some guy Gran didn't trust. He hit her at least once. Gran called the police, and from then on she blamed herself because she couldn't make Wenda see the danger. I can still hear her: 'If her father had been alive, they'd'a been calling the ambulance, not the cops. I was too much a coward; I let him continue to draw breath.'"

Her voice broke in short breaths. "Gran couldn't hold Aunt Wenda back. It was like she was on the edge of an abyss. Like I tried to talk Neanna out of leaving Atlanta. Now I know—"

She must have covered the phone or held it away, but I could hear her jagged breathing.

"Fran?" I hoped she could hear me. "Fran, I'll talk to you later, when I know something more. Okay?"

The phone clicked off.

I couldn't imagine Neanna's life and her losses, and I couldn't imagine Fran's grief. No point in telling Fran it wasn't her fault. Words weren't going to make her believe that.

I waited a few seconds, then picked up the receiver and checked for a dial tone. I flipped through my Rolodex—one of the few organized parts of my previous life I'd managed to maintain.

I dialed Rowly Edwards in Atlanta. I'd lucked into Rowly in February, during a frantic, misguided trip to Atlanta on another case, when he picked me up in his cab at the airport. What I needed now wasn't his cabbie skills or his country-music singer/songwriter skills. I needed his private eye wannabe skills. Last I'd heard, he'd finished his training course and had taken a job with an investigation firm to work off his apprenticeship. Who better to cover Atlanta for me?

His voice mail message said he was unavailable.

"Rowly, it's Avery. See what you can find for me on a guy named Dirick Timms." I spelled it for him. "His birthday is October 31. He was living in an apartment somewhere near Georgia

Tech. May have a record. See what he was up to last Friday night, if you can."

I talked fast to get all the information recorded and left my office number.

As I walked through what I was beginning to think of as Shamanique's office, she came in carrying the mail. More brochures from experts wanting to improve my office function or win my cases for me and magazines I needed to read to keep up in a field where I no longer played.

"Put the sales brochures in the recycling basket." I pointed it out under the desk. "Stack any bills to be paid with their envelopes in this top drawer." I hoped there weren't any. "Put the bill stubs and everything else in the to-be-filed basket. No, wait. Maybe we'd better have a new mail stack, so I can go through it first." I was still trying to think through the best work flow.

"Okay if I listen to my music?" She pointed to a tangle of delicate wires and an MP3 player.

"Sure. Oh, and a book should come today or tomorrow, about running a law office. Thought that might be helpful to read. When you run out of things to do, you can get familiar with that legal-research site. I left the Web address on your desk. I may get a callback from Rowly Edwards. You have my cell number if he needs to talk to me."

I could've put Shamanique on Dirick Timms's trail. If she'd worked for Edna, she was probably handy at skip traces. But Rowly was on the ground in Atlanta and could size this guy up without spooking him. It also gave me a chance to hear what Rowly had been up to lately.

I headed for the stairs to change into my work clothes. If I couldn't put in some billable hours on a case, might as well work off some of my rent.

The bells on the front door jangled about the time I got to

the top of the stairs. Something to help me procrastinate on cleaning the rest of the light fixtures, which would further delay my inevitable appointment with the wax rings on the toilets.

In the entry hall, Colin "Mumler" Gaines and the ghosters stood peering all about, through the doors into our offices, down the back hall, and up at the soaring staircase, watching me descend.

"Hi," Colin said. He gave a shy wave, his elbow at his side, his hand raised in a sideways salute. "We were wondering, is Mr. Bertram in?"

"I don't know. Do you have an appointment?"

"No, ma'am. We were passing by, thought we'd—"

Melvin picked that moment to swing open his French doors like a landed gentleman making his study available for brandy and cigars.

He got a wave from Quint and a handshake from Colin. Trini stayed closer to the front door, her hands intertwined in an awkward knot of fingers.

"Do you have a minute?" Colin looked from me to Melvin and back. "We had a quick question and you're the very people who would know."

Trini nodded her head in affirmation or encouragement.

Melvin hesitated before he stepped aside. "Come on in."

In the front room of Melvin's two-room suite, a leather sofa sat under the window opposite the French doors, flanked by two leather chairs. In the bay window that overlooked the wrap-around porch, he had two armchairs and a large pie-crust table that probably cost more than his Jeep. Though it was arranged for comfortable conversation or for reading, Melvin never sat in here. Too much on display, I supposed. He likely had a lavishly furnished den upstairs as well.

It made a nice gathering place for a visit that I expected Melvin would keep short.

The three ghosters sat on the sofa, reminding me of three blackbirds perched side by side on a fence.

"Mr. Bertram, we were wondering . . ." Colin indicated his fellow black-clad birds. "We heard that you arrange investments?"

Oh, this was going to be good.

Melvin settled in the club chair facing me. Colin sat on the end of the sofa closest to me, so I got the full effect of Melvin's response. He didn't say anything, but he didn't have to. I knew that expression. Melvin leaned back in his chair, his legs crossed, his tasseled loafers spit-shined, his gray slacks creased.

The kids obviously didn't hear what he didn't say, but to me the tension at the corner of his smile and the steel gray-blue gaze spoke volumes.

"Yes, I do arrange investments." He didn't lean forward with the intensity he shows when something catches his interest.

"We were wondering what it would take to attract investors for our project." Colin's excitement carried him to the edge of his seat. "You see, we have this idea for a TV series. We've decided on a name. *On the Ghost Hunt.* And Quint here even wrote theme music for it. Didn't you?"

Colin nodded to Quint as if urging a reluctant child to give a hug to the grandma who always pinched his cheeks. Quint rubbed his knees and started humming, *Tum, tum, tum-tum tum-ta-tum,* and bobbing his head in time to something that sounded like an off-pitch mix between *Mission: Impossible* and *Scooby-Doo.*

"This could be really big. We were talking about it with a couple of cops, and this guy said you might be interested, maybe to invest yourself or for somebody else. One of your clients."

I slipped my hand over my mouth, assuming what I hoped was an unobtrusive, thoughtful expression. This was too rich.

Oh, I was glad the bells on the door had beckoned me back downstairs.

"May I ask who told you I might be interested?"

"One of the cops."

"Oh?" Melvin let his gaze slide over to me. "Where did you meet up with this cop?"

"At the graveyard last night."

Uh-oh.

"Did you get some good film?"

"Uh—no." Colin's gaze danced from the Persian rug to his partners to the door. "Not really."

Quint came to the rescue. "We had set up and started rolling. You just tape, you know. 'Cause you can't ever tell what you might get."

Trini sat between her partners, nodding.

"Then we heard this noise. I almost levitated, it scared me so bad. Trini screamed. Man, can she scream."

His tone indicated he meant this as a compliment.

I knew where this was headed. With the hand covering my mouth, I dug my fingers into my cheeks to keep myself from laughing.

Colin picked up the story again. "This lady, dressed all in black, appeared outta nowhere. She had this air horn and she let 'er rip. Jeez, I thought it'd busted my eardrums."

"Then the police came," said Quint.

"Mrs. Amey," Melvin said, his voice businesslike. He looked like he was playing with a rough cuticle. He was avoiding looking at me.

"Yeah, man. How'd you know?"

"She lives in the graveyard, in the caretaker's house. She doesn't take kindly to people who interfere with the cemetery, especially at night."

"The dudes who suggested we film there sure didn't tell us about that."

"No way we wanted to disturb anybody."

"Or have the police come threaten us," Trini spoke up. "Said they'd arrest us. For trespassing and for vandalism."

She'd taken the warning to heart, that was obvious.

"Who suggested you film in the graveyard?" Melvin asked.

Colin shrugged. "Dunno his name. Tall dude, mullet. And one of his buddies. Stopped us on Main Street. Word's out about our project." He nodded, his spiky hair waving with pride.

Coughing really isn't a good way to disguise a laugh. I tried anyway. Melvin gave me a stern glance, one that said, *Don't get me started.*

"Do you have any usable footage so far?" Melvin asked.

The three faces told the tale.

"No. Nothing yet."

"Except the freaky lady dressed all in black," Trini said. "With the air horn."

"We got good leads, though," Colin said, preferring to look ahead to success rather than behind.

"Going to Moody Springs tonight," Quint said. "Like you suggested."

I started to warn them away from Moody Springs, given that Neanna's body had been found at the overlook not far from the springs, the same overlook reputedly used by the ghostly hitchhiker. Moody Springs was a little distance from the overlook, though, and I didn't want to encourage them by mentioning the recent death, fearing what the possibility of fresh ectoplasm might urge them to do. I didn't want Neanna's death to become a curiosity.

Melvin nodded, his look solemn—the only way he could avoid trying a fake cough of his own. "I should explain how difficult it is to get funding for movie or television investment. My clients, for example, would consider it too risky."

Crestfallen expressions replaced optimism on the three faces.

"Filmmakers often have to provide start-up funding on their own. I know that's not easy to hear, but you've already found a way to start, and that's better than most with your dream do. Lots of artists start the way you are starting. You may find funding is easier to obtain when you have something to show an investor, something to establish your credentials."

Their forlorn expressions softened.

"Street cred," Quint said.

"Starve for your art, man," Colin said, grasping the vision. "Gotta believe in it before anybody else will." He nodded, first to Quint, then Trini, who nodded in return. The optimism was spreading.

"Well, thanks for your help." Colin stood. "Gotta go get set up for tonight while it's still light. Scout locations, plan shots."

The three waved good-bye and loped out, pulling the door shut behind them.

I stayed in my seat, giving Melvin a mischievous smile. "Good fatherly advice there. Too bad they didn't quite hear it."

"Hear what?"

"You telling them to go home."

"They have to figure that out for themselves. Thought I'd at least plant a few seeds of reality. They might sprout."

"You always handle them nicely," I said, but I couldn't stay sincere for more than a moment. "Who knows? They might really have a hit series on their hands. Then you'll be sorry. You could have been on the ground floor."

He got up, stretched, and headed into his inner sanctum. Over his shoulder, he said, "Don't you have work to do?"

I'd once again climbed almost to the top of the stairs when I heard my phone. I took another detour back to my office.

Shamanique was hanging up as I closed the door from the entry hall.

"Wrong number," she said. "I got what you wanted on Nut Case." She handed me a printout. "Here's their schedule. Been in Charlotte. Good news is they're back here tonight for a show in Clemson. Opening for some band at Littlejohn Coliseum. You might could catch them there."

Not a bad idea. "Any tickets available?"

Her eyebrows came dangerously close to her slicked hairline. "You don't have to go to the concert. Besides, you don't want to."

"Why not?"

Her pitying look reminded me too much of her aunt Edna. "Headbangers."

"I thought they played some kind of acoustic music."

"Don't know about that. Maybe this guy does that on his own. But Drip Dry is headlining. They got their own cult."

"But if I want to see this guy—"

"Wait outside. He'll be through early. Slip some green to one of the security guards. Those guys don't get paid nothing. Give him a message for Pippen. Or find out where the band is staying."

I studied her with new respect. "You've done this before."

She just stared up at me from her desk chair, her eyebrows raised. What I didn't know, I couldn't tell Aunt Edna.

"Slipping past the guard is one option," I said. "Can you call—what were their names? Out at the Pasture? Ash Carter and Lenn Edmonds. See if either of them has a contact number for the band."

She pursed her lips, her only acknowledgment that I might have struck on a better plan.

I changed clothes and spent the next couple of hours soaking the crystal wall sconces in dishwashing liquid and rehanging the now-sparkling prisms on the hall fixtures. Once I saw the pattern for the pieces, the puzzle wasn't that difficult to fit together. I couldn't let it lie around for long, though; I didn't want to forget how to reconstruct it.

Shamanique came back to the kitchen as I dried and admired a clean sconce. I like having something to show for my labors.

"I called that Pippen guy, said you'd like to meet with him. He can do six, before the show. He'll leave a pass at the back gate. I might have given him the impression that you were thinking about hiring him."

"You might have?"

"Just said a friend of yours had met him. When he asked which gig, I said he'd have to talk to you."

"Okay."

"What? You think he'd've jumped at the chance to be questioned about what he'd had to do with a dead girl? Don't think so." She popped her head in a sassy side-to-side.

She was a quick study.

"Point taken," I said. "You heading out?"

"You better be, too, if you gonna make it to Clemson."

Almost five o'clock. I raced upstairs to change into jeans and a black V-neck tee that should pass for appropriate concert wear. I could add a touch of eye makeup and lipstick at traffic lights on the way.

With only summer-school classes in session and the day employees gone before five o'clock, parking wasn't too bad on campus. I still had a hike to the mostly underground basketball arena, with its mahogany steel exoskeleton. I walked halfway around the perimeter before I spotted a tractor-trailer rig parked on the side street. I'd never paid attention to the short drive that ran into the building or the massive door where equipment was off-loaded and groupies could hang out awaiting their favorite rocker.

The guard motioned me through after only a moment of skeptical study. His directions to the green room were easy to follow. The group gathered in the spartanly furnished room was low-key, not at all what I'd expected.

Several guys in tight, tattered clothes sat around with black-garbed young women, talking quietly or nibbling from the nuts, cheese, and fruit on trays around the room. It had the air of a family gathering before a football game started on television.

Nobody even glanced at me as I stood in the door. I reached and tapped the arm of a girl as she wandered past me. A sweep of jet-black bangs covered her black-edged eyes. She shook her head when I asked about Pippen and wandered away. Somebody cranked up a CD player.

My reddish-gold hair must have stuck out in the sea of deep-dyed black because before I could flag down someone else a shaggy-haired young man in a white button-down shirt approached me.

"Avery Andrews?" He leaned in close to my ear, the pulsing music loud enough to draw conversation close.

He cocked his head toward the door. "Step outside?"

I nodded and followed him into the hallway.

"Get you something to drink?"

"No, thanks. I won't take much of your time. Just some quick questions." I slipped a picture of Neanna out of my pocket—a kittenishly cute photo Fran said they'd taken on a trip together before Fran went away to college, a much kinder likeness than the morgue photo Fran had viewed to identify her sister.

"I believe she met you during your concert at the Pasture last week."

His eyes narrowed, wary. "Yeah?"

No need to waste time on a warm-up act. "She came from Atlanta to see your concert. She was a big fan. A guy said you met her, talked for a while."

"Yeah. Talked. That's all."

He didn't give the impression he trolled the loading dock looking for an easy lay after every concert, but he certainly was defensive all of a sudden.

"I wanted some idea how she looked to you that evening, what she talked about. I'm just trying to understand her state of mind that night."

"What's to tell? She was a nice kid, that's all. We talked about music, about where the band was playing next. She asked me to autograph a CD. That was pretty much it. Just a nice kid."

"Did she seem drunk? Stoned?"

He shook his head. "Not that I could tell. Not when I saw her. But we talked maybe five minutes total. At the end of our first set."

"Did she seem depressed? Anything unusual?"

"No, but I didn't know her. How would I know what was unusual? What're you getting at?"

"Her sister hired me to find out who she saw, what went on that day." I looked him in the eye, wanting to gauge his response. "She died that night."

He drew back, his brows knit in concern. His surprise seemed genuine. "What happened?"

"The police believed she shot herself."

"No." The word came quiet, involuntary. He stood mute a moment, studying my face. "She was such a nice kid."

"Yeah. Her sister isn't—willing to be convinced that she killed herself," I said. "She's asked me to look into it. Anything you could tell me would be a help."

He kept shaking his head, studying the polished tile floor of

139

the wide, empty hallway. "I—just that she was sweet. Funny. Soft-spoken. Not sleazy. She didn't come on to me or anything. Lots do, almost like they think they're supposed to. She just really liked the music."

I let the silence settle on us.

He looked up. "She did say something about being on a quest. That the concert that night was the portal. Does that mean anything?"

"Yes." It didn't mean anything new, though—and nothing I needed to tell him about. "That's all?"

"Yeah," he said and bowed his head again, as if offering a benediction. He returned the photo to me.

"I just wanted to get an idea about where she was and how she acted that evening."

"Sorry I couldn't be more help."

Was his sadness real, or was he a professional performer, good at improvisation?

I'd let our conversation float gently with the current. Time to take the cross-examination in a different direction. "Where were you between 1:00 and 3:00 A.M.? After the concert." Sometimes it's best to pitch it hard and fast.

Pippen didn't miss the harder edge in my voice. His gaze met mine.

"Packing up my gear. I crashed in some no-tell motel down the road, on the outskirts of some little town. Alone." He added the last with emphasis.

"No nubile groupies?"

His mouth tightened. "At the Pasture? You're kidding. That cheap-ass operation attracts—I don't even have words to describe it. Rednecks wanting nothing but cheap beer buckets. Older women pretending clown makeup hides the sags and wrinkles. Sleazy guys ready to get it on with anything that looked like it would say yes." He shuddered. "Not a one of them interested in music. A sappy soundtrack for their sad lives, maybe, but not music."

Was he trying out new lyrics? "You saying you didn't have any fans there?"

"A few. Your—client, Neanna. And a couple of local kids."

"Thought you were supposed to be pretty popular." I was trying to goad him. In this well-lit, empty hallway, I didn't have a bailiff to back me up if the witness got angry, and the crowd in the green room looked too mellow to come to their own rescue, much less mine.

He fixed me with a controlled stare. "Not with the rednecks and rejects at a place like the Pasture."

"So why'd you play there?"

"Favor for a friend. A guy who plays some backup for me was supposed to do it. He had a better gig come along, but he didn't want to break his contract, get a bad name in the business. I was in the area, and the owner agreed to the substitution." He shrugged. "Like his clientele would care."

"So how did your fans find out you were playing there?"

"My Web site. I asked them. Said they knew where the Pasture was, so they came. Everybody else in the area just waited for the date here, I guess."

He had an answer for everything. Was that because the truth usually offers answers or because he was well rehearsed?

"When did Neanna leave? Was she alone?"

"How should I know? Just because I had so few fans there doesn't mean I was keeping tabs on them. I was working. The house band and I started jamming on some redneck music the crowd enjoyed. I wasn't paying attention to your friend." His tone wasn't as annoyed as mine would have been.

I handed him my card. "If you think of anything else."

141

"Yeah." He glanced absently at the card and slid it in his hip pocket.

"Thanks."

I walked around the circular hall back to the loading ramp. The guard held open the door for me and wished me a good night.

I stood under a floodlight, breathing the warm evening air. So where did that leave me? She hadn't appeared drunk, drugged, or depressed. She hadn't hooked up with her musician idol, if the musician could be trusted. She hadn't left with Skipper, if he could be trusted. Taken at face value, the interviews told me she'd listened to a concert, which had probably moved from some of her favorite music to an updated version of "Rednecks, White Socks, and Blue Ribbon Beer." Then she'd left, driven to a scenic overlook, and shot herself. At an impossible angle.

The more I thought about it, the outlandish experiment Rudy and I had talked ourselves into made sense. Tomorrow could be interesting.

Thursday Morning

My cell phone rang at seven the next morning. Only my dad calls that early, mostly because that's not early to him.

"Hullo?" As I spoke, I realized my breath reeked from the Mellow Mushroom garlic and cheese pizza I'd had the night before in Clemson. I'd walked from the coliseum to the former frat house and sat there mentally processing what I didn't know about Neanna.

"Missed you last night," Dad said.

"Last night?"

"At Emma's soccer game."

"Ah, man. I forgot all about it. Something came up at the last minute."

"Just checking to make sure you were okay."

"Ran down to Clemson to interview somebody. Darn. I'd been looking forward to it."

"She was looking for you." He was quiet for a long pause. "It's awfully easy to disappoint a seven-year-old. Sometimes we forget how big things are to them."

His words were gentle, but they hit me in the chest like a fist.

"I feel awful. Something came up, for work. I completely forgot." I was offering him grown-up sounding justifications. Nothing that excused it in my mind—or Emma's.

"She'll understand. Just worried that something had happened. That's all. Talk to you later, honey."

I lay back in the bed, sick at my stomach. Emma always seemed so matter-of-fact and in charge, but she was a kid. How could her aunt Bree—her toddler mispronunciation that had become a nickname only she used—let her down? As I lay staring up at the soaring ceiling and the deep crown molding, I wondered what I'd heard in my dad's voice. His words hinted at more than an abstract fatherly observation. Who had disappointed him when he was seven? And how? How sad that he still remembered whatever it was.

Missing the soccer game wasn't the big deal. Letting Emma expect me and then not showing up—that was the big deal. I needed to make it up to her. Maybe lunch would be a start.

The sooner I got to work, the more time I could free up later. I threw back the sheet and headed to the shower.

I didn't hear Shamanique come in, but when the phone rang at eight-thirty, she answered it.

I'd made it to the entry hall with my cup of tea when I heard her say, "Avery Andrews, attorney-at-law. May I help you?" Pause. "May I say who's calling?"

That sounded professional.

"Avery! Oh, there you are. Rowly Edwards for you."

Yelling from the outer office was not so professional. We'd work on that.

I took the call in my office.

"Rowly! How are you?"

"Wondering why ever' time I hear from you, you got yourself mixed up with some bad number."

"You mean to tell me Dirick's not the president of the Atlanta Jaycees?"

"Ha. Unless that stands for Juvenilely 'Carcerated instead of Junior Chamber of Commerce."

"A record, huh."

"Not all juvie, either. Started young, hadn't stopped. Property crimes, mostly. Graduated to domestic violence—two charges, two different ladies."

"Gosh. How old is he?" I hadn't imagined him old enough to get in that kind of trouble that many times.

"He's twenty-one."

Violence usually escalates, takes time to build, both in a person and in a relationship. Dirick Timms wasn't wasting any time.

"Do have some good news, though. Or maybe only good for Mr. Timms. He couldn't have been in your neck of the woods causing problems last Friday. He has the best kind of alibi."

"Locked up?"

"Bingo. High-speed chase, cold-cocking an officer at the side of I-285. Five-car call-out for backup. DUI, stolen vehicle, drug paraphernalia, intent to distribute. You name it. Locked up and not getting out anytime soon."

"When was all this?"

"Thursday night, a week ago."

"You sure it was him?"

"Don't have two of them in the system. Not a common spelling. His age sound right?"

"Yeah." How had Neanna gotten mixed up with him?

"So how come you looking for this loser?"

145

"Just a good girl who likes bad boys, I guess."

"Hope that's a client you're talking about." He chuckled. I could picture his Adam's apple bobbing up and down along his Ichabod Crane neck.

"I'm afraid so. Actually, her sister is the client. The girlfriend ended up dead. Sister doesn't want to believe it was suicide. I'm starting to agree with her."

"Least she had a sister who cared about her. Lots don't."

Even when they did have family who cared, it was often impossible to pull them back from the edge, once they'd gotten swept into a violent relationship. Had Neanna gone back to Dirick and hidden it from Fran? Or had Dirick sicced some of his friends on her trail?

"Rowly, you think there's any way he could have gotten to her even while he was in jail?"

"You talking a hit or something?"

Sounded crazy, especially when spoken in his thick drawl. "She is dead," I said.

"Maybe," he said. "If he's in a gang. Don't know about that, but I can sure check."

"And could you quietly check out Neanna's family. Her grandmother raised her. Her grandmother has a cousin you can talk to." I explained the family dynamic, the aunt's death, the suicide that might not be, and Fran's reluctance to trust private investigators.

"Heck, I hang around with P.I.'s now. I can see why she's reluctant," Rowly said.

"Gran's cousin might be able to give you a different perspective on the family. I'm especially interested in why Gran kept a scrapbook and where she got a gruesome death photo of her daughter, Neanna's aunt Wenda."

"Can you send me a scan of that?"

"Sure." That photo was proving a more popular share than Labor Day family picnic photos.

I gave him Fran's phone number and address. He could get contact information on Gran's cousin and perhaps charm Fran at the same time—provided she was as much a sucker for his wiry straw-colored hair and scarecrow physique as I'd been when I met him.

After we said good-bye, I picked up an employee handbook and noncompete agreement lying on my desk. Last week, as soon as they'd contacted me, I'd reviewed a new start-up company's documents. I'd scribbled my comments and corrections in the margins, but hadn't taken time to draft a transmittal letter or invoice. Those kinds of details always bogged me down more than the actual work did.

I carried the file to Shamanique. After just one day, I was really beginning to like having her here.

"Could you draft a letter? Here's the contact information. Tell him my comments are on the draft itself, ask him to let me know if he has any questions, and thank him for letting me be of service. Blah, blah, blah."

I scribbled a dollar figure on a sticky note. "Also prepare an invoice for this amount. There should be a sample form on the computer."

I'd transferred my files to my laptop and moved the desktop onto Shamanique's receptionist desk. Might as well find out if she knew how to use it.

My calendar had only two appointments for today: one I'd made last week to have lunch with Emma at computer camp and one for an afternoon trip to the auto-salvage yard. Last night, on my way back from Clemson, I'd stopped by Wal-Mart in Seneca just before it closed to get some supplies for my junkyard trek.

I called Rudy and got his voice mail.

"Hey. Pun over at the junkyard has a wrecked two-door Civic on the lot. He said I was welcome to shoot the windows out of it. Care to join me? I'm heading over about one-thirty."

As I passed Shamanique on my way to the kitchen, her fingers were flying over the computer keys. She declined my offer of some ice tea. As I returned with a tall glass clinking with ice, who should yet again be jangling the front door closed but Colin, or Mumler or whatever his name was, and his merry band of ghosters.

"Hey! Wait'll you see what we got last night! You and Mr. Bertram will be amazed!"

He was even more animated than when he'd reported his run-in with the motorcycle gang. Quint carried a computer bag slung over his shoulder, and all three of them stood looking at me expectantly, Colin shifting from one foot to the other.

"Um, let me see if Mr. Bertram is in his office."

His outer door was closed but unlocked. He sat in a pool of desk-lamp and computer-screen light in his dim office.

"They're ba-a-ack," I singsonged.

He blinked at me and closed his eyes, feigning weary resignation.

"They can't wait for you to see what they got. You'll be amazed!" I mocked Colin but in a quiet voice. I didn't want my joke to carry into the hallway.

"What is it?"

I shrugged. "I'm only the receptionist. My guess is, they've captured some ghosts."

He remained at his desk and just stared at me.

"You know you'd hate to miss it, if they really got something on film."

He rolled his eyes upward but pushed his chair back and followed me.

Quint had unpacked his laptop and had it balanced on one arm, booting it up.

"Come in," Melvin said, sounding as if he was glad to see them. Breeding does tell.

Colin almost danced on his lanky, Mr. Bojangle legs.

"That was a great lead you gave us. Absolutely incredible. We haven't slept all night."

Punch drunk. Didn't want to be in his head when that wore off.

"Moody Springs. What a perfect name! That place is really spooky late at night, for sure."

Trini nodded, her face solemn, her dark eyes large.

"But worth it," Colin said.

Quint's laptop hummed on Melvin's coffee table. I took a seat on the sofa, ready for the show, while Melvin pulled the heavy drapes on the eight-foot windows behind us. I was certain he had no intention of investing his or anyone else's money in this cinematic venture, but the installments had been entertaining.

Quint turned the large-screened laptop to face the sofa and knelt beside it to start the show. Colin and Trini sat in the club chairs.

I felt Trini's anxious gaze. I glanced at her and smiled.

"This is unedited, of course," Colin said. "We cut out the boring stuff, when nothing was happening, but this is still raw."

The screen showed a stretch of two-lane blacktop and, on the left of the screen, a broad, rough-paved pull-off.

Moody Springs. I recognized the CCC-constructed stacked granite wall lining the parking area and thought I could make out the steps cut into the hillside leading to the picnic tables scattered in the woods. It brought back memories of hauling grocery bags full of marshmallows and wienies and picking our way up the steps. Kids laughing, deep dappled shade, my family and friends, my childhood. And the nasty water in the fountain from the spring, the essence of rusty iron.

"We set the camera facing up the mountain," Colin narrated.

The film—is that what you call it when it's digital?—jumped, indicating one of their fast-forward cuts. The sky had darkened into dusk, the thick trees melded into a single darkness, the white line of the highway glowed.

A pickup truck came around the curve at the top of the frame, driving slowly. Its blinker signaled a right turn. The driver pulled off onto the verge some fifty yards from the camera, at the far end of the picnic area parking.

The passenger door opened, the dome light inside backlighting the driver who sported a gimme-hat and bushy hair. The driver, sitting bolt upright behind the wheel, turned toward the open door and waited until it closed. As the truck pulled off, passed closer to the camera, and disappeared from the computer screen, its color became more discernible—a dark blue or brown, rather than black.

The screen once again showed the original scene: empty pull-off, empty road, ominous solid line of trees. No one had been visible in the passenger seat. No one had gotten out of the truck. No one stood at the side of the road.

The camera shot began to swing slowly to the right, the lens focusing in tighter on the opposite side of the road.

"See it?" Colin asked.

Quint, still on his haunches beside the coffee table, pointed to the center of the scene. "Do you see it?"

I squinted at the screen. Melvin too leaned forward.

A faint mist swirled at the roadside, like fresh car exhaust on a frosty morning. But this wasn't a frosty anything. The air would have clung pungent and sticky, a normal, warm June night.

The smoke curled white-gray for a few seconds, faint against the almost black trees. Then it evaporated into woods I knew dropped immediately down the mountainside.

"Did you see it?" Colin leaned toward Melvin, trying to read his face. Quint fiddled with some buttons on the laptop, the scene running backward until he could replay the scene.

On the screen, the truck door closed as the driver, sitting stiffly behind the wheel, bid farewell to someone—someone who wasn't there. When the interior light clicked off, the driver fell into shadow.

The truck pulled away, leaving empty pavement. The camera zoomed in on the smoky dance of fog. I detected no skip in the picture, nothing to indicate that anything had been edited or deleted.

"Any idea who was driving the truck?"

"Naw," said Colin. "Didn't see there was any reason to flag him down until it was too late."

My head flooded with rude questions: Couldn't you jump in your car and chase him? Didn't somebody get his tag number? Seemed important to know who or what opened the door and got out.

"Ectoplasm," Quint announced. His compatriots nodded gravely. Melvin and I just stared.

"You know. A vortex. This is incredible. Usually all you get are orbs, which is the best we'd hoped for. But to capture a vortex or vapor event on camera. This is unbelievable. The only thing better would have been a full apparitional manifestation, but those are really rare."

Quint could tell from our faces that we weren't among the converted. His voice grew more animated. "Are you familiar with the various manifestations?"

I shook my head and knew he would explain.

"Most paranormal researchers consider themselves lucky to

capture orbs on camera. A round ball of light representing a concentration of psychic energy."

"Most of them are friendly," Trini said.

"Some aren't," Quint added with a sober face but no elaboration.

"A vortex is a heavier concentration, usually stationary, where the energy takes an elongated form. Then there's vapor—what's probably a moving ghost or possibly a spirit."

"If you're really lucky, you get a full manifestation," Trini said, scooting her skinny backside to the edge of her seat.

"Many documented sightings, relatively few photos of full manifestations," Colin said. "Some think an ectoplasmic event indicates that a ghost is moving toward or capable of a full appearance."

Trini said in a near-whisper, "Or about to fade away forever."

"Like a lost radio signal," Quint added.

Colin nodded. "Which leaves us with a dilemma. Do we set up at the top of the mountain, where he enters the car? Do we drive up and down the mountain ourselves, hoping he'll flag us down? Or do we stay with this location?"

From his kneeling position, he looked around at his troops, planning the assault on the hitchhiking spit of fog.

"Full moon next week," Quint intoned as if pronouncing an incantation.

"Wish we had instruments. Maybe we could've told whether it's building strength." Colin sounded wistful.

"Equipment?" I couldn't resist asking since he so obviously wanted to pique Melvin's interest. The equipment he coveted undoubtedly cost money.

"Professionals use an electromagnetic field detector to record energy fields and such. And infrared cameras. Mostly stuff you can get at an electronics store."

"Professionals?"

Melvin had obviously picked up on the wrong part of Colin's description.

"Altogether it can cost over a thousand dollars."

Melvin kept Colin pinned with his gray-blue gaze, the merest shadow of a bemused smile at one corner of his mouth. "I suppose a notebook, to record car tag numbers and such, would be useful, too," he said.

"What's next?" I asked, to cut off Colin's silent plea and Melvin's gentle gibes.

"That's another dilemma. Do we continue with Moody Springs since we had such success there? Or do we move on to a new site? Maybe we've got all this site has to offer—at least until the full moon or a rainy night, when this manifestation should be stronger."

They'd got everything except the name of the truck driver who'd watched someone open the truck door and disappear. Who was that guy?

"If we had a second video camera," Colin said, "that would solve everything."

Another not-so-subtle hint.

"Did you get anything at the Heath house?" I couldn't resist asking, wondering when the sheriff's deputy had gotten their camera back from Max and the motorcycle guys.

"We might have captured an orb there, near the second-floor balcony. But . . ." Quint shrugged.

"That's no good," Colin snapped.

I wanted to ask if it included footage of Max or Do-Rag threatening to beat the crap out of them, but that would be rude.

"We do have some rough footage from another site last night," Quint said, his ponytail swaying with his movements, "but I didn't have time to edit it.

"Sometimes you just shoot blind and see what turns up. Too dark to see at all clearly what happened out at the railroad track."

"Railroad?" I asked.

"Mm-hm," Colin said. "The train light that comes without a train. Quint here may be the only person who's stood his ground on the track to film it. He's a plucky guy."

He clapped his friend's shoulder. "We'll just have to study it, see what we have. I'll be glad to come show you, when we get finished," he said to Melvin. He clearly didn't assume I had money to invest in his ghoster pilot.

"What about the crybaby bridge?" I asked. I knew Rudy would rather they didn't mess around the overlook above Moody Springs.

"Haven't checked it. Haven't had time to do any validating research on that yet."

I glanced at my watch. We'd reached my morning quota for fun. "I've got to go. Special invitation from my niece to eat lunch with her today. Can't miss that. Grammar school cafeteria food. Mmm." I tried to approximate lip smacking.

Melvin gave me a look that said *traitor* as I excused myself.

Lunch with Emma's computer camp was an unprecedented honor. It turned out they'd invited parents today, especially those who used computers in their jobs. I was Emma's parental stand-in. Fortunately I didn't have to talk about my career, just show up and eat corn dogs and yellow cling peaches.

Emma looked up from her computer and gave me a gap-toothed grin when I appeared in the doorway.

"Class," the teacher announced. "It's time for lunch. Let's line up."

To me, she said in an equally slow, stern tone, "We were to meet the parents in the cafeteria."

Emma shot me a commiserating smile, not too embarrassed to claim her errant "parent."

"Hey, kid," I said when she joined me in the hall. "I'm sorry about last night."

She looked puzzled a minute, then nodded. "That's okay."

"It was work. I completely forgot."

"They don't even keep score, you know." She looked no more concerned about my lapse than she was about me being scolded by her uptight computer teacher.

In the cafeteria, we picked up our box lunches and sat at the long, munchkin-short tables. Emma sat beside me silently studying the other kids like a red-haired Jane-Goodall-in-training. Did she sit and stare every day? Or was she looking at her life through my eyes? Knowing Emma, age seven going on seventy, she spent every day studying them because it made no sense to try to interact with this life-form.

The noise level in the cafeteria drowned out any attempt at conversation, so I joined Emma in staring at her campmates as they spewed food and chattered incessantly at me and Joel's dad, an insurance salesman who made sure I had his card. I didn't reciprocate.

Emma could never be bothered with learning names, but I quickly realized she had an alarmingly accurate talent for description. Truth be told, they were a strange bunch. One little black kid—the most normal kid I saw—had his hair twisted in little balls all over his head, which explained the nickname Knothead. Emma had told me about a girl who looked like Frankenstein, which I thought was a mean thing to say. Not so. As soon as I spotted the little girl with straight black hair, flat face, and deep-set dark eyes in skin so pale it had the luster of a frog's belly, I had to bite the inside of my lip to keep from laughing.

Joel proved to be fascinated by me—just as he obviously was with Emma. But equally obvious, he was afraid to talk to her, so I became the bull's-eye target for much of his lunch and all of his bad jokes. His dad egged him on by laughing, a peculiar hyena snort. I noticed he wasn't wearing a wedding ring and felt a sudden, intense kinship with Emma. Not wanting to inadvertently encourage Joel or his dad, I too mostly sat and stared, and periodically scooted my squat little chair away from the line of fire. Didn't anyone teach these kids to chew with their mouths closed?

Had my grammar school class been like this? I didn't remember it like this at all. I remembered Rudy and L.J. and my best friend who'd moved away the next year. I hadn't met Cissie Prentice until third grade; she'd been a boy-crazy flirt even then. I remembered myself as exactly the same person I was today. I wasn't aware that anything inside had changed. I looked down at Emma with an odd sense of déjà vu.

That had been the same year L.J. took to smashing me up against the brick bathroom wall for fun and sport. I guess Aunt Letha's right: People don't change, they only get more so. That didn't bode well for Joel, Frankenstein, or even Knothead.

I pulled out of the teachers' lot at school with a better appreciation for how underpaid teachers are, and with some amazement that Emma loved school enough to spend part of her summer in computer camp.

I parked outside the Law Enforcement Center's employee entrance and rummaged around in the back floorboard for my hiking boots. From the usually quiet street that bordered the parking lot, I heard a familiar buzzing sound. Donlee Griggs on his scooter. His six feet seven inches topped with a ludicrous round, glowing orange helmet lent a circus-clown air to his balancing act on the tiny scooter.

Where was his girlfriend? Without her matching pumpkin head smashed into the small of his back, he looked . . . alone.

With my car door open, I sat sideways in the seat and finished tucking my pants legs into my boots and tying the laces as Rudy, dressed today as a civilian, ambled down the exterior steps to join me in the parking lot.

"That's quite a fashion statement," he said. "Something you learned while you were off in Greenville?"

I made a face and swung my legs back in the car.

"You ever been to Pun's junkyard?" I said. "You're going to wish you weren't wearing those spit-shines you got on."

"You're telling me you know all about junkyards?" Rudy climbed in the passenger seat, reluctantly consenting to ride with me only because neither of us wanted to make this appear an official visit.

"Restore and maintain a classic car, you learn a lot of things. I've spent enough time out there that he agreed to let us come play in one of his cars."

I'd tagged along with my dad over the years when he went out looking for parts. Pun knew more about what had gone into refurbishing the Mustang we were riding in than anyone other than my dad.

Pun's junkyard sat on the edge of town, mostly hidden by a twenty-foot-high barrier of red tips and the natural swell and fall of the land. As I drove through the rusty chain-link gate, we could see the fields spread out before us as if they'd been planted to produce a bumper crop of rust and shiny chrome and rainbow colors.

I got out to greet Pun, who stood in the door of the battered lean-to that served as his office.

"I hauled it 'round yonder." He pointed down the dirt-and-grass track, then crooked his thumb to the left. "In front of a dirt bank. So stray shot won't fly around."

"Thanks."

"What'cha doin' with that one with you?"

He pointed a greasy knuckle toward my windshield and Rudy.

"Protection," I said.

He snorted. "Never heard tell'a somebody wanting to shoot out win-der glass for the heck of it. So whatever you want to call it. Keep him away from my cars." Again with the knuckle.

He turned without waiting for a response.

I folded myself back into the car, popped the clutch, and drove away before glancing at Rudy.

"So why didn't you tell me you and Pun have bad blood? What's that all about?"

Rudy's turn to snort. "We've had to come execute administrative warrants a few times—somebody junking a new car to collect insurance or stripping a stolen car."

"Pun chops stolen cars? No way you're telling me that."

"No. But all junkyards end up with stuff—just like pawnshops do. We gotta check it out. Pun, he's got to take it personally."

"If I'd known hanging out with you was going to disgrace me with my only connection for keeping this forty-year-old car running, I wouldn't have invited you to my party."

"That could've been a blessing. This isn't my idea of the ideal party spot."

We were winding our way along a weedy aisle of debauched car carcasses, headed toward a hillside that had been bulldozed flat on one side to make room to stack cars.

"So when are you letting me in on what you've got planned?"

I stopped beside a gray Honda, the hood and engine missing, the upholstery torn.

"We're going to put a bullet in a head and see which way the glass shatters."

Thursday Afternoon

The Civic coupe Pun had towed into position for me had met its demise when someone rammed its front end into an accordion shape. Just as I'd asked, he'd situated it with the driver's window parallel to the red dirt bank.

Despite the front-end damage, the passenger compartment was intact, the right-side door worked, and the window glass was undamaged.

From the Mustang's trunk, I drew out a plastic shopping bag and Exhibit One for our demonstration.

"What the hell?" Rudy stood, his hands on his hips, his mouth open, staring at the white foam head I'd stuck on a thirty-inch dowel nailed to crossed slats.

"Thought it would help us position the shot, if we had a

head. Other than mine." I had a sore spot behind my right ear where the gun muzzle had hit me yesterday.

The head, intended as a wig model, could slide a few inches up and down on the dowel so we could get it into the right position. I was proud of my handiwork, despite Rudy's derision.

I crawled into the passenger seat, wedged the ends of the crossed slats under the back of the driver's seat cushion, and pushed the head down an inch or two, trying to approximate Neanna's height by measuring it against my own.

I leaned back. "How does that look?"

"Like somebody's got too much free time on her hands."

I rolled my eyes. "About where her head would've been?"

He bent over with that awkward stiffness common in former high school football players gone to seed, his hands on his thighs. "Yep. 'Bout there. So?"

"The gun." I held out my hand for the gun Rudy was supposed to bring from the evidence room.

He held a fake suede gun case, but he wasn't unzipping it.

"You plan to shoot the head."

"Yep."

"Why?"

"To see what happens. To the driver's window."

Rudy was being purposely obtuse.

"Perfectly safe," I said. "See? The dirt bank will stop the bullet."

"Okay. But what are you going to do about the flying glass?"

From my plastic bag, I pulled two pairs of safety glasses I'd borrowed from Dad's workshop.

He still just stood staring down at me. Finally, he cocked his head. "Get out. I'll do it."

My turn to stare. I gave in. What did it hurt to play along with Mr. Macho?

I climbed out, flipped the front seat forward, and slipped into the backseat.

He shook his head. That wasn't what he had in mind, but he too decided to give in.

The Honda wasn't as low-slung as my Mustang, but the passenger seat wasn't as far from the dash or the roof, so it was a snug fit for Rudy.

"Miz Smarty, what about ear protection? This'll be—"

I reached over the seat, presenting two bright yellow foam earplugs pinched between my fingers.

"Cheesh." He took them, though, kneaded them into thin cylinders, and stuck them in his ears.

"You'd better close your door," I said.

He tried, unsuccessfully, to turn a baleful gaze at me, but gave it up in favor of flipping down the visor and eyeballing me in the mirror.

"We want the conditions as close as possible, don't we?"

Rudy slammed the door. He looked like a bear stuck in a refrigerator.

He grunted as he twisted in his seat and tried to place the gun muzzle behind the ridge indicating the mannequin's right ear. He studied it a minute, then grasped the barrel and handed me the gun.

"You'd better do it. To get the right angle."

I took the gun grip. "Like this?" I braced my arm along Rudy's headrest and tried to mimic the impossible angle I'd tried yesterday on my own head.

"Yeah. Let her go."

I gently squeezed the trigger, concentrating on not letting the muzzle shift.

The shot deafened me, even with the earplugs. I'd involuntarily closed my eyes.

The eerie white head leaned over in the seat, with only a small hole surrounded by a gray-black spatter of gunshot residue.

The window glass in the driver's door also had a hole and was crazed into frosted glass, but it was still intact.

I looked at Rudy in his visor mirror. We both looked back at the window.

"So. What does that prove?" Rudy asked, his voice tinted with frustration.

"That cookies don't always crumble the same way twice." Disappointment and the metallic smell of burnt gunpowder left a sharp taste in my mouth.

I toyed with the idea of getting Pun to haul out another Honda, but I squelched that thought. I'd already pushed the bounds of propriety and goodwill.

"It was worth a try," I said with a shrug in my voice.

"Yeah." Rudy grunted as he unlatched the door and climbed out. I slipped out of the backseat and walked around the rear of the car.

On the ground glinting in the sunlight were a few pebbles of safety glass. Nothing but bits, forced loose by the rush of air pushed ahead of the speeding bullet. Very few glints. Just like the crime-scene photos. I bent over and picked up three of them, arranging them in the palm of my hand.

Rudy watched me over the roof of the car. I took one more look at the shattered window, held in place as the safety glass designers had hoped, in a crazy quilt of pebbles rather than in shattered, scarring shards.

"Ready to go?" Rudy asked.

I nodded.

He took a step back and closed the passenger door.

Then it happened. The driver's window crumbled before my eyes. Myriad tiny bits pinged, falling endlessly. With the crazed glass gone, I could see the foam head, the left side facing me blown into shreds by the bullet's exit.

I stood spellbound. The glass continued to tinkle as bits sifted down. Inside the car. Except for a few stray pieces that bounced off the window jamb, the glass had fallen inside the car. Just like the crime-scene photos.

Rudy came around the front of the car and stood near the front tire, studying our handiwork.

"It happened when somebody closed the door," I said, feeling deflated, disappointed. I'd hoped we'd learn something I could offer Fran. What, I wasn't sure. The glass falling inside the car wasn't sinister. It hadn't happened because of some mysterious shot from outside the car, as I'd secretly suspected. It had happened when someone closed the door.

"When who closed the door?" Rudy said. "That's the question."

I jerked my head up. Reality struck like a blow. "Those pictures were taken when the investigators first arrived on scene. The window was already shattered by the time the first officer arrived."

"Had to be."

We both stared at the open car window and the foam head, reordering our earlier versions.

"So somebody else was there," I said. "With her. Somebody got out and closed the door."

Rudy pursed his lips. "There's a chance somebody else found her and didn't report it."

"They opened the door, looked in, closed it, and drove away without reporting it? Any strange fingerprints on the door?"

"Just smudges," he said. He didn't sound convinced by his theory.

We looked at each other without speaking. I crossed behind the Honda to my car. Rudy climbed in beside me.

In silence, we drove a distance between the stacks of cars before I could turn around. As I returned to where the Honda sat, Pun stepped out into the road waving the foam head like a South American tribesman with an enemy's shrunken head on a stick. The mannequin was huge compared to Pun's head—and had almost as much hair.

"Take this with you. Jeez. I have enough trouble keeping good help around here without you leaving stuff like this behind. Scare the shit outta somebody."

"Sorry," I called through the window as Pun jammed the head in at Rudy.

"Least you could'a done was shoot some rats while you'uz out here. Make yourself useful."

"Thanks, Pun." I waved and pulled slowly away before he could launch into another diatribe.

Once on the highway, I had to pull off again in front of a long-boarded gas station. I was shaking.

"Somebody was there. With her." I turned to Rudy.

His face was somber. "It's possible."

"She couldn't hold that gun in that position, Rudy."

"Okay, probable, then. Still not certain."

"She didn't kill herself, Rudy."

The certainty of it washed over me. I gripped the steering wheel. I'd never had a response like this, shaking as if from fear or exertion.

"You okay?" Rudy asked after a moment. "You aren't going to throw up, are you?"

I shook my head. "Can I see the crime-scene photos again? All of them? And do you have—can you find the file on Wenda Sims?"

"They're still looking," he said.

I shifted into first gear, eased the clutch out, and pulled onto the road. Disappointment was not mixing well with my adrenaline overload.

"I've got a call in to Vince Ingum," Rudy said. The one who worked Wenda Sims's case. Retired to Myrtle Beach, old sumbitch. If he hasn't fallen off a deep-sea fishing boat, he'll probably call me back today or tomorrow."

I underestimate Rudy sometimes. He'd been busy.

We drove back to town in silence. I dropped Rudy off and went back to the office, still trying to process the implications of what we'd witnessed.

Shamanique stuck her arm straight out as I walked in, waving a phone message slip. She didn't take her eyes off her computer screen.

It took me a moment to digest the note. "This all Rowly said?" He'd called from Atlanta.

"Yes'm. He wanted to make sure you knew about that."

"He got this from the cousin?"

"That's what he said."

An unnecessary cross-examination on my part. I was reading directly from Shamanique's note. Her handwriting was neat, she'd time-dated the message. I was simply having trouble taking it in.

I pulled the pocket doors to my office closed and slumped into one of the armchairs in the window, staring at the note.

Gran bought life insurance on Neanna—$200,000. N. signed it over to Fran. Paid in full for one year, starting last May. N. made Fran her beneficiary. Call me.

Two hundred thousand dollars. Why hadn't Fran told me how much? And that the policy was recent? People had been killed for a heck of a lot less. Crazy possibilities swirled in my head. Was Fran's "money is no object" attitude an act? A ruse to draw me off the trail?

Who really says, "Money is no object"? Nobody. Not even people with lots of it. Especially people with lots of it. Could she afford to be generous with the investigation because she was counting on the insurance money? Was she using it like a broken branch to obscure footprints on the trail? Or to ease her conscience for being around to collect it?

Who buys a $200,000 life insurance policy on a young woman who's bouncing around in dead-end jobs? Why?

I dialed Rowly's number and got him on the second ring.

"Hey, it's Avery. A good time to talk?"

"Sure. How'd'ya do?"

"Got your message about the insurance. Anything else you can tell me?"

"Yeah. Miz Sidalee Evans—the grandmother's cousin—told me about the policy. She thought the whole thing was a sin and a disgrace. She had sermons on several topics, but I won't preach 'em at 'chu."

"Thanks." Rowly and his rural Georgia accent always raised a smile.

"One important thing. Said Neanna was pure furious when she found out about it. Neanna said that's about what she'd expect, her own Gran wagering on when she would kick off. Said she'd see what she could do to oblige her. Guess you know about Neanna's mom Marie and her aunt Wenda—Gran's only two children?"

"Yeah."

"Miz Sidalee thought buying the insurance was right creepy. Said the grandmother couldn't afford the premiums, even if it was for term insurance."

"She bought term life insurance on Neanna?"

"Yep."

My early-warning system—a knot in my stomach—twisted

on me. Why term life insurance? It didn't accumulate any cash surrender value or act as an investment Neanna could use later. It simply insured her life, as long as the premiums were paid. It served no other purpose.

"Anything else I need to know?" As if that wasn't too much already.

"Nope. Thought you'd want to know about that quick as possible. I've been invited to tea with Miz Sidalee this afternoon, so I'll fill you in on that."

"Thanks, Rowly. Got to mull on this a bit."

Life insurance on a young woman from a family plagued by young deaths. While she was young, the term-life premiums would be low—lower than whole life insurance. Only as she got older would the premiums increase. If she got older.

Gran died first, leaving the policy behind, paid up for a year starting in May. Neanna made Fran the beneficiary. Then she's dead. Made to look like a suicide.

Why was Fran stirring up questions about the death? Why hadn't she just collected her check and accepted the obvious?

I reached for the phone and hit redial.

"Rowly. Me again. When was the policy first taken out?"

"Don't know exactly. Why?"

"Can you find out? And find out how the suicide exclusion reads?"

"Know where you're headed. I'll get back to you."

I stared at my neat desktop. Shamanique must have been in here straightening things. She hadn't moved any of my stacks—thank goodness. My whole filing system depended on positional memory. The office was definitely neater, though, and I appreciated her initiative.

I tried to conjure up an image, an impression of Fran. She'd seemed earnest, sincerely saddened by her "sister's" death. On the other hand, I'd been fooled before. Sociopaths make great liars. I'd had no warning signals, no reason to doubt her. Did the size of the insurance policy give me a reason now?

I hit redial again.

"Rowly, one last question. Any information on Fran French's family? In particular, does she have money?"

"Hoo-wee, I reckon. Her dad and granddad developed half of northeast Atlanta. She seems to have a knack, too. Owns her own sports marketing firm, you know."

"And it's successful?"

"I should say so. I can see if there are any cracks, though."

"Thanks. Just checking my perceptions. Through bugging you for a while. I promise."

I replaced the receiver. That explained Fran's understated elegance, her self-assured expectation that she'd get what she asked for. But some people who once had money are good at pretending they still do. I'd let the jury stay out a while longer on that, until I heard back from Rowly.

Talking to Fran on the phone would serve no purpose. I needed to eyeball her when I asked my questions. I'd check with her, see when she'd be back in Dacus.

I slid open the doors to my office.

"Shamanique, any word from Edna about Mr. Mart?"

She turned in her chair to face me, her chin down, her head cocked. I saw that flash of family resemblance.

"I wouldn't be bothering her with questions, if I was you."

I stared without reply.

"She don't like folks bird-dogging her while she's working. She said she'd let you know."

I nodded. Not much else to say.

When Shamanique turned back to her computer screen, I noticed a familiar font and screen color. The South Carolina case reports search system. At least one of us was gainfully employed.

Back in my office, I slid a file folder from the stack on the front corner. Inside was the copy of the photo I'd found in the liner of Neanna's car.

The tiny blood spots had photocopied as sprinkles of black dots. I sat in the sunlight, studying it.

Something about it didn't look like the recent crime-scene photos Rudy had shown me of Neanna's death. The tone was washed out, not the stark light and shadows exposed by the police photographer's flashbulb, so it had more depth, particularly in the shadows. Could the crime-scene photographer have used a different flash technique? Did film and digital photos look different? The newer photos had all been in color. Were they all black and white in 1985?

All that still begged the question how Gran had gotten this photo.

Who could've taken it? As soon as that question arose, one answer followed. Who routinely snapped photos of the worst moments in people's lives?

I slid the photo back in the folder and clamped it tight under my arm as I headed out the door.

Thursday Afternoon

I untucked my pants legs from the hiking boots I'd worn to the salvage yard but didn't waste time going upstairs to change into walking shoes. I sure needed a longer walk than the two blocks to the newspaper office. Too sedentary of late, but the two blocks would have to do for now.

Alice Vann, the real power behind the Dacus *Clarion*, greeted me at the chest-high desk where she took orders for restaurant menu printing jobs, accepted copy for ads, and complaints from people who didn't have anything better to do.

"Walter's in back, either setting up a circular or yakking with one of his fishing buddies." She rolled her eyes. Walter, the editor, and Alice had been married to each other and to the newspaper for longer than I'd been alive.

I'd debated with myself on the way over, to make sure I

wasn't violating any confidences in showing the photo to Walter. He was, after all, a newspaperman, even if he spent most of this time printing menus and sales flyers. I couldn't think of any prohibitions against showing the picture, and I knew he'd be discreet.

Alice flipped up the countertop to allow me access to the inner sanctum. The familiar nose-tingling chemical smells grew more pronounced in the large rear workroom.

Dad, wiping his hands on a rag and heading for the door as I entered, stopped short.

"Hey, hon. What brings you in?"

"Hey. Needed to ask Walter a question. Got a breakdown?"

"Naw." He wiped around each cuticle. "Just time for a little adjustment on the paper feed."

Dad lives for something to fix, especially anything that involves grease and moving parts.

"You got something on your sleeve," he said.

I raised my arm. Something crusty. "I ate lunch with Emma's computer camp today." No need to explain further.

"You coming for supper tonight?"

"Hadn't thought that far ahead." I paused. Maybe I should ask Dad about the window glass in the car. He's an engineer. It would have to wait, though. Too much explanation for now.

He mistook my silence for hesitation. "Don't feel you have to. Don't even know what your mother has planned. She might be off saving the world somewhere this evening. You know how she is."

"I'll let you know, okay?" I smiled. The First Fruits Food Bank or the English as a Second Language Bible Study might not save the whole world, but they did save parts of it.

"Sure." He smiled down at me, his blue eyes clear as he peered over the glasses that perpetually sat down on the end of his nose.

My dad's natural lack of curiosity meant that he continued on his way without hanging around to see what business I had with Walter, conveniently saving me from having to answer difficult questions. His immunity to idle gossip made him the last person anyone expected to buy a newspaper to entertain himself in his early retirement.

Walter, his fringe-rimmed bald head gleaming and his perpetual scowl oddly welcoming, stood with both hands in his pockets.

"What'cha need, girlie?"

"You recognize this?"

I held the photo up in front of me, my fingers framing the edges.

He leaned closer, his head cocked back to study it through his bifocals. He tilted his chin down and pursed his lips, squinting at me with his fair-sky eyes, waiting for an explanation.

"Remember the Wenda Sims murder? In 1985?"

His attention wandered away from me and the photo, his gaze unfocused as he searched his mental file cabinet.

"Girl found dead in the graveyard. They never solved that one."

"Might this be a news photographer's photo?"

"No." He shook his head, his mouth crinkled in distaste. "Wouldn't have any reason to take a picture like that. Who wants to see that on the front page of their hometown newspaper? Parents want to see little Johnny's name in the article about the church league game and that a good time was had by all. Not that."

"But mightn't a photographer have snapped it, just—because?"

"No." His headshake grew more insistent.

"But how can you—"

"Be so sure? Because I was the photographer then. And the feature writer and layout guy and about everything else."

Duh, of course.

"Even if I'd been on the scene before the cops got there, I sure wouldn't have spent film on something like that. That's just not decent."

No, it wasn't decent. That was a good way to describe it.

"Disrespectful. If that were my daughter, I surely wouldn't want someone capturing that on film." More head shaking, slow and sad.

"You think maybe another newspaper took it?"

He pooched out his lips in a bowknot. "Anything's possible, I suppose, but I don't remember anybody else showing up until later. Especially back then, nobody could print something like that, so why shoot it?"

Good point.

"Any need in me asking how you came by that?" he asked.

"A client."

"Someone with a kinky eye for keepsakes, if you ask me."

I looked down at the picture, seeing it with some of his perspective. Somebody had a kinky eye, for sure.

"Was everything you shot then in black-and-white?"

"Yep. We developed our own film, of course. Didn't have time to mail stuff off, even if it was just a weekly paper. Black-and-white was cheaper and easier."

"That makes sense." I couldn't see Alice running to drop off film at the five-and-dime store. "Thanks, Walter."

"Keep us in mind, you get a story you can tell." He absent-mindedly smoothed the front of his heavy black apron and turned back to his printing job.

I waved to Alice and stepped carefully down the canted granite block that served as the front stoop. Head down, I wandered along the narrow sidewalk across from the back of the courthouse, musing on the photo I carried in my file folder.

Made sense that news photographers in 1985 still used black-and-white film. I imagined police photographers used it for the same reason—more clarity and easier to process in-house. Wouldn't want to freak out somebody at a commercial film developer with gruesome close-up crime-scene shots. I wanted to see Wenda Sims's case file. I was certain the photos in that file had been stark black-and-white. Clinical. Not obliquely flash-lit with artistic angles.

I stopped, opened the folder, and stared at the photo. What was it that seemed so—demeaning, insulting? Even though it revealed nothing sexual, it felt obscene, like a violation. Walter had seen it, too. Something about the angle of the shot, looking at her from beyond her slightly parted knees up toward her slack face, her lips apart in a caricature of a breathless sex kitten. Maybe it was her half-lidded eyes, the unseeing half circles of her iris visible only because of the intimate angle.

In the sun, with the hazy heat thick in my lungs, I shivered. The most likely photographer? The murderer. Nobody else made sense. So how had Neanna's gran gotten the photo? The questions circled around. For Neanna, had the answer been deadly?

Late Thursday Afternoon

I nodded at my stone-faced guardian angel as I poked up the sidewalk at the office. Wish she could fly me in some wisdom on her wings.

If I'd noticed the battered VW microbus parked on the street, I'd have hurried inside.

Melvin appeared as soon as the doorknob bells stopped jangling.

"Just in time, m'dear." His tone carried a smirk.

"Huh?"

"Trust me, you'll be mad if you miss this." He used the same teasing invitation I'd offered him on the ghosters' last visit as he ushered me into his office.

Colin, Trini, and Quint were back in their familiar spots. Colin had taken a seat on the sofa, flanked by his aides-de-camp.

The heavy brocade drapes that some interior designer from Greenville had dipped into Melvin's wallet to have custom-made were once again drawn against the late sun, and Quint's laptop sat open on the coffee table.

"Could you replay your footage for Avery?" Melvin asked, indicating nothing but sincerity, unless you knew him well enough to detect the teasing undertone.

"Sure." Quint slid off the sofa onto his bony knees.

"Not our footage, exactly," Colin said. "This is someone else's. But we personally went out and captured the EVP."

"EVP?" I asked.

"Electronic Voice Phenomenon," Colin said, clearly proud of whatever that meant.

From a perspective in the middle of a railroad track, the computer screen showed a twin rail disappearing into the distance along a berm that sloped off with grassy sides. The two solid walls of dark trees merged with the tracks in the distance.

The sky and trees blended in shades of dark, the rails glistened as though absorbing all the available light. A beautiful tableau.

As I scanned the screen, wondering what I was missing, a pinprick of light appeared in the middle of the tracks. Not back where the tracks disappeared, and not close to the camera. Somewhere midway between identifiable and gone.

I expected it to move toward us. I expected a train. Logical, I thought. But it stayed put, swinging slightly from side to side, slowly, sending a signal.

Melvin leaned forward, his elbows on his knees, watching the screen. "Who gave you this film?"

"The two dudes. They said we needed to go out to the track, check it out ourselves."

"What two dudes?" I asked.

Colin shrugged. "We started talking at lunch the other day."

"We've had lots of people interested in our research," said Quint.

Melvin and I exchanged glances.

"So you got some more film like this?" I asked.

"No-o, but watch here."

Just then, the light blazed bright, fixed on the camera. Then clicked out. The screen showed only shadows of dark, now deeper as daylight faded.

"No visuals, but we got an audio recording."

"Where was this filmed?" I asked.

"The train track heading south out of Dacus," said Colin.

"Just the other side of the crossing, near the sawmill."

"Pretty isolated there," said Trini. "Just the little road that crosses the track, hardly even a two-lane."

"What's supposed to cause the light?"

"The guys said it was a switchman trying to warn the engineer that the switch is frozen, that he's fixing to wreck," Trini said in her breathless near-whisper.

"He keeps coming back because he was late that night, he was working on the switch and couldn't repair it and he didn't make it onto the track in time to warn the engineer. So it crashed."

"When was this?" Melvin asked.

Colin shrugged and looked at the other two. "In the sixties sometime?"

"We haven't had time to do the background research on it," Quint said.

"But we did go stand in the spot, where these ties are thrown about," Colin said.

Quint flipped to a still shot showing a jumble of old railroad ties strewn along the sides of the low embankment.

I snuck a glance at Melvin.

"We don't know for sure if these were left over from the accident," Quint said.

"But this is the spot where the dudes who made the tape told us to go. This is the spot where the light actually appears, where those other guys filmed it."

"The ties looked burnt," said Trini.

I didn't ask if they knew what creosote looked like—or if they'd ever smelled charred wood. But from nothing more than the photo, I was sure I could tell the difference. The railroad company had been recently repairing sections of the track.

"What's this audiotape?" Melvin asked.

I wasn't certain why he was feigning interest: curiosity for the absurd? Melvin wasn't one to string along the gullible just to be mean or make fun of them. The same did not apply to whichever good ol' boys sent them in search of a haunted railroad, in a place that had never witnessed a train wreck, at least that I'd heard of. I'd certainly never heard of a lonely brakeman with an eternal flame. Somewhere in North Carolina, yes. Not here. Somebody was tweaking these kids—somebody besides Melvin.

Quint pulled a miniature digital gizmo from his backpack of tricks and held it aloft. As we sat in silence, he pushed a button with a dramatic flourish.

I recognized Colin's voice. "Are you here? Can you hear us?" He sounded as if he were at a distance from the microphone.

Silence followed. Colin asked again, "Can you hear us? Are you here?"

Another silence. Quint held the recorder like a beacon lamp. The three listened, Trini's eyes wide, watching Melvin for his reaction.

Then we heard it. A scratchy voice, like a pie tin scraping on metal. "Have you found it? Have you found it?" the voice pled.

On the tape, Quint's voice said, "Did you hear anything?"

"I don't know," Trini whispered.

"Play it back and let's see," Colin said on tape.

"A spirit voice," Colin interrupted the tape, matter-of-fact.

"I take it you couldn't hear the voice when you were standing there?" Melvin asked.

"No." All three chimed in.

"Not the words, really," said Trini. "It was a total shock when we played it back."

"There's one more bit," Colin said.

Quint hit the play button again.

"Tell us what happened," Colin's voice said, again at a distance.

"Get away! You'll be killed!" the voice rasped.

The digital machine then went silent.

"We asked more questions, but that was the final reply," Colin said.

"You called this what, an Electronic Voice Phenomenon?" asked Melvin.

"EVP," Colin said with a nod.

"This is just a digital recorder, like a dictation machine?"

"Standard equipment these days for our kind of investigation," Colin said. "Along with an EMF, a still camera, and video. I like to take Polaroids, too. Sometimes the old stuff works the best."

Melvin stayed quiet, encouraging him to continue.

"Spirit voices can sometimes be captured on digital recorders or videotape. No one is sure why, but investigators often don't hear anything during the site visit, only when the tape is replayed."

"Sometimes you have to really listen to make it out, what with all the static," Trini said.

"You're saying you didn't hear that voice when it spoke?"

All three shook their heads, more insistent this time.

"Not really," Trini added. "We heard a noise, but we couldn't make it out. But that's what you do. Take it and listen to it until you can understand it."

"Standard procedure," said Colin. "We used the EMF— Electromagnetic Field Detector—to test the area. Ours isn't very sophisticated, but we found a spike at one particular spot close to the ground. So we placed the recorder on the crosstie at that spot. Just like the guys who shot the video said, when we asked the question, we heard some faint rasping sound. So we played it back."

"That's the way it works for most people," said Trini. "They'll ask a question and it's like the universe speaks back."

"Or, more precisely, the accumulated energy of an intense event, imprinted on the area, speaks back," said Colin. "One researcher suggested that these events may be recorded on iron found in the area of an event, like the ferric oxide used on tape recordings. Of course, it has to have been magnetized in some way."

"Replaying like a video on a loop," said Quint.

I wondered if the universe always sounded as though it needed a throat lozenge, or if the cosmic video had replayed so often, the tape was worn. I didn't speak my random inquiries out loud to the universe.

· "Is this EMF detector the same thing used to check for electrical interference around electronic equipment?" Melvin asked.

"Yeah," said Colin. "Most standard equipment in our field has been adapted from other uses."

"We want to go back and try to re-create the video the two guys made there, capture the light on film for ourselves. They said certain nights around the gibbous moon worked best, so we'll have to postpone that inquiry."

"But we're very excited," said Trini.

"There have also been sightings of a headless guy walking the tracks in that area," Quint said. "Getting that on film would be bigger than that Bigfoot video."

Melvin bowed his head, and I knew he was biting his lip. Melvin knew there was no point in arguing with a true believer.

"So what's next?" I asked, drawing attention away from Melvin before he gave himself away.

Quint rocked forward on his knees, turning the laptop toward him to power it down. "We're going to the Freed house tonight. Down from the Baptist Church?"

"Night is supposed to be the best time there. Really the only time to capture orbs."

"We haven't been able to get permission to go inside," said Trini, "even though it's abandoned now."

"There are reports of a full manifestation there."

"On the stairs," said Trini. "A weeping woman."

I'd weep too if I had to spend eternity dodging the ectoplasmic version of celebrity paparazzi.

"The orb activity outside is supposed to be incredible," said Trini.

"So we're going to check that out after dark."

"Incredible," said Melvin with no trace of a grin. He stood as Quint packed his computer. "Thanks for sharing your latest find."

He ushered them out the door like a gracious host and rejoined me in our mutual entry hall, shaking his head.

"Why're you egging them on?" I asked. "You're not really thinking about investing, are you?"

"Of course not. And how am I egging them on? They stop by, I watch their show, and I'm polite." His mild indignation covered his mischievous grin.

"You're not the only nine-year-old boy in town having one over on them."

Melvin couldn't contain it any longer. He laughed. "I half expected the next answer to be, *Where's my head? What have you done with my head? Boo!* Just like those old campfire stores."

"Melvin, it isn't funny." But I was grinning. "Okay, it is funny."

"EMF detectors." He snorted. "Why didn't it dawn on them it might be picking up a wireless microphone somebody put on the tracks?"

I stared at him, almost embarrassed for the ghosters. "You think that's what it was?"

"Makes sense, doesn't it?"

"Somebody could get hurt, them wandering around all over the place in the middle of the night."

"Not as long as they have sense enough to get off the railroad tracks when a train comes."

I gave him a chiding frown, a weak imitation borrowed from my mother and Aunt Aletha.

"Admittedly, there's every indication they wouldn't have sense enough to come in out of a shower of ectoplasm, but it's harmless. They're having a good time. Heck, considering what's on television these days, they'll very likely sell at least an episode. What's the harm?"

"It's all fun right up until somebody gets hurt." I did sound like my great-aunt Letha.

Melvin just shook his head. Something about his grin and his sense of mischief hinted that, indeed, a nine-year-old boy was locked inside this responsible, buttoned-down adult.

As soon as I came through the French doors into Shamanique's office, she said, "Aunt Edna called to give you an update. She's surveilling Mr. Mart's house. She thinks she has it figured out."

"Did she just call? Can you get her on the phone for me?"

"Nope." Her earrings rocked to emphasize her headshake.

"Said she'd be away from the phone all afternoon. You want to leave her a message?"

"No. She didn't give any details?"

"Nope."

"Darn." I was thrilled she'd found something to help Tolly Mart, and I wanted details. At the same time I was suddenly worried. Did Edna know enough about wiretap laws and surveillance not to cross a line into trespass or breach of the peace? I knew Edna was a professional, but lawyers have been held liable when investigators crossed that line. I needed to talk to Edna, without sounding as though I doubted her skills, which wouldn't be easy, given how prickly she can be. On the other hand, she'd been at this awhile. Maybe I needed to relax.

"Thanks," I said and strolled into my office. No e-mails, no phone calls. Nothing else to do on Tolly Mart's case until I talked to Edna.

Best to turn my anxiety into something productive. I needed to change the wax rings on the toilets, and I'd come to the end of a long line of excuses.

I passed Shamanique's desk. "I'm going to be working on the toilet down the hall. Repairing it," I explained when she shot me one of her quizzical looks.

Upstairs, I changed clothes, got my tool belt and cleaning supplies from one of the pantries downstairs, and set to work. First I cleaned the floor and the toilet thoroughly, then unscrewed the ancient bolts that held it in place and called for Shamanique.

Months earlier, when working on the cabin's toilet, I'd discovered that how-to manuals often omit key pieces of information. Experienced do-it-yourselfers know that once the nuts were unscrewed and the toilet bowl loosened, you need to secure the bolts or they wind up under the house, often in an inaccessible place. Novices—the kind who resort to reading how-to books—really need that kind of information.

Fortunately, I was officially experienced—after commando-crawling through the spiderwebs under the lake cabin in search of lost bolts.

Shamanique wordlessly joined me under the stairs, serving as plumber's assistant by holding the bolts in place until I could secure them with masking tape. Before she returned to her desk, she studied me with a look that clearly asked why I didn't hire this done.

I slipped a wrench in the pocket of my overalls, unwrapped the slimy, sticky wax ring, and wondered who'd forgo this sense of accomplishment by calling a plumber?

As I worked, I mused over the Mart case and the simple will that had wandered in last week and the court appointments that usually resulted in simple plea agreements. I was generating some cash flow, but what kind of lawyer life was this? Had I collected all my trial experiences and honed my skills in complex cases just so I could come back here and pick up cases the other attorneys didn't want to fool with and be berated by a stick-up-his-butt Family Court judge? Thinking about the berating from Judge Lane made me wince. I flushed the toilet. At least I had something to show for today's work.

I hung up my tool belt. Shamanique had gone home at five. Through the leaded glass windows in and surrounding the front door, I could see that dusk had started to settle in. It would be dark soon. June days were long, but never long enough.

Dark. Damn, I'd been fretting over the wrong thing.

A shot of adrenaline pushed me to the front door just as Melvin came out of his office.

"Fixed the toilet," I said as I swung open the heavy door.

"Great," Melvin said, eyeing my orange T-shirt, denim farmer's overalls, and scuffed tennis shoes. "Where're you headed now?"

"For a walk. Got to check something out."

"Mind if I come? Been inside too long today."

"Um, sure." I made a hurry-up gesture. "Our ghoster friends might be in a spot of trouble."

It wasn't dark yet. Maybe we could head them off.

I picked the route. It was only a few blocks, and arriving on foot seemed like the least intrusive plan. We crossed Main Street and turned left without a question from Melvin. He didn't even complain when, two downhill blocks later, we passed the Feed and Seed and started up one of the steepest hills in town.

The occasional car whizzed past. I tried to disguise my shortness of breath from Melvin but couldn't hide it from myself. The setting sun didn't pull the temperature down, and the humidity wrapped around my face and bare arms like a warm, damp blanket. I needed to get back to walking every day, even when muggy weather sapped my resolve.

A horn honked, the sound racing toward and away from us as it passed. Melvin threw up a wave without even glancing to see who it was. Not much point, given that it was dusk. Even with a thirty-five-mile-an-hour speed limit, the cars were moving too quickly, especially those headed down the hill and back up toward town.

As we neared the crest where the street narrowed to two lanes heading out of town, the shrubs alongside the sidewalk opened onto the front lawn of the Baptist Church.

We crossed the street just past the church. I hoped I was mistaken about the address of the tourist home.

As it turned out, my premonition about an impending breach of the peace became audibly real as soon as we turned the corner.

We had the residential side street to ourselves, but angry voices announced that we weren't alone.

As we stood on the deserted sidewalk, I thought of calling out a question and seeing who answered, but neither Melvin nor

I had brought an Electromagnetic Field Detector or digital recorder to pinpoint the disturbance. I stifled a nervous giggle. This really wasn't a laughing matter. If the altercation was what I feared, I could end up in front of Judge Lane in big trouble.

Melvin glanced down at me. We drew even with the end of a driveway shared by two houses. The picture came into focus for both of us.

On the right of the drive stood an elegant French mansard two-story. On the left stood a rambling three-story with peeling lapped wood siding. Knee-high wrought iron fencing leaned higgledy-piggledy around the weedy yard and overgrown nandinas.

In the middle of the drive, battle raged. One-sided, to be sure, with every indication that the weaker side had resigned itself to defeat.

The players were familiar, the relative positions predictable. I should have foreseen this. Somewhere in my brain, I'd subconsciously put together the proximity of the old Freed house and Mr. Mart's tourist home, prompting my not-so-mysterious premonition. If only I'd put it together sooner or walked up the hill a little faster.

Melvin's three ghosters huddled together, elbow to elbow, the backs of their knees pressed against the Freed house's short iron fence. Before them, her hands on her hips, Edna faced them down.

The ghosters' anxious gazes darted, one after another, in our direction. Trini's tense expression melted with relief.

Edna spun around. "You know these three?" she barked. "Maybe you can tell me whether they are liars or just stark staring lunatics."

The three stood frozen, offering no defense or explanation.

"Caught them skulking around taking all manner of photos of this house here. Claim they know you."

The disbelieving accusation in her voice rang so harsh it almost forced me to deny any knowledge of the ghosters.

Melvin stepped up in their defense. "Yes, ma'am. We can vouch for them. They're conducting research for a possible film project."

Edna's right eyebrow shot up. "Somebody"—she glared at me, then at the ghosters—"needs to be telling them about trespassing and interfering in other people's work."

She turned back to Melvin and me. "I'm setting up equipment and testing. Whatever it is they're doing, it's interfering with my equipment."

She gave an exasperated sigh and asked Melvin, "Can you take them somewhere else?" She sounded like a mother begging a neighbor to take her pesky kids off her hands for a while. Something about Melvin had an unexpected calming effect on her. "I can't be out here on the sidewalk arguing. I got work to do."

Melvin looked from Edna to the ghosters, who still huddled together. Quint shifted the strap on his bulging messenger bag higher on his shoulder, and Trini hugged her backpack to her chest. All three eased around Edna to join with Melvin's protective aura.

"Sorry," said Trini.

"Yeah," said Quint.

Edna gave one curt nod of acknowledgment and a shooing motion as Melvin led them over to the sidewalk.

Edna rounded on me. In a hoarse whisper, she said, "If you want to keep your client out of jail, you better clear out. No telling, it might already be ruined."

"This is Mr. Mart's residence," I said.

"Yeah. His wife's not here right now, but she will be. I don't need the neighbors across the street calling cops and reporting trouble."

"Edna, I have to ask. It could be my head on the judge's chopping block. You know not to trespass on her property."

"Not her property, is it?" Her voice was angry. "Her name's not on the deed. Got his permission, the owner's permission, and Miz Freed's permission." She nodded toward the peeling white house beside us. "That's all I need."

"Where—I thought Mrs. Freed was—" *Dead* seemed a harsh thing to say, standing there beside her house.

"She's in the Lenny Dell Annex. My aunt used to take care of her."

A local nursing home. "Oh," I said.

Edna's pursed lips and her cocked head telegraphed clearly the challenge she wasn't going to throw down: *You didn't think I knew my job, did you?* I felt the need to explain.

"I learned the ghos—the kids were coming to the Freed house tonight. I didn't make the connection with the tourist home until a few minutes ago."

Why did I feel so inadequate and out-of-step around Edna? Was it some leftover childhood memory of May Ellen, who'd helped care for me when I was a baby, who'd loved me like I was one of her own? As the stories went, May Ellen also didn't mind popping a red mark on my chubby toddler leg. Was that what I remembered around Edna? A sense of high standards, of demands I wasn't quite achieving?

Or was it something else? The challenge Edna exuded couldn't be all residual or imagined. Did Edna have her own reasons for having to prove herself? What was the chip on her shoulder?

Whatever the explanation, it was time for me to back away and let her do her job.

"Thanks, Edna. I'm so sorry about the—interference. I'd hoped we could get here before . . ."

She spun on her heel and melted into the gloom at the far end of the driveway.

Friday Morning

The next morning, Shamanique was her usual punctual self. When I heard her come in, I rushed to dress in my usual office uniform—khakis and a white button-down shirt, the sleeves rolled up. Doesn't set a good example for the boss to wander downstairs late to work in the ratty Clemson T-shirt she'd slept in.

I stuck my head around the door. "Want some toast?"

She shook her head, the new braids and beads in her hair dancing happily. "Maybe some tea." She pushed her chair back and joined me on the short trek to the kitchen.

From the cupboard, Shamanique got the green tea bags she'd brought, disdaining my English Breakfast tea and other well-caffeinated varieties.

"So," she said, getting her kitten-and-flowers mug from the dish drainer. "Hear you had a hot date last night."

Her voice had a singsong tell-me-more note.

"Huh?" She'd obviously talked to her aunt Edna.

She raised an eyebrow and cocked both her head and her hip. "With the cute old guy next door? Why didn't you tell me you two were—"

"Uh-uh," I said, my hands held up in what could be seen as either a stop sign or a defensive gesture. "Don't even go there. We just took a walk, to check on some—protégés of his."

"Oh, come on. You know he's cute. In that preppy sort of way. You both live here. You telling me there's—"

"Nothing. Absolutely nothing. Strictly business." When Shamanique had first arrived, I'd suspected that underneath the polite *yes, ma'ams* lurked someone less docile, someone who could be related to Edna Lynch and, at the same time, could get herself in trouble with the law. She was beginning to lose the façade.

She stared at me a moment and apparently saw I wasn't making false protestations. She shrugged. "Whatever. So you got something lined up for tonight?"

"What's tonight?"

"Friday?" She drawled it out, as if to a slow-wit. "Date night? The weekend?"

I snorted. "Hm. The weekend. Probably Sunday lunch with my great-aunts. And some work around here." Or at the lake house. The usual excitement.

"Man, you need to get out. Good-looking woman like you don't need to be sitting at home when you can get a man to buy you dinner. Maybe go dancing."

I thought of the Pasture, full of stale odors, scarred furniture, and desperation. That was the dance spot that came uninvitingly to mind.

I waved her off. "I got plenty to worry about without adding a guy to the mix." Fortunately I could go home or to my great-aunts' or Lydia's to bum a meal—or I could pay for dinner myself.

The electric kettle whistled and she unplugged it. "You telling me you aren't dating anybody?"

"Not right now," I said, pouring water in her cup and then mine. "It's complicated."

She shrugged, apparently taking the hint. I hadn't dated—anything more than a casual working dinner with an acquaintance—in too long to remember. My life had been busy: I'd made partner in a large firm, then resigned after I blew up at a lying witness during a trial; I'd come home for a temporary refuge that had become quickly permanent, then gone to Charleston to help Jake Baker with a big case. I'd been busy for the last few years, especially the last six or eight months here in Dacus. Besides, if I hadn't found any serious dating or marriage material in Columbia or Charleston, what did Dacus, the little town I'd left after high school, have to offer, other than idle entertainment? And I did mean idle, as in local members of the hunting, fishing, and tobacco-spitting club.

"If the right guy comes along, I'll know it," I said. "Until then, no need to waste my time or some guy's money." Or risk another broken heart.

Shamanique gave me a pitying look. For one so young, she'd mastered Aunt Edna's silent expressiveness. "Honey, there's always a good reason to use a guy's money. That's about all some of them are good for. Trick is finding one with some money. Too many of them got their eye on your purse along with your other things."

She stirred some honey in her mug and eyed with suspicion my artificial sweetener.

I followed her down the hall, dunking my tea bag. The dating scene undoubtedly presented different challenges for the two of us—very different. In my case, if there'd been any good prospects, they'd moved away or were already married. The ones who'd stayed seemed to gather in a small-town hill-country fraternity specializing in hunting and fishing, with football, stock-car racing, and golf thrown in for variety. A woman in the beauty parlor last week, when I went to get my hair trimmed, was talking about how glad she was her husband had something to do every season of the year now—the best was when he was gone off hunting, but locked in his den with the TV remote was almost as good, she said.

From watching my great-aunts—two who had never married—I judged single a better option than that, even if a guy who could hunt and fish had skills and could feed the family. He might even be able to rewire electrical outlets. But getting his attention could take longer than learning to do it myself—which reminded me I needed to stop by the hardware store for a sink washer.

The phone rang as soon as we entered the reception room. Given how much I hate phone calls, just having somebody answer the few phones calls I got was proving worth her salary. I liked her directness and her spunk, though I hoped she'd satisfied herself on the topic of my love life. Her chattiness made me appreciate all the more Rudy's reticence on personal matters.

"One moment please," she said in her cheerful phone voice. Covering the receiver with her hand, she mouthed, "Rowly Edwards?"

I nodded and carried my tea into my office.

"How'do, Miss A-ver-ee?"

"Grand. Take it you have some news?"

"Another long chat with Miz Sidalee Evans yesterday." He said her name as if it ran together, Sidely. "A fount of information, she was. And more than willing to talk. I also got a little more on Dirick Timms, the boyfriend. Not a gang member. I wondered if maybe he could'a had somebody helping him, lending him cover. He's a punk, true enough, but a loner, by all accounts."

"Not even the other punks like him, huh?"

He snorted. "Like as not. Oh, and from the little I've dug up, Neanna had for certain broke it off with him."

"Really." That gave me pause. "That's too bad, in a way. I'd had him picked out to play the bad guy."

"Don't mean he isn't," said Rowly. "He moved on to another girlfriend, but that don't mean he was ready to let go of the old one. Word is, he's not averse to slapping girls around."

"That's what made me vote him most likely culprit." That and the fact that lightning had struck twice. Neanna and Aunt Wenda both attracted dangerous men into their lives—and ultimately into their deaths.

"He still could'a gone after her. Got drunk or tweaked out, decided he'd been wronged and decided to fix it. Wouldn't be the first ex-boyfriend or ex-husband to want to right a wrong done him."

"Yeah, but he'd be the first to slip out of the Atlanta jail and slip back in to do it."

"True enough." He paused. "But who's to say he was her only bad boyfriend?"

That was a thought. "Any mention of another one?"

"Nope, but she headed outta here on a crazy whim. Maybe some guy was part of that."

I thought about Skipper, her boyish hitchhiker. Did he know something he wasn't telling? Was he hiding something I couldn't see?

"What did Cousin Sidalee have to say?"

"Over mint tea and these little powder-sugar balls that make one heck of a mess unless you poke the whole thing in your mouth, she had plenty to say."

"Oo, the buttery kind with chopped pecans?"

"Uh-huh. They were good, but hard to be dainty with. She didn't seem to note the mess. She was just glad to have company. You know how it is with folks of a certain age. They get lonely, don't get too many new stories or new listeners."

I could see Rowly puffing little clouds of powdered sugar as he chewed the nut teacake balls, his Adam's apple and his brown-thatch hair both bobbing as he nodded in time to her story.

"So what'd she 'llow?" I asked. Talking to Rowly, with his deep drawl, deepened my own drawl.

"She talked a lot about how devastated Gran—everybody called her that—was over her children. The first daughter running off, lost somewhere in drugs or craziness. The other one, Wenda, murdered. Sad enough to lose your child, but to such as that, and to have both of them gone in bad ways."

Rowly's tone summed it up with words I could imagine in one of the country songs I knew he wrote.

"She loved that granddaughter of hers. Seemed determined to fix whatever had broke with her own two, even to the point of asking the French family to take Neanna in when she herself got sick. Seemed to be working, too, right up until Gran died. Thank goodness she never knew it didn't keep working."

"So why'd she have such a large insurance policy on Neanna? That really freaked her out when she learned about it. Frankly, it would freak me out, too."

"Ready for this?" Rowly said. "Miz Sidalee had fussed at Gran about spending money on the premiums. Miz Sidalee didn't think it right to spend that money when Gran needed it for herself. But, in Gran's words: 'This is the only way I got to hold her here. God knows I could use the money, but He ain't gonna give me two hunnert thousand dollars, else I might stop relying on Him. So if He won't give me the money, He'll have to keep her alive.'"

"That's—" I didn't have a word to describe my reaction to it. The theology was more than a little cockeyed, but who was I to question the methods of a desperate woman?

"Crazy?" Rowly supplied a word.

"Not to her, apparently."

"I reckon." Rowly's tone oozed judgment.

"The policy was in effect when Neanna died and the premiums were paid up."

"Yep."

I searched my memory banks, reordering information Fran had given me, what I believed about her. Why hadn't she mentioned that she was Neanna's beneficiary?

"Is the insurance why Fran French can afford to be little Miss Money's No Object?" I asked. "Is she using blood money?"

Rowly knew we'd be remiss not to cast a skeptical eye on everyone involved.

"No, not hardly. Truth is, Miss French's family's got plenty of money. That insurance payoff—when it comes—wouldn't pay to air-condition one of their houses."

"Those are her dad's houses, though, aren't they? Not hers."

"True enough. Still, she hasn't put in a claim for the money, and the girl's not hurting. Got her own trust fund, from her own grandmother. Following the money this time doesn't lead far."

"Her grandmother, huh?" The dichotomy between Fran and Neanna, the two "sisters," and the two grandmothers who'd played—or tried to play—fairy godmother struck me.

"Yeah. One other thing. Miz Sidalee talked—at grave length—about how hard Gran worked to find out what happened to both her girls. Finally she found Marie, the oldest, but not the way she'd hoped. Gran went to the library and studied up in the computer classes after states started posting Jane and John Doe descriptions of unidentified bodies. Miz Sidalee said Gran could 'googly' anybody.

Made me laugh. Googly. I like that word. Like that song about goo-goo-googly eyes."

"Dear Lord. Imagine searching for your daughter on Jane Doe sites."

"That's how she found her. On a Web site out in San Francisco. That's how she learned she was dead."

No wonder Fran disdained private investigators. Gran had been left to do on her own what they didn't do.

"The strange part," said Rowly, "was Gran quit pushing to find out what happened to Wenda. She just stopped. No more calls to the police or the newspapers to stir up stories. No more scrapbook—mostly because there were no more articles. She just stopped."

"Did Miss Sidalee know why?"

"At the time, Miz Sidalee thought it was a good thing she stopped, that Gran needed to put it behind her so's she could heal. When she thought on it later, she saw it wasn't so good. Gran got that picture in the mail, the one you sent me. That scared Gran, made her worry about the same thing happening to Neanna. So she stopped. Miz Sidalee saw it once. Said Gran thought it meant Neanna, even though she was only seven at the time, would be leaving her too and it scared her."

"Did she have any idea who sent it?"

"No, but before that picture came, Gran was always pestering the newspapers to run articles, especially on the anniversary. She even tried to get it on one of those TV shows about solving mysteries. She loved that one show, but not so much after they wouldn't do the story. Said they were nice enough, but still."

The murderer had sent the photo a year after the murder. If he'd wanted to scare Gran off, it had worked. The photo was eerie, but not gruesome, and Gran didn't sound like the kind of woman who would back down easily, especially when she was fighting to protect her brood.

Worried about the same thing happening to Neanna. Had the photo arrived with an explicit threat? Had the murderer finally, twenty-three years later, made good on it? What if these weren't his only victims? Had other families received sick mementoes from him? A chilling thought.

"Thanks, Rowly. Send me a bill. This has been a lot of help. I can't thank you enough."

"Sure you can—just let me know how it comes out."

"Will do."

I shuddered at the words "how it comes out." So far, I had a murderer with a long memory and a long reach, one who didn't mind threatening little old ladies with macabre memento mori. One who was close to getting away with murder—for a second time?

Friday Afternoon and Evening

I finished drafting a simple will for a couple, friends of my parents—and hoped they hadn't sought me out thinking they needed to help a charity case. They'd be in Monday to have it signed and notarized. That's something I needed to put in motion for Shamanique. Having her serve as notary would be more professional than paying a teller from the bank to come on her lunch hour.

The rest of the afternoon, I worked upstairs cleaning my two-room apartment. I still hadn't unpacked many of my boxes, unsure whether this home would be permanent and worth the effort.

My summer clothes hung in the closet or were folded carefully in a few of the drawers in the dresser I'd first hauled out of my grandfather's attic when I was in high school. A few books sat on the built-in shelves that ran under the large windows in both rooms. The packed boxes sat stacked in the corner of what would ideally be my sitting room. What a genteel concept: a sitting room.

Years before, someone had put a doorway between these two rooms, so I didn't have to go into the hallway to move from one room to the other. The luminous marble bathroom, complete with a decadently deep, claw-footed tub and shower, opened off the bedroom.

My rooms sat at one end of the second floor, opposite Melvin's suite of rooms. Like our offices below, mine were on the left of the stairs and Melvin's were on the right. The stairway continued to a third floor of smaller, cluttered rooms—perhaps once the children's rooms—and on to the attics.

Had Melvin's grandmother and grandfather used these suites as separate bedrooms? Maybe they'd filled the third-floor rooms with children, then wisely decided to stay away from each other. I'd never asked Melvin how many siblings his father had.

It struck me, as I squirted tub cleaner around, that Melvin's grandfather and mine would've known each other. They'd lived blocks apart. Had they served in civic clubs together? Did they like each other?

My cell phone rang, Shamanique calling to say I had a phone call downstairs. I needed a better phone system than this—but originally I hadn't had a receptionist or an assistant. I also hadn't wanted—still didn't want—the office phone ringing upstairs. I was determined these rooms would be a haven, a place where I could forget that my office and my work were literally under my feet, beneath my pillow, all the time.

I thundered down the wide oak stairs and into my office.

Rudy said, "It's official. No file on Wenda Sims."

I groaned and flopped into one of the armchairs, trailing the extra-long phone cord across the floor from my desk.

"Thank the County Council who wouldn't cough up the money for secure storage until the old courthouse was crowded and crumbling at the seams."

"So that's it, huh? Somebody gets away with murder, because the evidence was thrown into a Dumpster full of sodden, moldy papers and photos."

"Not exactly."

"So? What'd you find, Mr. Brilliant Detective?"

"Not what. Who. Vince Ingum. The guy who retired to Myrtle Beach. He returned my phone call."

He waited in vain for an admiring murmur of appreciation. Then he sprang his biggest surprise.

"He has copies of the file, along with the crime-scene photos."

"You're kidding?" Now I was awed and admiring.

"Talked to him this morning. Said that case was his one regret. Forty years in law enforcement, that's the only murder he never solved."

"So what's next?"

"I'm going to see him tomorrow. Said he'd meet me in Columbia. You game?"

"Sure." I immediately craved a chicken-fried steak at Yesterday's, but it was their meeting; I figured they had their own favorite spots, maybe one featuring barbecue and rebel flags.

"Can you leave about eight? That'll give us plenty of time, in case we want to stop for breakfast or something."

In other words, Rudy knew he'd be hungry and knew a good place to eat on the way.

"See you then."

Melvin met me in the hallway as I headed back upstairs.

"You just missed our new best friends," he said.

"The ghosters?"

He nodded. "They came by to thank us for rescuing them last night from, as they said, that witchy little crazy woman. I told them I couldn't take credit for that."

He eyed me with suspicion, as if he hadn't quite believed my story about not foreseeing the collision until it was too late.

"They also came to issue a very gracious invitation to the two of us for this evening."

"Uh-oh."

He chuckled. "Well said. They're going to film a campfire storytelling session at Yellow Fork Camp. Ghost stories, of course. For background."

"Yellow Fork?"

"Somebody's rented it for the summer, to host a series of summer camps for kids. Unfortunately, a prior commitment prevents me from attending the evening's festivities."

I started to decline, but the possibilities for both hilarity and disaster struck me at almost the same time.

"I reckon somebody ought to go keep an eye on things." And I did like bonfires and storytelling.

"Who better?" he said, his arms open, palms up. "If that witchy little crazy woman should materialize, for instance, you'll have the proper counterincantation."

"Seems to me your charms are what enchanted her." Edna wasn't what I was worried about. A bunch of screaming kids with whittle-pointed marshmallow sticks and the ghosters—who needed anything else to fret over?

"The festivities commence at nine o'clock," he said.

"Isn't that past the crumb-crunchers' bedtime?" It would push up on mine, if I was heading out with Rudy in the morning, but the more I thought about it, the more I was both repelled and intrigued. "I'll let you know what you missed."

He smiled. "Take good notes."

"You can wait for the movie version."

I went back upstairs to finish my bathroom cleaning, dusting, and vacuuming. The nice thing about a small abode: It allowed a quick trip to a sense of order. I left the unpacked boxes pushed close against the wall. Those could stay put for a while longer—mostly winter clothes and a few books. Easier to dust without all that stuff anyway.

The mugginess persisted, hinting at either rain or more heat. I reminded myself, as I dressed in a short-sleeved knit top and shorts, that this weather was tame compared to the humidity and heat we'd find in Columbia tomorrow. I laced my walking shoes, grabbed my purse, and, at the last minute, grabbed my camera, though I didn't know why. After supper at my parents' house, I headed up the mountain as the air began to cool slightly.

The rutted dirt road to Yellow Fork turned off the two-lane and wound through the woods to a jumble of weathered gray buildings looking much as they had when I'd come in March to visit what I'd hoped would become a corporate client. They'd decided to pack up and move on. The place now teemed with kids, running and tagging each other and jumping and chattering. The counselors—identifiable only because they were taller than their charges and slightly less red-mud-tinged—seemed remarkably immune to the chaos.

I walked over to the closest counselor, her dark silk hair braided into a pigtail, her arms and legs bark-brown with the kind of tan my Scots-Irish genes can only covet.

"Hi. I'm Avery Andrews. I was invited up to the bonfire and storytelling?" With an earnest smile, I hoped to convey not only my purpose in coming but that I wasn't a pervert or someone with evil designs on her campers. Her tired expression said she couldn't care less. In fact, she might have paid me to cart off two wildly screaming boys practicing their best cartoon ninja kicks on each other.

The counselor waved absently toward the picnic tables at the edge of the woods, close to the mess hall. I nodded my thanks—no opening for conversation with the banshees wailing—and strolled toward the shelter and tables. I'd come early, wanting to get here before dusk made it difficult to find my way.

Two male counselors, both lanky and thin with the loose-jointedness and slouch that serves as a uniform for guys their age, paid me no heed as I slid onto a picnic bench and watched them put the finishing touches on the wood stacked for the bonfire.

I was content to slip into the background. Before long, the frenetic activity and the decibel level calmed as though a mystical hand had passed over the campers. It took a moment for me to spot the cause.

A sheriff's patrol car pulled slowly around the rough-paved drive. All the boys stood in awed attention, staring at the car. The girls kept chattering, I noticed, clustered in small bunches, heads together. But even they followed the patrol car's progress.

The deputy rode with his window down, his arm resting on the window frame, offering a cool-hand wave to the kids as he drove past: Chief Deputy Rudy Mellin.

Who'd invited him? I wondered.

As he parked, some of the more audacious kids ran over to his car, peered around him to study inside the car, and when he got out, stood with their heads cocked back listening to his every word and staring at his gun.

Two on the fringe of his groupie gathering mimed shooting at each other. One clutched his stomach and fell back in a puff of red dust, his legs straight up in the air before they thunked to earth.

Rudy chatted with his entourage as he made his way across

the large central yard to take a look down the slope toward the ball fields. He then strolled at a magisterial pace around the perimeter and sat at a picnic table twenty yards distance from mine, the kids still giving him their rapt attention.

No need to interrupt them. I kept my seat, my chin in my hand, listening to the chatter and laughter, smelled the pine tar and the lighter fluid, felt the air take on a clammy coolness as the sun began to disappear behind the thick trees. I hoped there'd be marshmallows.

About the same time the glow of the fireflies appeared, the ghosters pulled in, driving their honest-to-goodness Scooby-Doo van.

By the magic of an unseen hand, everyone began to drift to-gether without an audible or visible signal. As dusk passed full into dark, the bonfire caught through the kindling and blazed, and the kids drew in around it, whether from the primitive mes-merism of fire or a conditioned response to the promise of scary stories and toasted marshmallows.

Trini saw me and waved, but Colin and Quint were too busy setting up their camera shots. Their handheld giant flashlight would scare the ghosts away if they weren't careful.

As I followed their progress, I noticed other adults had gath-ered. A cluster of guys lounged at a picnic table on the opposite side of the bonfire from my perch. To my surprise, the motley as-sortment was soon joined by PeeVee Probert and Donlee Griggs. For the second time in two days, Donlee had appeared without his pumpkin-helmeted girlfriend. Even more surprising was see-ing gigantic Donlee and his scrawny best buddy, PeeVee, up here partaking of wholesome family entertainment. Tap's Pool Room was their usual haunt. Who'd been responsible for the guest list at this wingding?

PeeVee hitched his jeans up as he sauntered over to the crowd of misfits. Something wasn't right with that group. I wasn't believing they'd driven up the mountain to listen to ghost stories. As I studied the half-dozen men, I got my first clue: they'd chosen seats facing the ghosters and their cameras, not the log where the storyteller would sit.

I winced. Word was surely out about the ghosters. Of course it was no surprise they'd attracted sightseers. I recognized several in the bunch as members of the Ghouly Boys, my pet name for the police-scanner addicts who rushed out at the first word of a bad wreck or other opportunity for gore. I'd seen the others around town or knew them from criminal court docket day at the courthouse. Unless this summer camp session was designed for the children of once and future convicts, I had a sneaking suspicion the ghosters had replaced car wrecks and drownings as the entertainment top bill in Camden County.

I couldn't see what was so entertaining about watching the ghosters at work. Colin knelt in the dirt and climbed on picnic tables, studying his light meter and camera viewfinder. Trini stood around holding the hubcap-sized flashlight until Colin finally ordered her to switch off. Quint bristled with an assortment of straps and bags.

The kids weren't paying any attention to Colin's artistic posing. They were seated on the makeshift board-and-rock benches encircling the firepit or setting marshmallows on fire, watching flicks of sparks dance into the air like fireflies freed from the netherworld. I really wanted some marshmallows, but this wasn't my party.

The weathered wood on which my rump rested creaked as Deputy Mellin wedged himself on the opposite end of my picnic bench.

"Surprised to see you here, Deputy."

"Not the least surprised to see you. You're pretty easy to entertain."

"I'm not the only one." I nodded across the fire and the circle of kids to the isolated misfits. Donlee towered over the huddle, swaying slightly, eyes bright with the firelight.

"Donlee ain't quite right," Rudy said, "but those other guys ought to know better."

"You're thinking what I am." A statement, not a question.

He gave one curt bob of his head and crossed his arms on the table.

I kept staring at one guy in particular, the one who was doing the most talking. His close-cropped hair and oxford shirt set him apart from the scruffier members of the group, but I couldn't place him.

"Who's the guy regaling the Ghouly Boys?"

Rudy didn't have to ask for a description. "Cuke Metz."

"Cuke?"

"Short for Cucumber. Don't ask me to explain that one."

I kept staring, trying to place him.

"The fellow you ran into in Maylene's?" I said finally.

"Yep."

"He sure seems to be the center of attention over there."

"Got better sense than to be hanging with those guys."

"You need to get those guys reined in," I said. "Before somebody gets hurt."

Rudy huffed. "I was fixing to tell you the same thing about your little ghost-hunting friends. They're big buddies with your friend Melvin." He said "friend" like a bad word.

"What you want to bet those are the guys that sent them out to see Max and the motorcycle gang?" I asked.

"Oh, that's an easy bet."

And likely put the ghosters on to the "haunted house" next door to Edna's stakeout. They couldn't have known Edna would be there—or we'd have heard their inebriated cackles and howls from some hiding place when Edna chewed out the ghosters. No, they'd mostly pulled their pranks at a distance. They'd had something else planned for the ghosters that night, and I shuddered to think what.

The video of the haunted train track and the swaying light and the raspy EVP tape-recorded warning came to mind. Among the ones gathered across from us, who was smart enough to create the video and the disembodied voice? Then again, it would be a mistake to underestimate the creativity of a bunch of guys who want to pull a stunt. For some of them, drunk is better than sober when it comes to planning and execution. Ask any dean of students on any college campus. The same guys who flunk physics can get the dean's car up in the bell tower.

"Can't you say something to those guys, before somebody gets hurt?"

Rudy didn't have time to commit to anything. A man with wiry strands of gray hair sprouting unruly all over his head and stringy leg muscles ambled into the center of the campfire half circle.

"Our storyteller tonight has been a huge hit with all our campers this summer." He gave an introduction that not a single kid cared about. Bring on the spooky stories.

A woman stepped up to take the stool, her back to the fire. She was as round as she was tall. Dressed in gauzy black skirts and scarves, she seemed to float rather than walk.

She started with an old campfire standard. As I listened to her tell it, the familiar story gave me a renewed thrill, her husky voice and gentle movement first hypnotic, then shocking as she bellowed, "Give me back my bone. Here! Take it!"

The younger kids all screamed. Even some of the counselors jumped, then smiled sheepishly.

The nervous laughter died, and she leaned close, her voice now soft, forcing us to lean close to hear.

"Some tales are just for fun. We know they're made up, and we love 'em for that." Her mountain drawl had the color and consistency of molasses.

"But some tales we tell because they're true and we need to know about them, because they're part of us, part of the first who came to these mountains. You've got to keep the stories. They're entrusted to you.

"The Native Americans who lived in these hills told stories about where they came from, how these hills were made. They believed a water bug pushed mud up from the bottom of the sea, stacking it a little bit at a time until it built up the land. Then a buzzard flew overhead, using its powerful wings to dry the wet mud. But it was such a big land, with such high mountains, that when the buzzard grew tired, his wings brushed the still-wet mud, leaving valleys and draws and places for rivers and waterfalls."

Even the Ghouly Boys had slipped with her into the story. Donlee sat on the tabletop, his feet on the bench, his chin in his hands, looking like a nine-year-old with a glandular problem. PeeVee, who normally danced from one foot to another like a wind-up tin toy, sat enthralled.

"Not all stories from these hills are lovely ones, though. Some are sad. Do you want to hear any sad stories?"

The kids sitting between me and the storyteller shook their heads in silent no's.

"Some are love stories. Do you want to hear those?"

Vigorous headshakes were accompanied by giggles and a few retching sounds.

"Some are truly, truly scary. Do you want to hear those?"

Enthusiastic nods and cries of "Yeah!"

"Now, think about that. You'll have to leave this toasty bright fire and walk all the way back to your dark cabins along those dark, dark paths through the dark, dark woods. Are you sure it's a good idea? You really want those stories?"

"Yeah!" A chorus of yells.

She shook her head and sighed, resigned to serve their choice.

"Very well then. You must understand I can't be responsible for what happens. I told your counselors that. They're the ones who'll have to explain to your parents if—well, if anything happens. You've come to these hills. Some part of these hills will now be part of you. I can't be responsible."

She paused. I felt myself draw in closer, savoring her offer to be a part of something unknown.

"Some who've lived here have thought the mountains themselves were bewitched. Just over that rise there, people from ancient times reported hearing cracks and groans from the mountain itself. Other times, people have seen wisps of smoke float up. Some have tried to explain it away, saying it was from a campfire." She waved over her shoulder to the bonfire and the smoke that rose from the glowing logs.

"Others said it was nothing more than gases released as plants decayed, or that it was stray bits of fog. Those who saw the smoke and heard the groans believed no such thing. Some believed souls may be trapped within the mountain, bound by ancient curses. Other, more practical people say these old mountains are just settling in on themselves, worn down and tired."

She looked from one firelit face to another. "Have you heard any strange sounds at night? Groans or sighs from the ground itself?"

The headshakes were jerky and slight.

"Seen any wisps floating about in the trees?" She paused. "Yet?"
The shoulders of two girls in front of me drew up, as if they'd both felt a chill.

"Keep your eyes open," she said, "and be careful, because you will see and hear. Oh, you certainly will."

Quint sat on one of the ankle-high board seats in the front row, to the side of the storyteller, catching her profile on film. He hunkered with his knees in the air on either side of the tripod, lowered to what had to be its shortest setting.

Colin didn't sit still. He moved from place to place, probably capturing shots they could cut in later.

Trini held a still camera and seemed to be snapping shots without even looking through the viewfinder. She mostly faced the crowd, but I also saw her wander off into the trees, snapping at random. Trying to catch some free-floating spirits?

When the storyteller finished, her stories left us just where the counselors wanted their little campers: satiated and happy and ready for bed. And so was I.

Rudy and I sat on our opposite ends of the picnic bench in companionable silence while the campers filed off into the night. Some of the boys still had the energy to goose each other and the girls chattered endlessly, in the way of girls, as they ambled off in opposite directions.

I kept staring at the Ghouly Boys across the circle. When Cuke Metz turned his head to his right, I recognized him and almost popped out of my seat. Cuke Metz. Suddenly I could picture him with a hat pulled over his thick curls. That's where I'd seen him. Driving a truck at Moody Springs. A truck with no passenger. The pieces tinkled into place.

I didn't have time to say anything to Rudy. Trini and Colin came rushing at us in a flurry.

"You won't believe what we got!" Colin was dancing.

Trini swung one leg over the bench and straddled it beside me, holding the digital camera. Colin huddled behind us.

"Look." She held up the camera display.

On the tiny screen, I could see me and Rudy, our chins in our hands, looking like a woodland remake of American Gothic. We were framed at opposite edges of the photo, in what looked like a snowstorm of bright, round white balls.

"Orbs," Trini intoned.

The picnic bench creaked as Rudy stood. I heard his knee pop, and he groaned as he stretched and came behind me, leaning over to see the source of excitement.

I handed him the camera and, over my shoulder, watched his expression. I didn't want to miss the look on his face.

Reflected in the firelight, I saw what I expected: not awe, but puzzlement.

"The lightning bugs?" Rudy asked finally when all Quint and Trini offered were expectant stares.

"Those are orbs," Trini said, almost reverential.

"A manifestation of coalesced residual energy," Quint offered by way of logical explanation.

"Those blobs of light?" Rudy jabbed his finger toward the back of the camera and asked in his best noncommittal cop tone.

"Yes." They both nodded, seeing the dawn of understanding, one who was beginning to see the light.

"Those are bugs."

"Lightning bugs and dust don't photograph like this," Quint said. "As you can see, there aren't that many bugs flying around here. We've studied all the online examples by other researchers. We know the difference between natural and paranormal phenomenon."

Quint reached for the camera, both palms extended, retrieving the sacrament from an infidel, one clearly not ready to join the believers in fully partaking.

Quint turned back to me. "You are *surrounded*," he pronounced.

Trini nodded.

"You've drawn forces to you. We've never seen such a manifestation."

"Never been in the damn woods near full garbage cans on a summer night," Rudy muttered without benefit of sotto voce as he wandered toward the dying bonfire. Maybe he'd toast me a marshmallow.

Quint and Trini ignored him and gathered on either side of me, earnest in their excitement.

"Once Colin sees this, I'm sure he'll want to interview you," Quint said.

"And film you," Trini added.

"Do you have any idea why you would be the center of such activity?"

I bit the inside of my lip, hoping I looked like I was ruminating rather than stifling the giggles.

"I have no idea," I said. "Probably just a fluke."

"We'll definitely want to study you," Quint said. I was glad Rudy had walked away. I didn't need to hear about this for the rest of my life. Queen of the Fireflies.

Glancing around, I spotted Rudy, his hands in his pockets, having a casual chat with a couple of the Ghouly Boys. I didn't want to interrupt that or attract the attention of Donlee, who was hovering at the edge of the group, so I slipped away in the other direction back to my car, forfeiting any leftover marshmallows.

Orbs. I winced as I closed the car door. Wait'll Melvin sees the orb photos. There would be some more ribbing. Maybe it wouldn't last twenty years, accompanied by a nickname, the way it could coming from Rudy. But I could hear it now.

I needed to get home and get some sleep. If I was to be the center of a manifestation, it would be helpful if Gran would hover over me and tell me what happened to her girls. That's a haunting I would welcome.

Saturday Morning

The next morning, Edna called just as I climbed into the front seat of Rudy's unmarked patrol car, which had conveniently pulled to the curb in front of my house.

"Thought you'd want to know as soon as possible," she said without preamble.

"Hey." I mouthed "sorry" at Rudy, who signaled with a head shake that he didn't mind me taking the call.

"Got what you needed in the Mart case. Your client may want to press charges against his soon-to-be-ex wife in a criminal action."

"Do tell."

"I staked out the client's house, this time without any third-party interference."

The sarcasm in her voice did nothing to detract from her Joe

Friday firing-range delivery. A short, stocky black woman who wore polyester pull-on pants, she was an unlikely one to channel a hard-boiled detective.

"At approximately midnight, I observed through a telephoto lens a figure later identified as the subject, dressed all in black, approach the client's address by means of a gate in the back fence. She approached the phone box near the garage and proceeded by means of an alligator clip to attach a homemade phone-tap box onto the phone line. With a handset device, she then dialed her own home number and waited until the answering machine picked up. She dialed three more times on auto-dial before she answered with a second mobile handset and demanded to know who was calling. She then repeated the process fifteen times in the space of an hour."

"You're kidding. She called herself? Mrs. Mart called herself from his phone line."

"Yes. She repeated the process again at 2:00 A.M. and again at six."

"And this shows up on the records as though he's calling her?"

"Egg-zactly."

"You witnessed all this?"

"And captured it with time-stamped videotape and still shots with a telephoto lens, clearly showing the tap apparatus attached to the line and the identity of the person conducting the tap."

"That's absolutely wonderful. I can't believe she had the nerve to pull something like that."

"The only surprise with folks should be when they don't surprise you." Edna had completed her report and reverted to her more typical homiletics.

"I suppose I should inform Mr. Mart before we turn your evidence over to—who? The solicitor?" Personally, I wanted to nail the witch's evil hide to the barn, but I'd never married the woman and he had. However, she'd committed a crime—a federal crime.

I doubted it would be up to Tolly Mart what happened to her at the hands of a criminal prosecutor.

That was a heart-warming thought. I wouldn't want to be the soon-not-to-be Mrs. Mart when she appeared before an irate Judge Lane. She might rather be arrested by the feds and forego that honor.

"I'll have Shamanique call the judge's clerk and schedule a hearing," I said. "He'll likely want you to be available."

"Certainly," she said.

"Thanks, Edna. This is really terrific."

"Of course."

I was certain Edna liked getting compliments as much as anyone, but she always did a good job pushing away any act of familiarity.

I left a message on the office answering machine for Shamanique, asking her to request a hearing, on Monday if at all possible. I'd see Tolly Mart later this afternoon—tomorrow at the latest. Always in a hurry to share good news.

I settled back in my seat with a grin of satisfaction.

"Can't tell me, counselor?"

"No. Not yet." Oh, how I wanted to. "Hope you'll have the pleasure of serving a warrant soon, or hauling someone out of Judge Lane's courtroom on contempt charge on Monday."

"Ah, the things that make your day, counselor."

I stretched my legs out in the super-sized floorboard, content with how the day had begun—or how the night had ended, in Edna's case.

Rather than turn onto the bypass around Seneca, Rudy drove straight into downtown.

"You haven't eaten breakfast, have you? Thought we could swing into Betty's Hungry House before we hit the road."

I wasn't about to complain about stopping for a cat's-head

biscuit slathered in butter and jelly. Knowing Rudy, it would be an appetizer for wherever we were having lunch in Columbia. Maybe I could run behind the car part of the way.

Rudy turned onto the residential side street and parked in the grass-and-gravel lot.

As we slipped in the door of the shambling building that showed years' worth of patched-together growing pains, a waitress changing out the coffee filter gave Rudy a nod. We took the only empty booth in sight, at the front window close by the register. Rudy sat with his back to the wall.

The air was smokier than I liked, but the biscuits—truly as big as a cat's head—made up for any breathing difficulties.

Rudy ordered his usual—three plates of food. "Don't tell my wife. She's been getting on me lately."

He rubbed his belly and settled sideways in the narrow booth, watching the bustle near the cash register.

"A'course, she's been getting on me about a lot of things lately." He wasn't talking directly to me. He was just talking.

"What's she getting on you about?" Sometimes friends just need to talk, not necessarily be heard.

He brushed an imaginary crumb off the table. "I don't know. She's chewin' my ass about running for sheriff."

"Wow. So you are thinking about it."

"Hell, no. She wants somebody in the family to be sheriff, she can run herself."

"Why's she want you to run?"

"Money. Better hours, she thinks. And prestige. Thinks it would raise her up. Tired of me being second banana, she said. But it's really more about her. She wants a boat."

He fell quiet.

"A boat, huh." Not the time to rib him that I didn't know a boat went with the job.

He watched the restaurant rather than me, in that way guys have when they're talking about something important and personal.

"Not that I've ever seen her swim. And she sure as hell don't want to fish 'ner nothing. She wants to hang out at the marina and the boat parties. Invite people out."

"You like fishing." I tried to keep any sarcasm out of my voice.

He turned to me, his eyes two squints. "Too busy fishing drunks outta the water to enjoy boating." His tone encircled that last word with contempt.

I didn't like knowing Rudy wasn't happily married. Maybe he was and this was just one of those minor marital stumbles, though pushing him to be more and better didn't sound minor. Not the kind of thing I'd want a spouse pushing me to do.

I changed the subject. "Do you like working with L.J.?"

The plates appeared quickly in front of us, dealt out like cards by a Vegas dealer. The steam rising from my biscuit carried warm comfort.

"Must," he said, chopping his liquid egg yolks into his grits. "Can always move on if I don't."

We fell to eating, me in buttery bliss. I wished I could find a graceful way to suggest Rudy take some precautions to protect his credit if his wife had designs on improving her lot in life. I'd seen it get awfully expensive for another husband just before his divorce—and ruinous for his credit rating.

We ate, Rudy quickly, me with plenty of time to savor the soft biscuit and its crisp crust. Even without Aunt Vinnia's home-made marmalade, this was good.

Not until we passed Irmo on the outskirts of Columbia did we talk about the reason for our trip.

"I forgot to tell you," I said. "You know about the $200,000 life insurance policy on Neanna."

"Yeah. Still can't fathom what a girl that age with no children or husband needs with that much insurance. Hell, I don't have that much insurance. Mostly because my wife keeps joking that if I had enough insurance, it wouldn't be a sad day for everybody when I die."

I left Mrs. Rudy Mellin's joke alone. "You won't believe the reason Neanna's grandmother took it out. Gran's cousin said Gran hoped it would hold Neanna here, keep her safe. Said God wouldn't ever let her have $200,000, so this gave God a good reason to let her keep her granddaughter."

Even though he was flashing along in the fast lane at probably eighty miles an hour, Rudy took his eyes off the road to see if I looked like I was joking.

He snorted. "Guess the joke's kinda on her, huh? Didn't get to keep either one."

"No." The whole thing grew even sadder in that perspective.

"You said this Fran woman has money of her own. You think that's a lie?"

"No. She really has money."

"Nobody ever has enough, do they?"

I had no answer to that.

We got to Columbia with time to spare, but Vince Ingum, the cop who'd retired to Myrtle Beach, apparently still shared Rudy's ability to flout the speed limit despite his retirement. He too arrived at the restaurant early, approaching the door to Yesterday's from the opposite direction but at the same time we did.

Yesterday's was Rudy's delightful surprise for me—my favorite place in Columbia, where in over a decade as a loyal customer, I'd eaten only one dish: what they called Confederate Fried Steak, a chicken-fried steak recipe imported from Texas or Oklahoma. Homesteaders moving west had taken their Southern fried fanaticism with them and melded it into a new tradition when they found themselves in a place with more beef cattle than chickens. I was glad the mouth-watering delicacy had made its way back to South Carolina.

I studied the vegetable list so I'd be ready to order— cantaloupe and black-eyed peas. Then I studied Vince Ingum.

The waitress had seated us in one of the sheltered church-pew booths that lined the walls, brightened recently by new paint. The lunch crowd would begin shrinking soon, so we could use our enclave as long as we wanted.

Ingum wore his hair in a buzz cut. His bulldog jaw jutted out like a challenge, and his crystal-blue eyes were circled with a yellow edge. What Granddad used to call killer-dog eyes. Never trust a yeller-eyed dog, he'd said, mimicking the deep mountain speech from whence the warning originated.

Ingum's face was open, despite his spooky eyes and his aggressive jaw. His skin had the blotchy red-brown tone that Scots-Irish descendants get when they decide to become near-tropical sun-worshippers. I hoped he had a good dermatologist. His voice had the husky scratch of a former smoker and a warmth that drew you in, all the while he was watching you.

I wondered what he saw.

"So you're trying to get on one a-them TV shows, are you?" He directed the good-natured gibe at Rudy.

"Got to be easier ways than this."

"Yeah. Maybe they'll pick you to be on *The Bachelor*, so you can have your pick of a bevy of cat-fighting beauties. Oh, no, wait. You're already spoken for. Better stick with the police shows. You ain't smart enough for *Jeopardy*."

Even Rudy had to laugh at that.

"A'course, I got too damn much time on my hands, I'm knowing about all these TV shows. I'm just glad you're looking into this." His voice grew somber. "This case has haunted me every day since. I truly hated to retire and leave this jacket in the file cabinet."

"You said you had some of the file?" Rudy asked.

"Copies. Right here."

The waitress came to take our order. Rudy and Vince wisely followed my lead on the chicken-fried steak, but went their own ways on the vegetables.

As soon as the waitress left, Vince hefted a thick manila envelope off the seat beside him and slid out papers and pictures.

"A'course, this is nothing compared to the full file. I can't believe it's gone. Guess it's nothing compared to the files you gather now, what with your computers and DNA tests and forensics. All we had was flat-footing it around town asking questions and banging out reports with two fingers on manual typewriters."

"And taking pictures," Rudy said as Vince handed him some eight-by-ten black-and-whites he'd separated out from the papers.

Rudy sat beside me, on the outside of the bench seat. He'd had trouble sliding his football-player thighs between the end of the pew and the table corner, but once he'd cleared the corner, the pew provided plenty of room.

I looked over his elbow. The photos showed Wenda's body, though from a distance and straight on, not at the intimate angle shown in the picture we'd found. Close-ups showed her suitcases, her gashed, bloodless throat, the dried fall leaves scattered around the bench where she'd been displayed.

I caught Rudy's eye and asked my question by raising an eyebrow. He gave one nod.

"Mr. Ingum, do you recognize this?" I pulled the four-by-six photo from the envelope I carried. "Would this have been one of your officer's crime-scene photos?"

He slid his wire aviator glasses up to his forehead, holding the photo close, studying it for a long moment before he started shaking his head.

He turned his spooky eyes to me, softer and more liquid and vulnerable until he let his glasses slip back into place.

"Where'd you get this?" His tone was even as he stared at me.

"Gran—Wenda's mother—had it. Somebody sent it to her."

"Who the hell'd send something like this to a victim's mother?"

I would've hated to be the rookie cop who stepped in a cow pie on this guy's watch.

"That's what we're trying to figure out. Walter—at the *Clarion* office—said it wouldn't have been one of his news photographers. They wouldn't take that kind of shot."

"Sure as hell not one of ours. We couldn't buy Bic pens, much less fancy flash equipment. Not like these days, with computers and Kevlar and college boys, huh?"

He jabbed Rudy's arm with a not-quite-playful fist.

Something about Rudy was different around this man. He didn't pop back a snide comment, and I sensed a tenseness I wasn't used to from Rudy. Was Rudy reliving his rookie days? This guy would've been a tough one.

I had my own nightmare mentors from my rookie days, but Vince wasn't one of them, so I went on with my questions. "What do you remember about the case?"

"We didn't expect murders like this. Drunken brawls at a pool hall, drunk drivers flying off the mountainside, goofy kids trying some stunt on the lake, a husband hits his wife once too often and one of 'em ends up dead. Nothing like this, though."

He pointed a stubby finger at the photos in Rudy's hands. "First off, she was from out of town. That meant we didn't know the players. Weren't even sure who she was, at first. Then the short list of suspects didn't pan out. Couldn't shake anything loose."

I watched as Rudy turned through the photos once again. These photos had a very different quality from the one we'd found in Neanna's car. I didn't know quite how to describe the difference in the photos—the angle, the light, the clarity. Something.

"Cold cases, as everybody's fond of calling them these days, aren't solved by police work alone. Let's face it. Absent some breakthrough like DNA, unless the killer's caught for another crime or unless time works on somebody's conscience, somebody with enough courage to come forward, cold cases stay cold."

"When somebody decides to do the right thing," I said.

"Naw." He shook his head. "Civic-mindedness seldom factors into it. Revenge is more like it. More'n likely, he pisses off his girlfriend and she decides to tally up the scorecard."

"Who were your suspects?" I asked.

"Her boyfriend, Tank Smith, for starters. Not an upstanding citizen. Tank had recently taken to spending time in Camden County and had brought some of his trouble from Atlanta with him."

He sipped his ice tea. "Tank had an alibi we couldn't shake. Visiting in Tampa, with plenty of witnesses and at least one of those would've loved to see him in trouble. Never found the place she was actually killed and never found the knife, so we had no physical evidence linking him or anybody else to the body."

"Was he the only one on your radar?"

"Naw. When she'd visited Tank in Dacus, she'd met another guy. We heard there were some sparks, but he had an alibi, too."

"Lots of alibis wandering around," Rudy said.

"Yeah. I had trouble believing it myself. How often you got even one suspect with a really good alibi? The kicker was, this other guy had not one but two alibis. A friend swore he'd been with him at Myrtle Beach that weekend, staying in another friend's beach house. Down visiting the clubs, photographing girls at some bikini festival. The photos were real enough." He smiled at a pleasant memory.

"Later, we got wind that he'd been in Atlanta shacked up with some woman who was inconveniently married to somebody else. Never could shake loose a name for this mystery woman, and the witness, after we questioned her again, couldn't be sure it was that weekend. We felt okay about the Myrtle Beach story, though. Just enough detail but not too much. Nothing else in his past that was suspicious. In the end, we had a guy with two alibis—never had that before—and no leverage to either crack or settle on one or the other."

I didn't say, *So you got stuck on one guy and didn't look anywhere else?* "Anybody else on your list?"

"She'd hitchhiked to Dacus from Atlanta. That opened up possibilities all along I-85, from Alabama to Richmond. Again, nothing we could prove."

"She hitchhiked?"

He raised his eyebrows, maybe thinking I was shocked that a woman would do that.

"An odd coincidence. Her niece, the new victim, gave a ride to a guy," I said. "From Atlanta to Dacus."

He huffed, his brows together now. "Not a big fan of coincidences myself." He shot a glance at Rudy, who sat with his arms folded on the table.

"How did Wenda die?" I asked.

"Strangled, probably until she was unconscious. Didn't do the trick because then her throat was slit." He pointed to the dark line circling her throat. "She was killed somewhere else, cleaned up, and dumped here. Staged here would be more accurate."

"Anything—else happen?"

"You mean was she raped?" He barked the word.

A woman at a two-person table sitting just over the pretend porch railing from us snuck a glance in Vince's direction.

"She wasn't. She had no money in her purse, but she had a gas card. It was still there. Nothing else missing, that we could tell, unless she'd muled some drugs in for her boyfriend. Which, knowing him, was a possibility."

"Wenda's boyfriend was a drug dealer?"

"That wasn't what he told the IRS, but we had plenty of evidence that's what was going on with his friends up at the Pasture. Still was when I retired, for all I know."

"The Pasture?" I asked. I felt Rudy come to attention beside me.

"That's how her boyfriend Tank met Lenn Edmonds. He'd recently bought the Pasture. Lenn still have it?" he asked Rudy.

"On paper and in fact. Never made a bust there that involved him, though we're called there fairly regular. Rumors about bootleg whiskey, but the feds've never made a case."

He snorted. "Like they ever could."

He took a cornbread muffin from the basket. "Much as I might have wanted to pin it on Tank or even on Edmonds, her hitchhiking seemed the likeliest place she met her killer. Never safe, especially for a woman."

"Lenn Edmonds was the other suspect?"

"Yeah. The guy with two alibis. You know, I always liked Edmonds. Damn good football player, even if he didn't have sense enough to go to Clemson. He just has a way of surrounding himself with shady dealings. Part of owning a nightclub, I guess. That Ash Carter still riding around on Lenn's coattails?"

"Yep," Rudy said.

"Not much changes, does it?"

Lenn Edmonds. No wonder he'd stared at Neanna's picture. She did look familiar, exactly like somebody he'd once known. Exactly like someone he'd been suspected of killing.

"You ever get any leads on who gave Wenda Sims a ride from Atlanta?" Rudy asked.

"Naw. Not enough manpower to troll all the I-85 truck stops."

"Unlikely that a serial killer has been plying I-85 all these years waiting for her niece to appear," I said.

Vince fixed me with his pale eyes, but I didn't blink or apologize for my sarcasm. Wenda's killer had been going on about his life for too many years.

He fumbled with his tightly rolled napkin. As if he read my mind, he said, "I hated to leave with that case file open. Can't say I was sorry when her grandmother stopped calling me ever' whip-stitch to see what was happening."

The waitress appeared with a wagon-wheel-sized tray full of plates and slid them in front of us. Vince paused but didn't step away from his memories.

"Too many of the cases we handled were obvious, almost like the victims couldn't have stopped themselves if they'd tried, like they went looking for it. With her, even though she'd made some bad choices, she didn't seem like one who deserved it. I remember reading about an English case once, a body found in a steamer trunk. Commenting on it, somebody said, 'You'll never find a good girl in a trunk.' In my experience, that's true. With her grandmother watching over her, seems she would've stayed out of an early coffin."

I cut my first steaming piece of steak. My mouth watering, I paused to ask, "Why did Gran quit calling?"

He shrugged, putting his knife to his own cream-gravy-covered golden-crusted steak. "I don't know. She just all of a sudden quit. A little after the first anniversary. I remember because that struck me as sad, as if the warranty had run out or something. I told myself I'd call her, keep in touch. A'course I didn't."

He waved his fork at Rudy. "You know how that is."

His voice was somber. I knew I was glimpsing the soft underbelly he used gruffness to hide. I wondered if Rudy had ever seen it before, the vulnerability, the sadness. I knew he felt it himself. Did Rudy work as hard to hide it around his colleagues, or had he just not been at it as long?

The three of us chewed and thought our own thoughts.

"How is Miz Sims, her grandmother?" Vince asked.

"Gran—died." I shied away from saying *she passed away,* figuring he'd read euphemism as weakness.

"Mm. Sorry to hear that." He kept his gaze on his food. "How'd you come by that picture?"

I glanced at Rudy, not sure what he'd already told Vince, or what he was comfortable telling. Rudy didn't look in my direction or step into the conversation, so I blundered on.

"You know about Miz Sims's granddaughter, Neanna Lyles? She had it."

"And she's dead. Rudy mentioned it when he called. Hell of a note, itn't it?"

"Neanna's friend—actually, they've been raised more like sisters—came to my office when Neanna first went missing. Neanna's body had already been discovered, but they hadn't officially identified her yet or located the next of kin."

I paused, but Rudy forked in some drippy collards and seemed content to continue his observer's role.

"The officer at the scene initially figured it as a suicide. Rudy took me to the impound lot to see the car, so I could give a full report to the sister, Fran. We discovered the photo stuck in the car's headliner. They'd found her luggage ransacked, and a scrapbook Gran—Miz Sims—had kept was missing."

"A scrapbook?" His weathered fisherman's face wrinkled in a frown.

"Gran kept a scrapbook about the investigation into Wenda's death. She kept all the news articles about the case. She'd had that photo stuck in the front."

I'd slipped it back into the envelope and had moved it aside when the food arrived. We didn't have to see it to remember all too well what it showed.

Vince snorted. "Grandmothers clip stories about their grands accomplishments, but that's sure not what any grandmother has in mind for making her babies newsworthy, is it? I can see wanting to know what was going on, but why the hell she keep a creepy thing like that?"

I didn't point out that he'd kept the file on the case, his own version of a memory book. "I think she'd always wanted to pretend the family was normal. After what happened, this was the most normal thing she could do. Maybe she wanted to write the story, so to speak. Make sure it was told, that her baby wasn't forgotten." Maybe save her somehow, pull her back from the edge.

His snort was milder than I'd expected. "Wish to hell we could've written an ending for her."

We ate in silence for a while, then Vince asked Rudy what some of his old buddies were up to and what the latest uproars and scandals were, both in the sheriff's department and around Camden County. I half listened, watching their easy camaraderie, trying to fathom the dynamic between old hand and the once-Young Turk. I detected grudging respect on both sides—and some envy. Envy that one was free from the pressure and envy that the other was still in the thick of it.

As the meal wound to an end, Rudy got down to business, making sure he had names and spellings for Wenda's boyfriend and the alibi witnesses. Vince gave him all he had to offer.

"Call if you think of anything," Rudy said, clasping Vince Ingum's hand in a warm, bear-paw handshake as we stood on the corner underneath the restaurant's man-in-a-bathtub landmark sign.

"Will do, buddy. Good to see you. Keep me posted." He paused and fixed Rudy with his pale-eyed gaze. "Write her an ending, will you?"

Saturday Afternoon
and Evening

The trip home was quick. Rudy groused that tonight was his night to take patrol, so he wanted to catch a nap before he went on.

"I thought you were chief deputy. Aren't you supposed to be the big-picture guy? Don't you have minions?"

He made a rude noise. "A department our size, we're all minions. Besides, it was kind of my idea that everybody rotate through patrol. Nobody wants a boss who's forgotten what it's like on the road."

I didn't ask if Sheriff L. J. Peters was part of the egalitarian patrol-duty roster.

"Not a complete waste," I said. "It gives you something to complain about."

"It's good to remember how bad it is," he said with a snort.

We made it back home by late afternoon, with time to spare. I'd been toying with the idea of taking Emma up to the state park with me, maybe stroll around the lake and go to the Saturday night square dance. Too easy to get lost in the daily details and let time for those kinds of things just slip away.

Melvin strolled into my office as I finished making arrangements with my sister Lydia about picking up Emma, what she should wear, and whether I was planning to feed her.

"Square dance, huh? They still have those?"

"Yep." Any excitement from new arrivals over at the jail holding cell wouldn't happen until later that evening, after Rudy and the other minions started clearing from the bars those who believed every weekend was a holiday worth getting plastered to celebrate.

Melvin was obviously in a summer celebration mood of his own but with no plans and nowhere to go.

"You want to come?" I asked. "Just me and Emma. We'd love for you to join us."

I held open the French door to my office, hoping to lead him out so I could lock the doors and get upstairs to change into shorts and a T-shirt. I was certain the state's parks and recreation budget hadn't sprung for air-conditioning the huge barn since the last time I'd been there.

"I don't want to cut in—"

"We're leaving in twenty minutes. You'd better get ready." I waved him into the hallway and cut off his protests.

The phone in my office rang. I hesitated, not wanting to answer it but wondering if it might be Lydia or Emma calling. I shooed Melvin in the direction of the stairs and turned back to Shamanique's desk.

"Hey. Found Wenda's old boyfriend, Tank Smith," Rudy said without preamble.

"Already?"

"Easy to find them when they're dead."

"Wow. Really?"

Rudy must have felt the same disappointment that swept over me. Otherwise he wouldn't have felt the need to call.

"Stiffed a guy in a drug deal ten years ago in Atlanta. Got a knife through at least one vital artery for his trouble."

"Nice. I'd really liked the possibility presented by a bad-boy boyfriend."

"Might still be a possibility. It'll just be harder to unravel without him around to answer questions. And not as satisfying in the end."

Rudy believes in justice—swift and meaningful justice.

"We'll just get busy on his alibi witnesses. Maybe, now that he's gone, somebody'll be willing to tell the truth."

"Aren't you supposed to be napping?"

"Who says I'm not?" He clicked off.

Thanks to Rudy's call and my indecision about wearing shorts when I saw my deathly pale legs in the mirror, I was the one who ended up making us late picking up Emma. By the time I jerked on khaki slacks and rushed downstairs, Melvin was waiting, jingling his car keys.

Melvin refuses to ride with me, which was just as well since my Mustang's backseat was like riding in a hole for seven-year-old Emma, who wasn't tall enough to see out.

Not that she minded riding in the Mustang any more than I had at her age, but Melvin's Jeep wagon was more comfortable, even if I thought he drove like a sissy.

Emma had finished her supper and was waiting on the front steps when we arrived. As we began our climb up the mountain, she perched on the backseat with her headphones on, her head bobbing as she watched the houses pass and grow sparser until trees took over the scenery. "You missed it last night," I said to Melvin. "Do tell," Melvin said, allowing a half smile.

"Your little ghoster film group captured some great storytelling last night, but they seemed more excited about blobs of light that looked suspiciously like bugs."

"Blobs of light."

"Excuse me. Orbs. Pardon my shocking lack of precision with the terminology."

Melvin shook his head.

"It obviously wasn't an invitation-only event. Tap's Pool Room must have suffered a sharp drop in business last night because too many of his regulars opted to attend the storytelling and marshmallow roast."

Melvin took his eyes off the road for a fraction of a blink to see if I was making up my unbelievable story. Unbelievable, yes. Definitely not fabricated.

"Don't ask me what they were doing there, but Donlee and PeeVee and Cuke Metz and several of the Ghouly Boys showed up to watch the festivities and the filming."

"Uh-oh."

"My sentiments exactly. I suspect somebody in that group is the one who's been suggesting haunted sites to Colin."

"Couldn't be your buddy Donlee."

"Gosh, no. He's not smart enough. And PeeVee's status as the brains of that duo doesn't qualify him, either. My money's on Cuke, from what I've seen. You know him?"

"No."

"He doesn't seem to fit with the rest of that crowd, and he looks suspiciously like the guy who drove the truck on that Moody Springs video."

"You're kidding. You sure?"

I shrugged, not willing to swear to it.

"Did they cause any trouble last night?"

"The ghosters?"

"No, your buddies."

I snorted. "Right. My buddies. No, they were perfect gentlemen, which is what worried me. Not even drinking, so's you could tell it. But I don't get a good feeling about it. Your ghosters are too earnest. They're taking this way too seriously. That's when somebody could get hurt."

"Maybe not," Melvin said.

"Somebody—namely you—needs to have a chat with them. They seem to take you seriously."

Melvin cocked his head with the slow tick-tock of a metronome but didn't say anything.

"True," I said, playing devilish advocate. "All this nonsense might attract an investor for their film."

"Might get somebody hurt, too," Melvin said, coming around to my point.

At the state park, we left the car far away from the barn, even though we were early enough to pick a spot among the trees near the front door. The better to make our escape if the dance wasn't as much fun as we remembered.

The long sunlight and the balmy air combined to make the perfect ending to the week, a lazy late afternoon.

We didn't have enough time before dark or the dance to walk all the way around the lake that served for swimming, canoeing, fishing, and waterfront views for the thirteen scattered lakeside rental cabins. We wandered down to the roped-off swimming area with its coarse-sand beach and across the WPA-built spillway to check out the moonshine still they had on display and to soak up the quiet as dark encircled the tree-sheltered lake.

By the time we strolled back up the hill to the barn, the crowd had gathered and the music had started.

The doors on one side of the barn were open to let the massive fans suck air through the screens. Bleachers on either end of the dusty wooden floor could seat only a small number of local regulars and the campers who walked over from the cabins and the RV park, but the almost constant music made sure few people wanted to sit, drawing them to the dance floor.

Much hadn't changed in the years since I'd last attended a square dance. The live band, with a couple of members I recognized. Young men grown to look more like their fathers than they'd want to know. The fathers grown into grandfathers who took turns calling the familiar changes in the dance. The rhythmic clacking of the two-tone taps nailed into the bottoms of loafers and boots, thudding in a pulse. The campers loose-limbed imitation of the knee-jarring buck-and-wing step.

Emma was a dance-school dropout like her aunt—too boring, she said. She needed the regimen of tae kwon do, she allowed, but she'd learned enough in her toddler tap class that she was a quick study. Melvin was the one who really surprised me. He remembered even the seldom-called changes, and he charmed Emma when we showed her and a little camper about her age how to do a freestyle swing turn.

Emma was thrilled with the orchestrated steps, less than enthralled with holding a little boy's hand.

I remembered in a familiar rush the first time I'd come square dancing. A more experienced sixth-grade friend of mine had told me that holding hands with a boy wasn't so bad, that you'd be having too much fun dancing to notice. "Not like you could really catch cooties or anything," I whispered to Emma.

Melvin knew how to let me know that I didn't need to lead. When he slid his hand under my shoulder blade and guided me into a swing spin on our first circle-four, then quickly led Emma and her camper partner into a shoot-the-moon without missing a beat, I knew he'd logged some serious clogging time.

Had I seen him here, when I was in high school? Had he been one of the older dancers, one of the men who'd bent over politely to dance with the kids Emma's age and then swept away in a courtly promenade me and the other high school girls—still kids but, at the same time, hopelessly grown-up and awkward, in our own minds? I didn't remember seeing him or dancing with him, but his strong, sure lead brought back that tilting balance between goofy adolescent and fairy princess in a red-faced rush.

When the band stopped to take a break, Melvin grabbed soft drinks from the crowded canteen, and the three of us adjourned to a picnic table in the now-dark trees several yards from the barn.

The crowded dance floor and the frenetic clogging had left my sweat-damp shirt clammy in the humid night air. After the loud music, even the cicadas' and tree frogs' efforts to drown out conversation sounded muted.

We sat on the weathered tabletop, rested our feet on the splintery bench, and drank our icy Sprites in companionable exhaustion for a while.

"So the storyteller last night was good?" Melvin asked.

"Yep, she was. Somebody from over in Cullowhee. Think she might teach at Western Carolina."

"Did she tell some scary stories?" Emma asked.

"Some. You'd have liked them."

"Ah, you like ghost stories, Emma?"

She gave Melvin one of her solemn nods.

"How about the story of the ghost dog? You ever heard that one?"

"No."

Emma was sitting on the other side of Melvin. Without her

noticing, I had no way to warn Melvin that she took life seriously, more like her great-great-aunt Aletha than any seven-year-old should be. He was on his own, picking a path between what any jaded seven-year-old would find tame, and therefore lame, and what a seven-year-old girl in the dark woods at night would find the stuff of nightmares. He was on his own, but I would be the one in trouble.

"Back up in these hills, before people had electricity and before many people had cars to get around in, most folks had sense enough to be in bed—or at least safely home—before it got dark."

Melvin's rich voice had taken on a country lilt I hadn't heard from him before, the cadence that made a story sound authentic.

"Now days, we zip along in our cars and we have so many streetlights, even up here." He gestured toward the lights surrounding the dance barn and visible through the trees. "We can hardly see the stars, much less what else might be around and visible only in the dark."

"Like what?" Emma asked.

"Like ghost dogs."

Reflected in the light, I saw Emma's face scrunch up. She didn't look scared, just skeptical.

"Lots of stories around here about them. Like one about a fellow heading home from a dance. A storm had blown through, keeping people inside until the wind and rain passed. He'd met a pretty girl there and he'd stayed longer than he intended. A friend offered him a bed for the night, not wanting him to head off on the hour's walk alone.

"He waved the offer aside, said he had chores to tend to the next morning. His friends parted ways with him as they turned down the road to their houses. He had the long dark path to himself.

"A full moon was out that night, and he was thankful because

240

it lit things up almost as bright as day. Then, without warning, the moon slid behind a thick cloud, and he knew just how much he'd had to be thankful for when it had been shining bright. He prayed the cloud would pass, but he could do no more than pray and keep walking.

"He reached a place where the path forked. One path headed into some thick woods. He had some good reasons not to take that path. One, it led past an old graveyard, left by a family or church long gone. For another, the path crossed a high, lonesome footbridge over a deep ravine. Scary enough in daylight, hard to navigate at night with no moon.

"Unfortunately the other path took the long way around the woods, adding time to his journey home.

"He hesitated, looking skyward, trying to decide if the cloud would move away. He could see no stars. He was tired, in a hurry to get home.

"He took a step toward the dark trees. It took a moment for him to believe what his eyes saw. Blocking the path, between two thick tree trunks, stood a dog, glowing white as if a light shone on him alone.

"The man gave what he hoped was a friendly click of his tongue. 'Hey, boy. Good boy.'

"The dog bared its teeth and growled. Its eyes glowed blood-red. The growl rumbled low, as if drawn from the very pit of hell.

"The man didn't wait around to see if the dog stepped out from the shelter of the trees. He took off running down the long path as fast as he could.

"He glanced over his shoulder only once, to make sure the dog wasn't following, afraid to know and afraid not to.

"He saw no sign of the dog. Not once did he glance into the trees, for he feared the glowing white dog tracked him, waiting to pounce.

"He made it home in record time. The next morning, a friend stopped by his farm. 'Wanted to make sure you got home safely,' his friend said. 'Heard tell the wind blew a tree across the footbridge last night. We were worried that you might have gone that way and fallen into the river below.'

"The young man thanked his friend for his concern and waved him on his way. He didn't tell him or anyone else about the ghostly glowing dog until years later, when enough time had passed that he didn't mind if they ribbed him about it and when he no longer shook inside whenever he thought about it.

"When he finally talked about the dog, he learned of another man, not so fortunate. One night, years earlier, he'd taken the shortcut through the woods and, not being familiar with the area and having had a bit too much white lightning to drink that evening, he tumbled into the ravine and died.

"His body was found the next day when two men approached the ravine and found a large white dog. The dog ran down the steep slope into the ravine and back up again, showing them to his master's body."

"Did the dog die, too?" Emma studied Melvin with that quiet contemplation I so often get from her.

I hoped he remembered she was a little kid.

"No, not until years later. One of the men took him home and took very good care of him. Years later, after the faithful dog had lived a long life, the man buried him in the graveyard with his first owner. Apparently the dog continued to guard the spot, making sure nothing happened to another man."

"Did you know these people?"

"No. Not personally. I'm not that old."

She stared at him.

Melvin stared back, unfazed by her intensity.

"Do you believe ghosts are real?" Emma asked Melvin.

"Good question," he said, matter-of-fact in the face of her stoic inquiry. "Ghosts might be like other things; they're real if we believe in them. If we don't, they just slip away."

Emma studied him without comment. I was glad he was smart enough not to condescend to her. She doesn't respond to that any better than I do.

"You'd believe a ghost story if I knew the people?" he asked her. "How about this one?"

Part of me wanted to end the ghost stories. If she had nightmares, her mama would call a halt to fun outings with Aunt Bree for a while. The other part liked the gentle thrill and Melvin's rich voice from the other end of our dark table.

"When my very own grandmother was young, she'd passed the age when most young ladies got married. Everyone in church and around kept introducing her to eligible young men, but she wasn't having any of it. 'He's not the one,' she'd say. Everyone had decided she was destined to be an old maid.

"One day, she met a man from over in Seneca. He was a bit older than she was, though not too much. When he asked to come courting, she agreed.

"The whole family was surprised by that, but she offered no explanation. A few months later, after a scandalously short courtship, she accepted his proposal of marriage. She explained to her mother that she'd started having dreams when she was quite young, dreams about a man. She said she saw him clearly, and though she couldn't ever recall what they talked about or what happened in the dreams, she knew he was the man she would marry. When Granddaddy appeared in person, she said she knew, as soon as she laid eyes on him, that he really was the man of her dreams."

Emma stared at him a moment. Even with her head turned in profile, I could feel the full effect of the frown.

243

"That's just mushy."

"Hm. I thought girls liked mushy."

"Not so much," Emma said, hopping down from the picnic table. "I liked the ghost dog better."

She dusted off the seat of her shorts and looked at us expectantly.

The music inside had started again, so we abandoned our dark perch and made our way back into what now felt like a crowded steam bath.

Melvin asked Emma to dance. I climbed up the metal bleachers near the screened wall and sat to watch. With an apologetic plea of fatigue, I waved away a dance invitation—not a longtime regular I recognized but also not a camper. Seemed to be a lot of people in that category, people from surrounding counties. One guy told me he drove an hour from Anderson to get here every Saturday.

Melvin's comments about ghosts slipping away if you don't believe kept playing in my head, which brought to mind Gran and how hard she'd fought to keep her family from slipping away. Just by caring, by believing, she'd kept the investigation into Wenda's death alive.

Love could make the difference between investigators staying hot on the trail and a case gone cold. Someone who cared enough to keep the heat on probably kept a file folder out of the cold-case bin more often than law enforcement statistics admitted.

Gran's love had kept Wenda alive in Vince Ingum's mind—until someone had scared her off. That struck me as the coldest cruelty, forcing her own mother to let her go, to let her slip away.

Gran had held on to Neanna, though, for as long as she had mortal hands to hold her, until she was no longer around to see her slip away. The thought of the orbs around me made me smile.

If Gran was trying to tell me something, lead me somewhere, she was going to have to get her ectoplasmic act together.

Something about the tragedy that enveloped Neanna's whole family made me believe in the abyss. Who was that old New England preacher who spoke of God dangling sinners over the pit of hell? That preaching tradition lived on in plenty of Primitive Baptist churches in these hills. No wonder Gran feared the abyss. She'd watched her girls dangle. She hadn't been able to call any of them back from the edge, not her daughters Wenda and Marie, not granddaughter Neanna.

Emma charged up the bleachers to grab my hand, the music and chatter too loud for conversation. She'd found a camper her same size, one she could boss around the floor now that she was an expert clogger, so Melvin and I danced one last set.

Emma protested leaving early, but then fell asleep dangling in her seat belt before we'd driven more than a mile down the road.

Even with my melancholy ruminations about Neanna's family, I still felt a warm wash of nostalgia as well as pinging reminders from muscles and joints that I was neither as young nor as fit as I'd been when I first learned to clog.

When we pulled into their drive, Emma's dad Frank came out to carry her inside.

"Haven't seen her that pooped in a while." Lydia smiled as dad and daughter passed us on the front porch, Emma's thick plaited hair draped over her dad's shoulder.

"Our work here is done, then," I said and waved good-bye.

Some nights, I wished I had somebody to carry me in from the car. Heck, I really wished I could still sleep that sleep of the dead that comes so blissfully to little kids.

Melvin dropped me off in front of our office.

"I'm meeting my brother and we're driving out to his lake house. Going to get in some fishing tomorrow early."

"You should've said something! We could've left earlier."

"No, this is perfect. He wasn't going to be able to drive out there until ten anyway."

"Have fun. And thanks. You made Emma feel like quite the princess."

He ducked his head in acknowledgment, looking a bit embarrassed by the compliment. I closed the truck door.

The streetlights along Main lit up the front sidewalk, highlighting my eight-foot praying angel statue with a wash of white and shadow.

The deep porch lay dark on both sides of the massive leaded-glass-and-oak door. I seldom use this door, especially at night. Small-town living had dulled some of the caution I'd brought home from living in an urban condo and apartments, so I felt nothing more than mild frustration as I fumbled to get the key in the lock.

I felt the movement to my left before I saw anything. I spun toward the movement, my dance-tired muscles suddenly charged with adrenaline, my brain searching for and discarding defensive options. No gun. Rocking chair too heavy to lift. Door too temperamental to unlock quickly. Street deserted but well lit. Run into the street.

Facing the shadow, I leapt back toward the steps, not wanting to turn my back.

"Who's there?" The huskiness and threat in my voice surprised me. In a flash, I thought, *If this is the ghosters or another stunt, I'm going to stomp the mud out of somebody.*

"Don't—" The voice—a female voice—quavered. "Please come back. Please don't—he'll know I'm here. He'll kill me."

Saturday Night

I climbed back to the top of the porch steps, keeping myself in the streetlight as if that would keep me safe.

As my eyes adjusted, I saw her. Huddled behind one of the rocking chairs, I couldn't make out her features, her size, not even her hair color.

Her breathing was ragged. She knelt against the wall, halfway between curling up in a defensive ball and bolting in mad flight. She was scared. Very scared.

"Who? Who might see you?"

"Please don't stand there." She was crying. "He might drive by looking for me. He might see you. Please—"

Her voice melted into a strangled plaint.

I stepped into the porch shadow, my keys in hand. I kept my eye on her as I unlocked the door.

"Don't turn on the light." The strength in her voice came from fear, not command.

I pushed open the door and stepped to the side.

"You first," I said. "Go straight ahead and sit on the stairs. No one can see you there. Hurry."

In a crouch, her arms clutched at her waist, she darted in the doorway. I waited until she had crossed the entry hall. I wanted her far enough away that I had a fighting chance if she jumped me.

I followed her through the door and locked it, my movements fed by the adrenaline-inducing thought that an accomplice may yet lurk on the porch. Pretty elaborate ruse if they wanted to steal something, the calmer part of my brain chided me—especially given how easy it would be to smash one of the floor-length windows with one of the porch rockers and stroll right in. Except for computers, the pickings were slim, but burglars have to play the odds like everybody else.

I unlocked the French doors into my office and again stepped aside.

"Go to the right, into the back office."

The lights from outside illuminated the front rooms of the house so that even a stranger could easily avoid bumping into furniture. With no window coverings, any interior lights would create a tableau easily viewed from Main Street and the Burger Hut lot on the opposite side of the street.

She scuttled past me, still trying to keep herself invisible. She disappeared into the dark of my office.

"Wait there. I'll be right back."

I heard something akin to a whimper. Part of me wanted to go comfort her, find out what caused such palpable fear. The pragmatic part of me bounded up the stairs to my apartment and, moving easily in the familiar dark, unlocked the gun safe and slipped my .38 revolver into my waistband, leaving my shirttail out to cover it. No sense being stupid.

She sat in one of the wing-back chairs in the bay window of my office. I crossed behind her to adjust the drapes on the eight-foot windows, then switched on the floor lamp beside her.

The pool of light glinted on brassy highlights tinting her hair. She looked familiar. Dark roots, a tallow complexion, a too-tight blouse stretching over her heavy breasts, and a skirt too high on heavy legs. She was the picture of somebody still partying like it was 1975. Where had I seen her before?

I could smell the acrid odor of fear, the panicked sweat that I'd only encountered in the holding cell with novice offenders. Her red-rimmed eyes were framed with smeared mascara, her breathing jagged. Her cheek was red, the skin taut, and her throat showed angry red marks.

I pulled my desk chair around and sat to face her. I still wanted to keep some distance. Until I had this figured out.

"You've got to help me."

"I'm Avery." Best to lull her with the niceties.

She took another rough breath. "Cela Newlyn."

A battered gold cardboard box, like a treasured Christmas gift might once have arrived in, took up her whole lap. I still couldn't place her. The courthouse? Maylene's? No. Maybe just around, one of those faces.

"My boyfriend, he's going to kill me."

On their own, the words alone would have been melodramatic, even corny. Delivered with her shaky whisper, her hands trembling, the words made me look over my shoulder to make sure we weren't visible from outside.

"Have you called the police?" *Why the heck come here?*

She shook her head, wincing a bit as she moved her bruised

neck. "I was afraid he'd look for me there, wait for me outside. I passed your office, saw your angel outside. I remembered you."

I cocked my head, my eyebrow raised in a question. I didn't admit that I didn't remember her.

"At the Pasture. You came in early one afternoon."

Now I remembered. The waitress who'd been getting ready for her shift when Fran and I visited. The woman near the rear office with Lenn Edmonds.

"The guy you were with in the kitchen. He's your boyfriend?"

Her mouth and eyes wrinkled in a frown. At first, I thought she'd had a sudden spasm of pain, but when she spoke, I knew it was a look of confusion.

"No-o. You mean Lenn. No. Gawd, no. Lenn is egotistical, but he's a sweetheart. Too much a soft touch, you know? Lets women take advantage of him. Just my luck, never could get him to look twice at me."

She was thawing, so I let her keep talking.

"He's hit me before. This was different. I was really afraid he was going to kill me this time. He was—"

She started shaking uncontrollably.

I crossed to her and pulled an afghan off the ottoman beside her chair. She kept a fearful eye on my every move, but leaned forward and let me drape the wrap around her shoulders.

"Can I get you some water or something?"

She shook her head, short little jerks.

"How did you get away?" Maybe reminding her of her own strength would calm her.

"He got a call. He said he'd be right back and told me not to move. That's when I knew."

Her breath came in dry sobs. "I knew he kept his gun in this box. I was afraid he'd use it, before he had a chance to calm down. So I took it. I climbed out the window and ran."

"We need to call the police."

She shook her head, wincing openly with this more vigorous movement. "No, I got to think. I can't think clear."

She grabbed the box as it threatened to slide off her lap. "Here. Let me take that for you."

She lifted it, offering it to me without hesitation.

Despite its battered appearance, it was sturdier and heavier than I'd expected. I balanced it on my lap and lifted the lid. No gun.

"Did you look in here?"

She gave an abbreviated shake of her head. "I hate guns."

Five bullets rolled around in the box, the metal catching the lamplight. Shiny and fresh. Wherever her boyfriend was, he had his gun, and probably plenty of bullets.

What I saw underneath the loose bullets chilled me more than the missing gun.

I carried the box to my desk, feeling the weight of my own revolver hidden under my shirt, tugging the waistband of my pants. I tipped the box and let the bullets roll onto the desk.

In the box lay a cream-colored book with a faux-marbled vinyl cover, bound along the spine with frayed cords. Old English gilt embossed a single word: *Scrapbook*. On top of the book, cracked and worn, lay a photograph. A duplicate of the crime-scene photo we'd found hidden in Neanna's car. This one, though, lacked the tiny blood spatters that decorated Neanna's copy.

In sharp focus, I saw it. The artistic angle of the shot and the wash of lighting, uncharacteristic for crime scene or newspaper photographers. The photos lining the walls at the Pasture.

"Your boyfriend is Ash Carter."

She gave me a panicked glance.

"He's a photographer." I wasn't asking her. I was reminding myself.

She looked flustered by my sudden change in topic. "Why?"

"He took the photos on the walls in the bar."

"Uh-huh."

I used a pen to open the edge of the scrapbook. Just as I expected. Yellowed newspaper clippings. I let the cover fall closed. No need risking fingerprints or other trace evidence.

Ash Carter took all kinds of pictures, including bikini-clad girls at Myrtle Beach. The same man whose photography trip to the beach had supplied Lenn Edmonds's alibi had a photo of a dead woman, some shiny bullets, and a scrapbook.

I stood staring down at my desk, at the battered gold box, the cracked photograph, the scrapbook. The same man had handily provided an alibi for himself.

I turned the phone around on my desk and dialed Rudy's familiar cell phone number. I glanced at my watch and felt a tiny ripple of guilt at calling so late. Until I remembered he was on patrol.

Rudy barked into his phone—his tough-cop-in-charge voice. He listened without interrupting to my rapid *Reader's Digest* version.

"So he's probably carrying the gun," Rudy said.

"That would be my guess." I didn't want to further panic Cela by letting her know about the missing gun. She thought she'd brought with her some security. I stared at the faded gilt letters. Security was the last thing she'd brought with her in this box.

"His girlfriend's got bruises and he caused 'em?"

"Yep."

"He's out at the Pasture?"

"Or out—looking." I caught myself and glanced at Cela. Abusive relationships are unpredictable on both sides. I didn't want either a wave of panic or of nostalgic remorse to wash over Cela, pushing her to do something I couldn't control.

"You got bullets for that gun of yours, Barney?" Rudy's sarcasm protected us both from reality for a moment.

"You're the deputy," I countered, though no one would mistake Rudy for the scrawny Barney Fife of *Andy Griffith Show* fame.

"I got my other guys scattered around the lakes, because of those break-ins. It'll take a while to call somebody in. You sure you're okay there?"

"Sure." I knew as well as Rudy how dangerous domestic cases could get. "Keep me posted."

As I started to hang up the receiver, I noticed the blinking message light.

Three calls, all from Fran. The first announced she'd decided to drive back to Dacus for the weekend and had just checked into the bed-and-breakfast. By the third, she'd given up reaching me and had decided how to entertain herself for the evening.

"It's about ten o'clock," her last message said. "I'm going to drive out to the Pasture, see if I can find anybody who saw Neanna there last week. Too antsy to sit around this room. Hope you're not gone for the weekend. Call me."

My tongue tasted like dried sweat. My fingers stumbled over the keys as I redialed Rudy's number. It rang and rang. Not even his voice mail picked up.

I dialed again, hoping I'd misdialed the first time. More ringing.

I dialed my parents' house.

My mom, usually on the night-owl shift at home, didn't ask any questions after I told her I had someone who needed to check into the women's shelter.

"Pull around back, into the garage, Mom."

That way, we could smuggle Cela into Mom's van through the basement garage, out of sight of any spying eyes.

A part of me hoped Ash Carter was lurking outside or cruising the streets looking for Cela. Anywhere but at the Pasture waiting to ask Fran to dance.

I dialed Rudy again. Still no answer.

I pocketed my cell phone and turned to Cela. I struggled to keep my voice even. She didn't need to sense my panic, though I didn't know how she could help but smell it on me.

"Come on. We've got a garage under the house. My mom is picking you up. You need to stay in the shelter tonight."

I didn't tell her the spacious, bright underground garage had once housed the Baldwin & Bates Funeral Home two-car fleet of hearses. That wouldn't be a comforting picture.

While we waited, I tried Rudy's number again. Ring, ring, ring.

Mom arrived in record time, wrapped Cela up in her charitably loving care, and whisked her away to safety.

I closed the garage and left through the side door to the rear parking lot. I cranked the Mustang and barreled out the narrow drive that ran between the house and the shrubs sheltering the office from view of the corner gas station.

I couldn't raise Fran on her cell phone, but at least it switched me to her voice mail.

"Fran, it's Avery. Stay away from Ash Carter. I'll fill you in. I'm on my way. A sheriff's deputy should be there soon. Stay away from him. I'll explain later."

I threw the phone in the passenger seat, bore down on the accelerator, and concentrated on the winding country road out to the Pasture. Wouldn't do any good to wrap myself around a tree.

Late Saturday Night

Late night brought big business to the Pasture. In the main lot, cars perched everywhere without a crack to angle my car into. I parked in the lumpy, unlighted field across the road and hoped I wouldn't twist my ankle as I loped toward the long, low building hung in white Christmas lights.

The cigarette smoke had spent the evening gathering thick at the ceiling. By this late hour, it had sunk to head height, leaving the room with little view.

This wasn't the hot, open, brightly lit square dance barn. The low ceiling, the smoke scraping the back of my throat with every breath, the din of alcohol-fired voices and the band's chest-thumping beat, the women old enough to need more clothes than they were wearing—all closed in tight as soon as I walked in.

My lucky night. No cover charge for ladies before midnight.

I tried to find a vantage point from which to spot Fran. The sooner I got her out of here, the better.

Was Rudy already here? I hadn't seen a patrol car outside. Would he be driving his unmarked car?

I quickly realized that the long, flat room meant I wouldn't see anything if I stood in one place, but moving around presented its own challenges.

The closer I got to the dance floor, the more I noticed the appraising looks I was getting. This place probably didn't get much fresh meat.

I slipped past a man who had backed a woman up against a rough-hewn support beam, his hand propped over her head to corral her, his face in her uplifted one. A guy stepped in front of me, his shirt collar open so low I had a *Saturday Night Fever* flashback. He cocked his head in the direction of the dance floor.

I wanted to say, "Careful there, buddy. The heat's loosened your toupee glue," but he couldn't hear me anyway. I just smiled, shook my head, and mouthed "friend" while waving my hand in a vague direction.

That's when I spotted her. On the dance floor, her slender back arched in the tight embrace of Ash Carter.

She danced on her toes, but not in the good form she'd learned in cotillion class. She smiled, nodding attentively. He had a too-bright grin. His step faltered. The crowd on the floor could have been either the cause or what kept him from tripping in an inebriated heap. He clutched Fran even tighter, as though she were the stuffed bunny he'd gotten in his Easter basket.

I didn't want to panic him. I tried subtle means to get Fran's attention, like staring at her hard and trying to send her telepathic messages.

Finally, in a glance over his shoulder, she saw me and flashed me a genuine smile, followed quickly by a single shake of her head and a frown when I motioned for her to join me.

She thought she was on to something. More than she knew. The dried sweat from the square dance blossomed out in the heat of my sudden fear.

I couldn't do anything but stand and watch. And avoid meeting Bad Toupee's gaze.

This close to the dance floor, the song was recognizable if you listened closely for several bars—an up-tempo waltz, though few on the floor recognized the difference between a three- and a four-count box step.

Ash apparently hadn't seen me, and Fran wasn't pointing me out. She kept circling aimlessly in his clutch, smiling and nodding at him.

I sensed the disturbance before I saw its source. All kinds of straightening up started—women adjusting their skirts, patting their hair, men no longer bent over to enjoy the view rising from a décolletage belonging to another man's wife. Heads didn't turn but eyes followed the source: Rudy Mellin in uniform, his handgun and other fixtures plainly visible on his belt.

Did officers know the effect they had? They must. Probably why some of them accepted the boring parts and the poor pay.

I'd stayed back in the crowd, hoping Ash wouldn't notice me and hoping Fran wouldn't say anything about seeing me.

No avoiding Rudy, though. He didn't look happy to see me.

"I tried to call you," I yelled into his ear, not wanting to waste time being scolded. "Fran's back in town. She left me a message and I couldn't reach you."

I turned my back to the dance floor to talk to Rudy, hoping Carter wouldn't recognize me. Rudy had to bend over to hear me, yet I still felt self-conscious, not wanting anyone to overhear and spook Carter into something rash.

Without warning, Rudy pushed me aside and plowed through the drinkers and dancers.

The crowd closed back before I could follow in his wake. I glimpsed Fran's face, turned back as if looking for help, just as Ash Carter jerked her out of sight near the band stage at the rear of the dance floor.

I squirmed through the hot bodies, stepping on somebody's foot and getting smacked sharply by a gyrating man's exuberant elbow. I reached the rear hallway just in time to see Ash take an ineffectual punch at Rudy. In an easy move, Rudy cocked his arm back and clipped Ash on the point of the chin.

Despite all his Maylene meals, Rudy made the punch look light, effortless. Ash's eyes literally rolled in his head. He dropped like a sack of feed off a truck tailgate.

With one hand, Rudy scooped Fran behind him, away from Ash. He then stood over Ash, making sure he wasn't playing 'possum.

I joined them and slid my arm around Fran. She started shaking uncontrollably.

Everything had ended so quickly. Most of the people in the bar had no idea a murderer had been captured in their midst. My adrenaline overload burned out just as my brain realized how differently things could have ended. The claustrophobic smokiness in the dance hall did nothing to warm my sudden icy fear.

Rudy must have called backup before he came inside, because a burly officer with salty gray hair and too many immobile years behind the wheel of a cruiser appeared almost as soon as Rudy clicked his shoulder radio.

The two officers flipped Ash over and cuffed him as his eyelids fluttered back to consciousness. They hauled him up unceremoniously and out the front door, dragging his toes when he couldn't or wouldn't stand.

Fran and I followed, the crowd staying parted long enough to let us pass.

After they loaded Ash, still limp, into the back of Rudy's patrol car, Rudy turned, flexing his fingers on his bruised punching hand.

"We'll talk later," he said, his tone a portent.

The patrol cars pulled away, leaving Fran and me standing alone. I still had my arm around her waist.

I didn't bother asking where she'd parked. We could retrieve her car later. I walked her slowly through the large gravel lot, across the rough-paved country blacktop, and over the lumpy field to my Mustang.

She slid in without protest, the bucket seat roomy around her slight frame.

Sunday

Sunday breakfast with Rudy was not a pleasant affair. He'd called me at seven that morning and ordered me to put in an appearance at Maylene's. He was not happy.

I'd no sooner slid into the booth across from him than he lit into me.

"What the hell were you doing, charging into the Pasture last night? You know better than that. Blundering around like that could've gotten somebody hurt. Or dead."

That hit like a punch, but I knew he was right. "Rudy, I tried to call you. What was I supposed to do? Just hope you got there? Just hope you knew Fran might be in trouble?"

"Why not do what ordinary citizens do? Call freakin' 911. That's what it's there for."

"And tell the dispatcher what?"

Rudy glared at me but didn't reply.

The waitress sauntered over to take our orders, which gave us both a chance to cool down.

"I'm sorry, Rudy. Like I told you last night, when Cela Newlyn showed up with that scrapbook, it all fell into place for me. All those photos at the Pasture. The photography trip to Myrtle Beach that gave Lenn Edmonds such a good alibi. All of a sudden, I realized who took that carefully lit photo of Wenda. I realized that Myrtle Beach alibi protected Ash Carter as much as it did Lenn. Knowing that, Lenn's double alibi made sense. Then I picked up Fran's phone message about going to the Pasture. I panicked."

My rush of words stopped. Rudy stirred the gritty sugar against the bottom of his coffee cup before he met my gaze.

"Ash convinced Lenn he was helping him out," he said. "Seems Lenn's real alibi, the one Ingum only heard rumors about, was awkward. Lenn was shacked up with somebody else's wife. As it happens, the wife of the guy who staked Lenn with the money to buy the Pasture. Seems everybody loves a college football hero."

"So Lenn had good reason to be grateful when Ash came up with the Myrtle Beach alibi."

"They'd been there the week before. Everything was just vague enough to be believable. Stayed in the Edmonds family condo. No time-dated gas station receipts or that sort of thing, and no manpower to track all the loose ends down."

"But why did Ash kill them?"

"He's not talking, not about Wenda or Neanna. My guess, he came on to Wenda. She told him to get lost. He got violent. Ash has a problem sweet-talking ladies. As you found out last night."

"He hasn't learned anything about finesse despite hanging around with Lenn Edmonds all these years."

Rudy snorted. "Finesse? Hardly."

I thought about shop-worn Cela Newlyn and free-spirited Wenda Sims. I doubted Wenda would have given him a second look, especially if she'd already attracted Lenn Edmonds's attention. Unlike Cela, Wenda had been a woman with options in men, even if she didn't always have good taste. What had Cela put up with in the name of love?

Rudy's mouth set in a hard line. "We're just now finding out what a scary little shit Ash Carter is."

I waited for him to elaborate.

"We're checking on him, everywhere he's been for the last couple of decades. Starting to wonder if these were his only two victims."

"No." The word rushed out in a breath.

Rudy shrugged. "Don't know for sure. Some questions have followed him around other places he's been. Girlfriends who left town suddenly. That sort of thing. Both SLED and the FBI are involved now."

The South Carolina Law Enforcement Division, our state police. I shivered, remembering the photograph and how Ash had frightened Gran into giving up on her daughter. Had he done more than send the photograph? Had he threatened her? Or Neanna?

"You said Neanna had taken a lot of Xanax. You think he gave it to her?"

"Possible. If she wasn't used to taking it, that would guarantee she didn't put up much fight."

"All he had to do was hold her hand near the gun when he fired it."

The look on Rudy's face said he hadn't thought of that. "That would account for the gunshot residue. Or he could've just held the gun in her hand, fired into the woods, replaced the cartridge, and shot her. With the pills, alcohol, and pot, she'd have been little more than a rag doll."

"Why kill Neanna?"

"Why not? She was asking questions. Probably easy to entice her to meet him on the mountain, with the promise of information. More of a rush job than with Wenda. He took his time there, and he came close to getting away with it."

"Why leave Wenda on that graveyard bench like that? That had to be dangerous, taking all that time."

"Who knows? Because he could. Ash has always been a cocky little shit, as long as I've known him. Always thought he was smarter than everybody else."

I shivered at the memory of Fran dancing with him, his tight embrace. It had been just mildly creepy last night. Now it was terrifying. Everything suggested Ash Carter had more experience than we knew getting away with murder.

"Would he have killed her? Fran?"

Rudy raised an eyebrow as if to say, *What do you think?*

He reached to answer the buzz of his cell phone just as the waitress set down our plates of food. After a series of uh-huh's, he said, "I'll be right there," and flipped the phone shut. "Dangnation."

He slid out of the booth, signaling for the waitress. "Can you put this in a box for me?"

She didn't roll her eyes, at least not where he could see.

"Got to go. We'll talk later about you and that .38 of yours. You aren't registered to carry concealed." He stood over me as he fished bills out of his wallet, then strode off.

The waitress swept his plates away and carried two loaded take-out boxes to the register for him. I sat alone with my oatmeal and my thoughts.

Early this morning, I had driven Fran to pick up her car, and

264

reassured her that I'd keep her posted, given her Rowly Edwards's number in Atlanta so she could follow up with him, if she wanted, and sent her off to Atlanta with a hug. Nothing more I could do.

I'd relished the thought of Sunday alone, with my house and my office to myself. I hadn't realized how much I enjoyed not having to answer to anyone or fill an employee's task list. Then Rudy had called about breakfast and disrupted my sanctuary with specters of things I'd rather not think about.

As I took a bite of my lumpy oatmeal full of blueberries and walnuts, my cell phone buzzed. I half expected it to be Rudy with something he'd forgotten to lecture me about or Aunt Letha wondering why I wasn't in church.

Melvin's radio announcer voice was the last voice I expected to hear. "Avery, you might want to head up the mountain to Stumphouse Tunnel, if you're of a mind to help out our little ghoster friends, as you call them."

"I call them your friends, not mine."

"I'd call them in trouble."

"I thought you were supposed to be fishing."

"I am. Colin called my cell phone. How he got that number, I want to find out."

His tone implied he might suspect me, but he was wrong on that score. "Maybe they're psychic."

He snorted. "I just know they're getting to be a pain. Colin said they were filming at the tunnel and Sheriff Peters and the ambulance had been called. The reception was bad, so I didn't get the details. Don't know why I care, but I wouldn't wish L. J. Peters off on anybody." Melvin and L.J. had a history.

"Okay." A drive up the mountain was always preferable to chores. Still, I sighed for dramatic effect. "I'll go check on them."

The tunnel wasn't far. In horse-and-buggy days, taking a

picnic lunch to the tunnel had been an all-day affair, but fifteen minutes after I closed my cell phone, I pulled off the state road and swung down the double-back road to the tunnel.

The football-field-sized parking lot was jammed. I'd never seen so many vehicles here, even on the hottest summer days when people drive up to enjoy the natural chill of the never-completed railroad tunnel. I'd also never seen a fire truck here, or six pickups with mail-order flashing lights—members of the county's volunteer Rescue Squad.

Someone had removed the barricades that usually block the road up to the tunnel entrance, and the fire truck was perched at the top of the short, steep hill. I didn't smell smoke and suspected the fire truck had another reason for being here.

I ignored parking lot etiquette and blocked two of the Rescue Squad trucks. They wouldn't be going anywhere until whatever had happened in the tunnel had been milked for all its entertainment value.

Stumphouse Tunnel had been former vice president John C. Calhoun's key to a railroad that would connect the Charleston port with Knoxville and Cincinnati. He wanted to minimize Southern dependence on Northern trade as the economic ties between those two sections of the country tightened to the snapping point in the decades before the Civil War.

Unreconstructed Southerners still wistfully espoused, "If only the railroad had been finished in time . . . ," even though that had been little more than a pipe dream. True, only nine hundred feet of the six-thousand-foot tunnel remained unfinished when war broke out, but other Southern states had already managed to build railway connections with the Midwest. South Carolina's construction had been delayed thanks to much-ballyhooed and characteristically shortsighted intrastate infighting over how to fund the enterprise.

In the 1950s, Clemson College had found a more pragmatic use for the abandoned tunnel, which mimicked perfectly the temperature and humidity of the cheese-making caves in France. The Continent came to the Carolinas, and Clemson bleu cheese was born. Nowadays, the tunnel was again abandoned, except for the tourists—and now a mob of sightseers.

I climbed the graveled embankment to the plateau entrance to the tunnel. I was used to being alone here, or one of only a handful of other visitors. I always stop to breathe in the damp earth smell and commit to memory the uncountable colors of green. The first waft of cold air from the yawning black hole always came as a never-quite-expected jolt.

Today, I didn't anticipate a peaceful green interlude. Weaving my way past a gawking crowd planted on the old rail bed as if waiting for a parade to march out of the boxcar-sized black cave, my mild irritation evaporated in the heat, replaced by an ice cube of fear.

What had happened to draw the official and the idle in such numbers? Had the naive ghosters gotten into some serious trouble, something temporal and dangerous?

I eased between two men in hunting camouflage and past an imaginary line that encircled the opening at a twenty-foot distance. I didn't acknowledge their disapproval of my pushiness or give them a sweet smile. Both were probably pleased when an official voice barked at me.

"Halt!" The deputy I'd been looking for. He stood to the right of the entrance, in the shadow of the overgrown rocks. I gave him a smile and started to ask a question when another voice, echoing from the tunnel, interrupted.

"Might as well go ahead and arrest her now, dep-ity. She ain't nothin' but trouble."

Pudd Pardee, the head of the Rescue Squad, waddled into the

sunlight on his stumpy, spraddled legs, looking like some mutated mythological woodland character. All he needed was a leprechaun's brocade vest instead of a khaki work shirt with his name embroidered in an oval patch.

"Pudd." I sounded delighted to see him. And I was. "Is everything all—is anyone—?" What exactly did I want to know?

"This is takin' am-ba-lance chasin' to new lows, A'vry. What'cha gonna do, sue the state 'cause somebody dug a big hole a hunnert years ago? Don't want to break your heart, but nobody's even hurt. Yet." He paused for effect. "I get Cuke Metz down outta that shaft, I'm gonna make that ol' boy wish he'd fallen down that shaft and died before I got here."

Pudd referred to a broad, vertical shaft dug from the top of the mountain down into the tunnel, a 180-foot-tall skylight designed to provide light and air during the antebellum construction.

"Cuke? He fell down the shaft?" As soon as I heard his name, I flashed back to the campfire storytelling, the mismatched gathering of good ol' boys and ne'er-do-wells. "You say nobody's hurt." I didn't want it to be a question.

"Like I said, not yet."

"Have you—are there three folks in there, from out of town?"

Pudd pursed his meaty lips and studied me. "Nope." He nodded behind me. "We're holding 'em in the fire truck for the time being."

Relief and irritation vied for first place. With a glance over my shoulder, I could make out shapes in the truck's cab.

"Been lovely chatting with you, A'vry. But I gotta get around to the top of that shaft before one'a them nidgits drops Cuke on his dumb ass."

"He's still in the shaft?"

"Swinging there like a gong in a bell and begging for somebody to save him." Pudd hitched up his britches with the air of one donning the inevitable mantle of greatness, knowing he was the only one to supervise such a harrowing rescue.

I gave Pudd a half salute and trailed him back through the crowd to where his battered pickup sat parked beside the shiny red fire truck. Once he'd driven around to the top of the hill, I had no idea how pudgy Pudd planned to get from his truck through the rough terrain to the air shaft's upper opening.

The top of the hill had, in the 1850s, housed the imaginatively named Tunnel Hill, a booming metropolis of fifteen hundred people, one strong-willed Catholic priest, and seventeen saloons. It had been a one-trick town, home to the mostly Irish laborers who'd lucked into the backbreaking work of digging through solid granite with picks and black gunpowder.

Three completed air shafts had been dug through the top of the mountain. Today, standing at the bottom of the one remaining shaft was an eerie experience—part beam-me-up shaft of light in the darkness, part mystery. Water droplets always rained down the wide shaft. Far overhead, trees sheltered the shaft's opening, green in summer, stark in winter.

As a kid, I'd heard that one of the tunnel's fatalities had occurred in that shaft. A donkey being lowered in a harness for the day's work fell and killed both the donkey and the man below who broke its fall. I'd never read that story in any official account of the tunnel, but I still can't think about that ten-foot-wide shaft without imagining the risk of being lowered almost two hundred feet into the deepest darkness to begin a deafening day's work hammering granite.

It didn't take a genius to figure out that Rudy's campfire chat hadn't stopped Cuke Metz from getting himself in trouble staging another haunting for the ghosters.

I turned to the fire truck, climbed up, and wrestled with the driver's door.

The three ghosters sat inside, sweltering in the heat.

"Why don't you roll down the windows or open the door?" I asked.

Trini, sandwiched between the two guys, her hands clasped between her knees, said, "They told us not to touch anything."

"Come on." I motioned for them to follow me. I climbed around into the rumble seats behind the cab. At least here we might catch a breeze.

We attracted some attention from the crowd below us. Since my brush with fame, in the person of Pudd Pardee, and since they had nothing else to stare at but an empty black hole, some of them turned their backs on the tunnel to study us instead.

I leaned over close to the three of them, keeping my voice low to avoid curious ears.

"So what happened?"

They looked from one to the other, silently electing Trini as spokesperson.

"We were filming. Inside. We'd been told there'd been an accident when the tunnel was being built, that someone had fallen down the shaft and that people sometimes hear him."

"Or even see him," Quint added.

Cuke had probably figured it'd be too dangerous to lower a live mule down the shaft, so he'd changed the story and volunteered himself.

"At first, it was just cold and damp. And drippy. Water sounds everywhere." She sounded really spooked.

"Then we saw these legs."

"And a scream—"

"At first, we thought—"

Colin interrupted. "We soon knew it was real." He needed some face-saving, given the goofy stunts he'd already fallen for.

"We ran out to call for help," Trini said.

"From inside, we could see some guys on top of the shaft. But they couldn't pull him back up."

"Unreal."

They fell silent. I glanced over at the tunnel opening, a scant thirty yards away, the edges hidden and softened by vines, bushes, and weeds. The tunnel, from whatever vantage point—on the ground or high up in the fire truck—was black, solid, both ominous and inviting.

"We have it on tape," Quint said, almost apologetic. He proffered the camera.

At my nod, he switched on the miniature screen and scanned for the beginning.

On the replay, I watched and listened as they walked through the black tunnel toward the shaft of light. The dripping water was audible, but I could only catch some of their whispered words.

Their scuffling steps in the wet sand discernible at times on the tape, they walked toward the light that descended into the blackness. I knew from experience that the light was capable of illumining their path. However, the darkness around them was so complete, they likely hadn't quite trusted the light ahead.

Drips, scuffles, whispered words, dark and light. Not exactly compelling television.

"What the—" Quint's voice replayed loud with alarm.

The camera then picked up the sounds that had drawn Quint's reaction. An animal bellow, a plea.

The camera stopped moving.

"What is that?" someone—Trini?—whispered.

"Who's there?" Colin yelled.

In the truck, we all jumped at the unexpected volume.

"Help!" a loud bellow in the distance answered.

The camera continued to move toward the light shaft, sweeping slowly from side to side, perhaps scanning for threats.

As it drew closer to the light, the camera angle slowly lifted, drawn upward into the tall shaft. The wide mouth at the top of the mountain looked small from where they stood. The falling condensation sparkled in the bright sunlight and fell in shades of green, colored by the trees thick and far above.

The yells for help grew louder, more distinct.

What at first looked like a clapper in a bell hung halfway up the shaft. The two legs gave a wild kick as if clamoring for a foothold.

"Oh, dear," I said. That about summed it up. Cuke hung in the center of the shaft, at least eighty feet from the sandy stone floor.

The picture cut off.

"We went for help," said Trini.

We all sat silent.

"Sorry this hasn't worked out for you," I said after a time.

"Oh, it's worked better than we expected," said Colin. "Much better, thanks to Trini's scream."

"Oh?"

All three nodded.

"We stayed up last night brainstorming some plot ideas. We've decided to make a horror movie. All thanks to Trini's one helluva scream."

I remembered their awed mention of her scream after one of their adventures.

"Bloodcurdling," said Quint, giving her an admiring smile.

"The real stumbling block is distribution," said Colin. "I know a guy in Charlotte who quit his big bank job to get into movie production. He made a serious film, entered festivals and such before he did a DVD release. We figure the straight-to-DVD market will be a better route for horror."

The other two nodded enthusiastic confirmation.

"Another guy used to make movies around Charlotte. We're hoping to hook up with him. After you get some credits, you can get hired on film crews. Charlotte gets a good bit of filmmaking traffic, even big Hollywood work."

"That'd be fun," I said. Probably not lucrative, but fun. I'd never asked what they did in the rest of their lives when they weren't chasing their artistic dream. College students? Retail? Fast-food restaurant staff? Something with flexible hours, obviously.

"Bet you guys could make quite a horror picture," I said.

"You reckon that would be something Mr. Bertram would be interested in investing in?"

If persistence was the key to success, Colin had what it took.

"I don't know," I said. I sincerely doubted it, but why should I deliver the bad news?

Outside our perch in the fire truck, a loud cheer echoed out of the tunnel, and the crowd gathered below began to clap and chatter in a slow wave, no more certain than we were what had happened but taking it as a good sign.

With so many members of the Ghouly Boys present—the scanner addicts who don't have anything better to do than show up at car accidents hoping for gore—they might have preferred something more tragic just because it would make a better story when they were sitting around in the pool hall waiting for the next scanner call. But since it was one of their own who'd almost re-created the made-up miner's fatal fall, they graciously cele-brated the happy ending.

I was surprised to see Rudy exit the tunnel, waving his arms and yelling.

"Okay, I'm gonna have to ask you to break it up," he called. "Break it up. Everything's fine now. We just need to get him to the ambulance to be checked over. Let us have some room here."

The crowd milled about, condensing toward the edges of the drive, but nobody turned toward the parking lot or made a move to leave.

Their persistence was soon rewarded. Two men, one wearing a complicated harness that looked like a parachutist's apparatus, supported a third man—bushy-headed Cuke.

The crowd erupted in cheers and claps. No lack of enthusiasm.

Cuke, with what looked like blue nylon ski rope still knotted around his thighs and waist, waved his hand high overhead, acknowledging his well-wishers before he ducked his head with a sheepish grin.

If he'd pulled a successful stunt, nobody but his buddies would have known. A royal screwup, and most of the town's underemployed population turned out and cheered. Cuke Metz had to have mixed feelings about the contradictions of fame.

His escorts walked him through a cross between a ticker-tape parade and a perp walk toward the ambulance. Looking at the thin ski rope he'd dangled from, I had no doubt he was having trouble getting his legs—and more personal parts of his body—to function again.

Rudy came over and waved up at us. "You all can go home now. We may need to talk to you later." He gave Colin a nod for emphasis. "We know where to find you."

The ghosters exchanged glances, the official menace not lost on them.

I followed them to the ground and walked them to their van. Miraculously it was no longer blocked in by other cars.

"I've been meaning to ask," I said. "Mumler. That's an interesting nickname."

Colin gave me a pleased grin. "After the first spirit photographer. The man who first captured recognizable apparitions on film. During the Civil War, so many restless spirits were taken when they didn't expect to go. He helped comfort a lot of family members after their tragic losses."

"That's—interesting."

As Colin walked on ahead to the van, I caught sight of Quint and Trini as they exchanged glances. I raised my eyebrows.

"Nobody really calls him that," said Quint.

"Except him." With a gentle smile, Trini rolled her eyes.

I nodded. Not much else to say.

Back at my car, I wasn't so lucky. Cars had triple parked around mine. I climbed in, cranked the windows down, and sat in the shade watching people stroll back to their cars as if they'd just been to a church softball game rather than a near-death experience. Odd way to spend a Sunday. I wondered if Fran was spending the day with her parents.

I noticed a message on my cell phone. Lydia's voice said, "Frank's fired up the grill for hot dogs and hamburgers. Mom and Dad are coming, and Letha, Hattie, and Vinnia. Let me know how many hot dogs you want."

I hit redial. A family cookout sounded like just the ticket. I'd stop for a bag of marshmallows.

Missing and Unidentified Persons

According to the National Crime Information Center (NCIC), more than 50,000 missing-person cases were open in the United States in 2007, and more than 6,200 unidentified-remains cases were active.

In researching *Hush My Mouth,* I wanted to understand the search for missing persons and the identification of remains. I first became aware of the poignant realities and the staggering statistics when I met Dr. Emily Craig, the state forensic anthropologist for the Commonwealth of Kentucky.

Dr. Craig, a medical illustrator before she studied forensic anthropology with Dr. Bill Bass at the University of Tennessee's legendary "Body Farm," brings an artist's eye—and an artist's heart—to her work as a scientist. In her book *Teasing Secrets from the Dead: My Investigations at America's Most Infamous Crime Scenes*

(Crown, 2004), she talks about the power of the Internet in matching the names of the missing to the unidentified remains—and bringing murderers to justice.

The NCIC is a national clearinghouse available to law enforcement, but it has limitations. Sometimes missing persons aren't reported because family and friends don't know they are gone or are embarrassed to report they've run off. Because the database records information by code, it requires proper coding in both the missing-person report and the unidentified-remains report. So much of what identifies us as human beings, though, is in the eye of the beholder. Is the hair dark blond or light brown? Is she tall because she always wears heels? The most important identifiers—such as a tattoo or unusual teeth or habits—might be missing because someone forgot to mention them. Another problem, too, is that investigators can have overwhelming workloads that give a low priority to logging the information into the database.

Over the last few years, thanks to dedicated and tireless work by law-enforcement officials and families missing loved ones, resources have become available to the general public, not just to law enforcement. One of the best-known organizations, the National Center for Missing and Exploited Children (www.missingkids.com), provides a database of cases, an online support group for families, and resources for law enforcement.

Because NCMEC focuses only on children, the National Center for Missing Adults was formed (www.theyaremissed.org). This organization was promoted through the dedicated efforts of Kristen Modafferi's family in Charlotte when the lack of resources hampered them after their eighteen-year-old daughter disappeared in San Francisco.

Resources also exist to help give names to unidentified remains. The Doe Network (www.doenetwork.org) catalogs both U.S. and international cases. The site also allows geographic searches, and the list of resolved cases includes happy endings of families reunited, sometimes years after the disappearance. Many states also have individual sites covering unsolved cases in their jurisdictions.

Though the reporting sites—for both the professionals and the public—are far from complete, they represent a quantum leap in the amount and quality of information available. As a result, more of the stories have endings—some happy, some predictably sad, but closure nonetheless.